Egg-Shell Thin:

A Fairplay Novel Featuring Private Investigator Adrienne Hargrove

by Karen Harmon

PublishAmerica
Baltimore

First printing

While the main character in this novel, Adrienne Hargrove, is based on an actual private investigator living in northeast Louisiana and her business, The Investigative Network, and many of the places she visits throughout the course of the story are real, *Egg-Shell Thin* is a work of fiction. Any similarities to real people or incidents, other than those specifically mentioned above, are purely coincidental.

At the specific preference of the author, PublishAmerica allowed this work to remain exactly as the author intended, verbatim, without editorial input.

ISBN: 1-4241-3093-X
PUBLISHED BY PUBLISHAMERICA, LLLP
www.publishamerica.com
Baltimore

Printed in the United States of America

This novel is dedicated to the memory of my mom and dad, Al and Eileen Harmon, for teaching their children to love books by being readers themselves, and for inculcating in me and my brother and sister, Roger and Carol, the absolute truth that you can do anything if you want to bad enough.

ACKNOWLEDGEMENTS

I would like to acknowledge:

My son and gifted horse trainer, Rob Epperson, for his contribution to the writing of chapter eight and for believing in me, no matter what adventure I might be pursuing.

My daughter and poet, Jaime R. Wood, for writing the poem Egg-Shell Thin, and other poems used throughout my novels, and for always understanding in every way the truth of what it means to be a writer.

My dear friend and confidante, neurologist Dr. Mike Boykin who has helped me see how kind and gentle people can truly be, and for giving me the idea and information to help me use puffer fish toxin as a pivotal point in the novel. Without his help, this novel would not have been possible.

Professor Bill Ryan with the Creative Writing Department at the University of Louisiana at Monroe for his total honesty, even when it was painful; for telling me one hundred thousand times that you shouldn't have to plod through a novel, that the story must be woven and textured. Only with Bill's kind of honesty can a serious writer really grow. I'm thankful for his kind of friendship.

Author James Lee Burke, under whom I studied creative writing in the mid 80's, at Wichita State University, for seeing how important my writing was to me even then, as a very young and confused woman, and for encouraging me to focus on fiction rather than poetry, and for helping me see how to make a character come alive through his character, Dave Robicheaux. Jim's smiling face and classroom antics touched lives in ways only a teacher can.

Annette Kovac, the key to it all, who has helped me see life from so many angles, and most of all, for being my friend, without whom I'd still be looking for a main character. Through Annette I've come to recognize that being the authentic "you" is possible, and that it doesn't have to mean being perfect.

I want to thank:

My children and their spouses, Ronda, Robby, Roger, Timothy, Jaime, Eddie, Tanya, Mandy, and my grandchildren, Jeremy, Brooke, Heather, Robin, Rachael, Kori, Davis, Ashlyn, and Kaelyn, for their total love and support even if Mom/Grandmother seems a little off center a lot of the time. Without the love of any one of them, my life would be filled with holes.

My friends Elizabeth Emerson and Rachel Richardson for always supporting my endeavors, no matter the direction they may go, and for waking me up in nighttime creative writing workshops and daytime literature classes.

eggshell thin

Jaime R. Wood

the motions between
a parade and a massacre
and my mind's ability to
tell the difference

the reality of your life
and mine, separated by
three small degrees
making us neighbors
with billions of people
we'll never know

my marriage day
so close to death that
i stopped breathing
when i said i do
- the immense change
between closing my eyes
and enjoying my self-created darkness

our lives so full of illusions
some by choice are kept
cradled, some swept
away in search of the reality
we remember hearing about
in fairytales

it's all so eggshell thin

Chapter One

Adrienne Hargrove stood in the darkness and leaned on the rails of the Lea Joyner drawbridge that connected Monroe and West Monroe, Louisiana, and arched itself high above the Ouachita River. She stared at the lighted outline of a giant barge moving slowly down river in the distance. From time to time, it released its warning sound, a deep and lonely horn, reminding the sleeping cities on each side of the river that life moves on, even in the darkness. Without looking, Adrienne reached inside the shoulder bag purse that hung from her slender 5'9" frame, and rummaged around for her Virginia Slim cigarettes and silver Zippo lighter. She lit a cigarette and took a soothing drag, shaking her long, curly, blonde-frosted hair back from her forty-five year old face, dropping the Zippo back into her purse as she exhaled the gray smoke into the night air. A police car crept up behind her, and a young, attractive policeman with a flashlight stepped out, leaving the car running and his partner inside. He flashed the light toward Adrienne's face.

"You O.K. lady?" he asked.

"I'm a private investigator," Adrienne answered, turning toward him, and looking at his face silhouetted by the light in his hand. "Just coming in from a job and thought I'd catch a breath of fresh air."

He couldn't help but notice her super tight jeans and the turtleneck sweater that accented her generous bust. Only the lines carved in the smoker's skin of her face gave away Adrienne's age. The gold, wire-rim of her glasses reflected the light from the policeman's flashlight as it explored her face.

"Pulled an all-nighter, huh?" he questioned.

"Guess you could say that," she smiled.

"Mind if I take a look at your investigator's license?" the cop asked.

"No problem." Charming laugh-lines crinkled onto the corners of her eyes

9

as she faked a smile and pulled the wallet out of her shoulder bag. She handed the license to the officer and took another puff of her cigarette, lifting her chin high so that she could blow the smoke into the air and not into his face.

"O.K.," the cop said as he handed the license back to Adrienne. "If I were you, I'd go home and get some rest. Goodnight lady." He tipped his hat, turned off the flashlight pushing it down into its holder on his belt, and walked back to the police car. He looked over the top of the car at Adrienne before he climbed in, but she'd already twisted on her high-heeled boots with her back to him, and was bent over the rail of the bridge again, staring out across the water.

"Go home and get some rest," Adrienne chuckled. "If I wanted to go home and get some rest, do you think I'd be standing here on this bridge at two o'clock in the morning, asshole?" She flipped the cigarette butt over the railing and walked a few feet to the end of the bridge where she'd parked her car. As she started the ignition, she tossed her purse over her shoulder onto the floor in back and sat thinking for a moment about the warmth of the lights on the barge showing the giant vessel which way to go even in the darkness of the October night. She thought about the water that worked in harmony with the barge to move it peacefully along its way, not even seeming to notice the chaos of the world around it. What a contrast to her life. What a contrast too, to the information she had delivered to her client, Professor Mel Brighton, just minutes ago, standing here on the bridge. Information that would bring pain and chaos to his life for a long time to come. The proof of his wife's affair, in living color. A video of her with her lover in the back seat of a car in a grocery store parking lot.

"Not even enough class to rent a motel room," Adrienne mumbled.

Mel, a literature professor in his fifties, tall, handsome, dignified, well-known throughout the community, highly respected among his peers. Loyal and honest, one of the few men left who were, in Adrienne's mind anyway. What had he done to deserve this? Adrienne knew there was no answer. *Life plays some sorry ass games*, she thought as she tried to push the case, her work on it now completed, and Mel, to the back of her mind. *It's amazing how many people live half their lives in the sunshine and the other half in the shadows. There's no end to the evil we seem to be capable of perpetrating on one another.* Adrienne didn't know for sure that adultery could be classified as evil, but she did know that it was at the lowest level of man's primal instinct, the fulfillment of animal lust, no matter what the effect on others. For this, many members of the human race were willing to put their counterpart, their life partner, through a pain that could be compared with no other. Besides all she'd seen in the hundreds of adultery cases interspersed among the other crimes she'd investigated, she knew about that kind of pain firsthand.

Adrienne put her car in gear and pushed on the accelerator. She felt around the seat as she drove, fumbling for an open pack of cigarettes and a lighter, tossing notebooks and loose pieces of paper onto the floor or behind her back.

"Shit," she said as she pulled a cigarette out of a pack that had fallen on the floor, pushed in the lighter on the dash, and lit up just as one of the four phones laying around in various piles of notes rang. "Shit," she yelled again, tossing one phone to the floor while she pulled on the cord of another, moving it closer to her. "Hello," she said in a mockingly sweet voice, noticing the number on the phone that told her who was calling.

"Where the hell are you?" Andrew yelled into the phone. "You said you'd be home by midnight."

"I know, Andrew. This is a pretty deep case. It took longer than I expected. If I hadn't stayed, the whole night would have been a waste."

"Everything comes first but me," he yelled again. "You're some wife. Thirteen years of this shit."

"Andrew, it's how I make our living. What do you expect me to do?"

"What the hell do you care what I expect you to do? Forget it and bring me some lemon drops. How far are you from home?"

"About an hour. Where the hell am I going to get lemon drops at two o'clock in the morning?"

"Try a truck stop. I don't care where you gettem, just gettem." He slammed the phone down on the receiver.

"Shit," she yelled into the phone whose line was already dead. She jerked the cord loose from its connection, accelerated the car to seventy, and took another puff from her cigarette. Up ahead was a Pilot truck stop, and she pulled in. Getting out of the car, she stomped her cigarette out on the sidewalk with the ball of her boot and headed for the candy section. "Sour cherry balls, cinnamon drops, where the hell are the lemon drops?" Two sacks of root beer barrels fell to the floor. No lemon drops. She left and headed further up the road to the nearest Love's. Inside, she once again headed for the candy section. This time she was in luck. She grabbed up six bags, paid the boy behind the cash register, and headed for her car with its tinted windows.

Adrienne unlocked the door to her house, walked inside, and threw the keys on the counter along with the bags of lemon drops. She sat her purse on the bar and walked to the door of the bedroom.

"Andy, I'm home," she spoke in a tired voice. "Andrew?" He was sound asleep. She walked to the side of the bed and bent over. Not a sign of movement. "Shit head," she mumbled as she closed the door and walked back into the living room. "Give me one more thing to do and make sure it's at two o'clock in the morning. Once an asshole, always an asshole. I don't know why I keep humoring his stupid demands. Makes me stupid too, I guess." She kicked off her shoes, poured a glass of rich, red Cabernet Sauvignon, lit a cigarette and headed for the sofa. She laid her head back against the soft, hunter green leather, removed her glasses, and stared at the ceiling. Looking around her, she thought about how deceptively beautiful and peaceful this log house was with the soft golden glow of the natural wood that seemed to exude safety and security, and as she did so, her handsome client, Mel, crept back into her mind. She knew how he'd be feeling right now; that horrible burning in the pit of the stomach, knowing that tomorrow he'd confront his wife who was still playing the game, still sharing his bed, with evidence of her adultery. This was his only marriage. They'd been together twenty years. Mel would be sleepless, staring at the ceiling, close to nausea, lying stiff, making sure not to touch Camille even by accident as she lay sleeping with no idea what would be taking place in her life tomorrow. Camille, thinking the secrets were still her own, without the slightest clue that the unimaginable had happened, that her secrets were all on film, enough of them anyway to convict her in a court of law if it became necessary to go that far. Adrienne was the best. She left nothing to chance.

Is it possible to ever really know another person? She wondered as her thoughts ran back to her own marriage and how naive she'd been about love. She'd tried so hard to trust Andrew, ignoring all the signs as long as she could even though she'd been through it all before in her first marriage. Nearly everyday with Andrew, especially since the car accident that left him a partial invalid, had been a battle. She couldn't wait until it was time to leave on the days she had a case. She was the best private investigator in the state, and she loved her work. She loved the importance it gave her to other people, and she loved the challenge of somehow playing a part in bringing all the assholes running around out there to justice. Most of all, she loved that it gave her reason to stay away from home and from Andrew and his temper tantrums, and in some ways, it was a kind of personal, subtle revenge for the raw hands life had dealt her.

"Soul mates," she chuckled. "True love. Yeah, right." She thought back to her first marriage, to the abusive young husband who'd beaten her and battered their child.

"Broken ribs, a punctured lung, contusions to the head, probably slammed against a wall. Brain damage," the coroner's report had said when the baby boy died.

She'd left the infant with his father just long enough to go to the store and…He served three years in prison, and was free to go on with his life. Adrienne had never seen the man again, but the tiny boy's face never left her heart or mind for one moment of one day, nor did the guilt that held her captive, no matter how much she kept telling herself that she'd tried everything in her power to make a happy home. At times during those days she wondered if anything really mattered; would anything ever matter again. Then she met Andrew

For awhile Andrew seemed to be the devoted husband. His abuse was more subtle, but over time, just as destructive. Little put-downs here and there. Nothing ever quite good enough, not dinner or the house or her hairstyle or the clothes she wore. In time other telltale signs developed. Andrew was dressing more neatly, lost a few pounds, often left the house wearing new cologne with no explanation about where he was going, and he found more and more fault with Adrienne. Then the mysterious phone calls started. When Adrienne answered, the caller hung up. When Andrew answered, the pleasure on his face couldn't be disguised. Adrienne had hired an investigator to check things out, and after paying him $3000 with no results, discovered that Andrew and his lover had paid the same investigator $5000 not to expose their secrets. They'd been more careful then, more elusive, but it made Adrienne even more determined to get the evidence she needed for a divorce, and to be awarded the house she and Andrew had built together. The thought of losing her home over his infidelity, having to start over again yet one more time, had been just too overwhelming. To keep the house she'd have to prove adultery, so she began following him herself, and in no time documented the whole sordid affair. Adrienne decided then and there that she would get her private investigator's license and catch other unfaithful jackasses. And, that she would divorce Andrew. She followed him and his girlfriend one last time. She wanted the pleasure of confronting them together, to show them the video that had captured all, to smile when she told Andrew that she was headed to the attorney's office to file for divorce. But Andrew spotted her tailing them and ran. She kept them in view, but he lost control of his car as he tried to take a curve and crashed over the side of an embankment. He was in intensive care for months, and came out a partial invalid, both lungs permanently damaged by broken ribs. He would need an oxygen tank for the rest of his life. His lover was killed instantly. Adrienne tried not to be glad the woman had died. She struggled with her "betrayed wife" feelings and the dark side of her own nature that kept telling her they both got what they deserved. Her sense of personal guilt for following them, like the guilt that haunted her over the death of her infant son, took over again. Now, without her, Andrew would live in a nursing home for the rest of his life. Adrienne could no longer love him, neither could she leave him.

Forcing her consciousness back to the moment, Adrienne put her favorite music on the stereo; Rochmaninoff's Rhapsody. She dimmed the lights, breathed in the beautiful, flawless notes, and poured herself a second glass of wine. She opened the door to the study that served as her office and walked over to the aquarium to feed the fish. Two black and white Angel fish stood motionless, staring at one another as though they were about to kiss. their bodies looked like hand-painted plates with fins. An orange and white clown fish, her own personal Nemo, swam toward her and seemed to smile right at her.

"I'm glad you've got something to be happy about." Adrienne couldn't help but smile back, thinking how simple and innocent the little creature's life must be. She gave him a little extra food and turned off the aquarium light. The answering machine on the desk was blinking, notifying Adrienne that she had three messages. She pushed the button.

"You have reached The Investigative Network. Please leave a name and number, and I'll return your call as soon as possible."

Message number 1: "Yeah, this is Joe D'Angelo. Don't guess I'll be needing your services anymore. My wife came home today and TOLD me she's having an affair. SHE wants a divorce! Can you believe it? The man's my brother, my own fuckin brother. Who the hell can you trust if you can't trust your wife and your own brother?"

Adrienne shook her head, but not in disbelief. "Sick bastard," she mumbled to herself as she pushed the button for the second message.

Message number 2: "I need to talk to you," a woman's voice. "Please call Catriona Kirby at 967– 7722, but if it's not me that answers, please don't leave a message. My husband is a powerful man in the community, a doctor. I may be in danger if anyone finds out I'm calling you. Please, I need your help. He leaves for his office at nine every morning." Adrienne jotted the name and number on her desk pad and deleted the message from the machine. The woman sounded desperate. She'd call her after nine in the morning.

Message number 3: "Adrienne, this is Mel." Adrienne's heart involuntarily skipped a beat at the sound of the familiar voice. "Sorry for calling at such an ungodly hour, but I left you at the bridge not too long ago, and I thought maybe I could catch you before you went to bed. I'm going to get a divorce." He sounded less distraught and more in control of his emotions than he had at the bridge where he'd left so filled with humiliation. "I sure could use someone to talk to. I know your work on my case is over, but I was hoping maybe you'd meet me tomorrow evening at Cottonport Coffeehouse, just to talk…you know. We have so much in common. You've been such a stronghold for me through all of this. I don't know what I'd have done without you. I don't want to see that end, especially now…. The music starts at nine. It's jazz this week. I hope to see you there." His voice was deep and calm and persuasive.

Adrienne stood in silence thinking about the invitation and Mel…mid-fifties, dark hair, blue eyes, so handsome and intelligent, faithful to his wife for twenty years even through her alcohol abuse, and now this. He seemed so warm, so capable of love. She felt a kind of personal despair for all the years he'd wasted. She also felt an uncomfortable twinge of pleasure from his words and his mellow voice. She pushed the delete button and walked across the house to the room where Andrew lay sleeping. She glanced down at the man who was her husband. Mel's invitation rang in her ears. It wasn't exactly an invitation to bed. Maybe that thought hadn't even entered his mind. It had hers, she had to admit, several times during her work on his case, but she had always pushed the idea away. Part of the respect she'd felt for Mel all these weeks had come from knowing that he was different, that he had a code of ethics he'd lived by all his life. Now, she downed the glass of wine and closed the bedroom door, leaving Andrew alone in the dark. She'd sleep on the couch and think. There'd be nothing wrong with meeting Mel one last time to sort of tie up the loose ends. He probably didn't even know how attractive she found him. But she knew. She fell asleep feeling a strange excitement mixed with a twinge of guilt, and thinking about whether or not she would go.

Chapter Two

Catriona Kirby stood looking out the bay window that covered most of one wall in the breakfast room of her house. The huge Magnolia trees scattered over the smooth, flowing slopes of the five acre yard had lost their white flowers in preparation for the oncoming winter, but their leaves were still deep green and glossy. She could hear the motor of a small boat and the distant chatter of fishermen in the bayou behind the 8000 square foot mansion. Cypress trees sat on the edge of the bayou, and long, blue, skinny fingers of Spanish moss hung from their branches, some nearly touching the water below. Catriona recalled a fact from a college biology course she'd taken while getting her degree so long ago now, it seemed. *The moss is so beautiful, pretending to be a protective garment for the trees, but it's really a fungus choking the life from them.* She looked down at the Cypress knees, standing only four or five feet tall, covered with knobs and long, gray streaks of bark that made them look like little old rigid men staring back at her. She took a deep breath and waited for her husband, Dr. Galen Kirby, to leave for his office at the only clinic left in the small Louisiana parish. She tried to sound normal when she wished him a good day, but she relaxed only after he'd pulled completely out of the driveway. Moments later, the phone rang.

"Mrs. Kirby?"

"Yes."

This is Adrienne Hargrove from The Investigative Network. Can you talk?"

"Yes. Galen just left for the office," Catriona replied. "Thank you for calling. The maid will be here today. I need to meet you somewhere else. I can't take a chance on being overheard. Please, Ms. Hargrove, it's very urgent."

"You can call me Adrienne."

"At the foot of the Lea Joyner Bridge in Monroe, to the south, just before you enter Antique Alley. There's a coffee house called Reward Yourself. Ten thirty? "Catriona asked.

"I know the place. See you there." Adrienne placed the phone on the receiver, wondering about the anxiety in Catriona Kirby's voice. An adulterous husband? Maybe, but she sounded more afraid than suspicious. She remembered the woman's words that her husband was powerful, that she could be in danger if he found out. Found out what? Adrienne took a small key from the middle drawer on her desk and unlocked the cabinet where she kept her handgun. She was licensed to carry it in her line of work, but she seldom felt it necessary. Something about Catriona Kirby made her think she'd better brush it off and put it in her purse, just in case. Just in case what? She had no way of knowing.

Chapter Three

Adrienne sat drinking strong, black Colombian coffee in the corner booth across from Catriona Kirby who was sipping on a cup of green tea. She wanted desperately to light a cigarette, that always made coffee taste better, but she refrained for Catriona's sake. Through the soft morning light in the coffeehouse she saw that Catriona Kirby was blonde, blue-eyed, petite, and pretty, a woman in her mid-forties who definitely fit the image of the pampered southern bell. But there was something more intellectual about this woman, something in her eyes that was deep and knowing. Adrienne glanced at Catriona's attire, taking in the details with her investigator's nose. A tan, tastefully clingy, cashmere sweater flattered her creamy skin. A thin strand of pearls decorated her neck, and small pearl and diamond earrings accented her face. Adrienne glanced down at the nervous woman's hands and saw a wedding ring whose diamond must have been at least three or four carats. Her watch, of course, was Rolex, a slender gold band, a rectangular face outlined in diamonds. Her perfume, Adrienne decided, was White Diamond, but this woman was more polished than Elizabeth Taylor could ever dream of being. Catriona glanced nervously around the room before thanking Adrienne again for coming.

"I'm not sure where to begin," Catriona looked hard into Adrienne's eyes.

"Start with what you're afraid of," Adrienne replied.

"I know it sounds crazy, but I'm not exactly sure," Catriona sounded confused and anxious. "You see, I've been married to Galen for nearly ten years. I'm his second wife. He has two children, both grown now, by his first wife. I've always known he has a wandering eye, an eye for the ladies if you want to call it that. I'd heard the rumors before I married him, so I've lived believing that old adage about having made my bed, and now I must lie in it." She took a sip of hot tea and twisted the cup in her hands. "I've known about a number of his flings over the years, but I've pretended not to know, not to hear the whispers around the community or to notice the grins from the men at the country club as they poke one another and make jokes about it. Most of them have had their own flings. There's a kind of accepted silent code of ethics that the country club wives will tolerate this behavior. In some ways I think it's related to the old south and the days of slavery. Many of the plantation owners had concubines among the slaves. Even produced children with them. Of course the wives knew. How could they possibly not know when an occasional mulatto child showed up among the servants? It was considered to be none of their concern, and it was much easier not to ask questions. The wives were taken care of. They and their children were the heirs. People ignored it, pretended not to know. Even Thomas Jefferson had a black mistress. The whole country knew. You can be sure his wife knew too. Our culture accepted it then, and in many ways, the same acceptance of infidelity still exists among the well-to-do. Close your eyes and pretend you don't see." The pupils in her eyes narrowed and Adrienne watched as Catriona's mouth began to turn down and her eyebrows arched with something that was different from anger or betrayal, something that was closer to indignation or humiliation or some kind of disgust. Adrienne made a mental note of the story Catriona was telling, a story told with language that again made her realize that she was talking to an intelligent and well-educated woman. Still, these affairs being considered normal irritated her.

"Sounds like a code of non-ethics to me," Adrienne's sarcasm was wasted as Catriona continued her story.

"None of his indiscretions have lasted more than a few weeks, a few months at the most, until a woman he was involved with about five years ago. It had gone on for nearly a year when she suddenly died. I heard about her death totally by accident. A group of men at the country club didn't see me come in. I heard them say it was hard to believe I hadn't known about "that one" since it had gone on for so long. They were laughing, saying it's a good thing she hadn't died while my husband was in her bed. I left humiliated and angry with them, with Galen, with myself; and, I'm embarrassed to say, glad the woman was dead." Adrienne looked down at her coffee cup, surprised, too, remembering those same feelings from so long ago, feelings she thought she'd squelched forever. "You see, these are not women the men would want to be seen with or connected to socially, but I had been worried about this one. She was the only one who'd ever seemed to be a possible threat to my marriage."

19

Adrienne listened attentively, thinking about this culture filled with pretense that attempted to portray itself as refined and superior, with a separate set of women, a class they considered lower than themselves as mistresses on the side. "You say that was five years ago. What does it have to do with now?" She watched Catriona become composed again, allowing herself to regain what she probably thought was a charming expression, the kind of fake charm she'd become accustomed to displaying for the right people at the right time, that practiced beauty contest kind of charm. Adrienne wondered exactly what emotions were really going on behind the high-society mask, but she tried not to let the thought show.

"After the woman's death, Galen seemed to change for awhile. He spent more time at home, was more attentive to me. I tried to pass it off as some sort of despair over his involvement with the woman and concern about her death, but in actuality, he seemed more light-hearted, more talkative and relaxed than I'd seen him in a long time. It was hard to understand his behavior, but I wanted to believe that he'd been ready for the affair to end and felt some sort of relief, and so I convinced myself that's all it was."

"Again, what does that have to do with now?" Adrienne called over her shoulder for a coffee refill.

Waiting for the waiter to leave, Catriona continued. "It wasn't long, a few months, until he was back to his old self again. A new aid at the nursing home. Then the receptionist from an attorney's office. Someone else's wife in a trailer outside of town. I know it sounds strange, but they were no threat to me. None were the type to hold his attention for long. They were to pacify his ego that he could still get the attention of young women. That's all. I pulled back into my shell, pretending that everything was fine and going on with my life at the country club."

Adrienne thought about the picture the woman was creating. She could see that in a strange and twisted kind of way, Catriona was trapped. This was the only life she'd ever known. It was almost as pitiful as some of the wives she'd known who put up with all kinds of abuse because they didn't think there was any way out. Almost.

Catriona continued. "Then, all of a sudden there was someone new. I wouldn't have paid any particular attention, but Galen started sliding back into that same behavior as when he'd been involved with the woman who died. He was totally preoccupied with this new one the way he had been back then. He was gone for longer and longer periods of time. He bought her gifts." Catriona looked deep into Adrienne's eyes. "He doesn't know I know those things, but it's not hard to find out, not in this town. Then, rather abruptly, it all seemed to end. He was home more, more attentive, just like before. That's been just a few weeks ago, and then a few days ago, on the news, I heard that this young woman had died from natural causes just like the one he'd been involved with before. I couldn't believe it. Both young women in their 30's, apparently healthy, suddenly dead!" Adrienne watched as a strange, shadowy expression began to creep across Catriona Kirby's face. She lowered her voice to a near whisper. "My husband is the parish coroner; he did the autopsies."

Adrienne felt the blood rush to her head. "My God," she whispered.

Catriona continued. "I don't want to believe Galen could be a killer. He's a doctor; he saves lives! A lack of personal morals doesn't make a man a killer. But there's something terribly wrong with the whole picture."

"A license to practice medicine doesn't mean he's not a killer," Adrienne answered, bending over the table, close to Catriona's face. Something else was bothering Adrienne. If Catriona was convinced that her husband couldn't possibly be a killer, why did she say her own life could be in danger when she left the phone message for Adrienne? Something didn't quite click.

"I'm so confused. I don't know what to think." Catriona spoke barely above a whisper, waiting for the waiter to move far enough away again. "I've put up with his unfaithfulness all these years. It's expected in our social group. I saw it over and over again as a child growing up, even in my own parents. But now, I'm not sure I can go on. Somehow, I can't help but believe Galen is linked to the deaths of these women in some way, and I'm afraid he knows there's something bothering me. His behavior is too calm, too practiced, even for him...." She stopped mid-sentence. "I have to know."

"You'll have to start by doing nothing to encourage him to think you have any suspicions," Adrienne agreed with Catriona's fears, thinking back to the way her voice sounded on the phone message.

"The news report mentioned the child of this last woman. A little boy a few months old. It called him an orphan" Catriona continued "No one knows who the father is, or at least no one has come forth to say. It's possible its Galen's child. If it is and you can prove it...that would just be too much. It wouldn't matter about the deaths." She paused, aware that what she'd just said sounded horrible, but collected her self and went on without further explanation. "If I divorce him, will I be able to keep my home and get the alimony it will take for me to be comfortable? I know that sounds selfish and materialistic. I have a degree in biology from LSU, but I've never worked in my life. I wouldn't even know how to begin to start over, especially by myself"

"It's not my job to judge your motives," Adrienne pushed her feelings about the woman's total willingness to spend a lifetime living a lie, deep down inside where they wouldn't show, along with Catriona's comment that it wouldn't matter whether or not Galen Kirby was a murderer on the loose, still out there playing Romeo, as long as she could keep her mansion on the hill, and keep the alimony rolling in. She wanted to tell Catriona Kirby that in her own way, she was just as sick as her husband, but instead she said, "My job is to get conclusive evidence so you can get your divorce. In this state, adultery means you win and he loses all. You can get alimony for life, plus your home, cars, and every other luxury you're used to. If we can prove that kid's his, you can make him pay for your bottled water for life. But if he's involved in anyway with the deaths of these women that will probably surface too. You'll have to be prepared for it."

Still, something in all this didn't make sense. Catriona Kirby just didn't come across as a kept woman. There was definitely a piece missing to the puzzle. "I'll need to get more information. Where the girl friend lived, what she looked like, how you found out about her and so on, and I'll need a $2500 retainer. You OK with that?"

"Just tell me what you need to know and what I should do in the meantime. I have a separate savings account." Adrienne took mental note that Catriona had money of her own. The missing piece of the puzzle became larger. "I'll make the withdrawal this afternoon. Tell me where to send it." Catriona breathed a sigh of relief that Adrienne would take her case.

"I'll meet you right here at the same time tomorrow to pick up the money. After that I'll need you to call me on a phone line that can't be picked up on by cell phones, scanners, and so forth. I'll give you that number when we meet tomorrow. It's a secure number. I'll also bring you a phone I want you to use anytime you talk to me. It's a secure phone, too. In the meantime, just try to be as normal as possible. Don't let on that you suspect anything. Keep your routine as usual. Be sure you don't let any suspicions slip, but listen carefully to any gossip about this woman or her death. I need you to bring me a couple of good pictures of your husband; one close up so I can see his face, the other a full body so I can get a clear view of who I'm looking at. I'll check the newspaper files for any pictures of the women, and stories about their deaths. Be thinking of anything you can tell me, especially about this last woman. What was her name?"

"Susanne Jasper," Catriona's face hardened at the mention of the name. "The first one was Drusilla Gifford."

Let's start with where Susanne Jasper lived, when your husband was probably seeing her, how you know about the affair, and any other information that might help us connect the birth of the child with the doctor's presence.... I'd like you to leave now, before me, so I can be sure no one is following you. Be thinking of everything I need to know. Don't write anything down. Can't take a chance someone might get a hold of it. Just be thinking and remembering. I'll talk to you here, tomorrow." Adrienne watched as Catriona gathered her purse, straightened her sweater, and sauntered out of the coffeehouse, her head held high.

* * *

Adrienne took the long way home from her meeting with Catriona. She needed time to sort things out in her mind. Physically speaking, she and Catriona Kirby could pass for sisters. Catriona was more polished, appeared to have more formal education. She didn't smoke so her skin was smoother, but other than that.

Why would Catriona Kirby stay with a husband who'd been repeatedly unfaithful over their ten year marriage? What kind of culture accepts infidelity as a way of life? Catriona had said it was for convenience, for comfort, yet she had an independent air about her. Was it for prestige? For some kind of hidden power? Adrienne had seen a little bit of everything when it came to strange marriages, but this one definitely didn't make sense. If there were no feelings of love for the man, would she really have stayed this long for the sake of material comfort? Adrienne didn't think so, especially since Catriona had her own money, and the two of them had no children together. Something didn't seem right in this whole picture. "There's an egg-shell thin line between love and hate," She reminded herself. But as much as she wanted to disapprove of her, to disapprove of everything she stood for, there was something likeable, something almost familiar about Catriona Kirby. Some kind of innocence or inner strength or touch of integrity that she seemed to be holding onto, trying to bring it to the surface in an indescribable way. "Love. Sometimes I think it's the most devastating disease there is in the human race." Andrew came to mind, but Adrienne whisked all thoughts of him away. There were reasons she had to stay. Not excuses. She wasn't like Catriona Kirby.

Chapter Four

***Psychopath** - Mental disorder of unknown origin often manifesting itself in the form of aggressively antisocial behavior. People with this disorder are said to operate without the benefit of conscience, experiencing no remorse or feelings of guilt. No genuine emotion. Psychopaths observe and mimic emotions in order to fit in. While easily frustrated, having problems with anger management, explosive and potentially dangerous to others, psychopaths are often charming and attractive, and find it easy to disguise themselves. Deviant from all social norms, psychopaths are true aliens filtered in among the human race.*

***Treatment** - Attempted treatment and/or counseling and/or treatment with drugs, unsuccessful*

***Cure** - No known cure.*

***Cure Success Rate** 0%*

Dr. Galen Kirby unlocked the back door to his one-doctor clinic. He liked coming in through the back so no one would know he was there until the nurses and receptionist arrived later. Inside the narrow back entrance were two small windows covered with slatted blinds, effectively shutting out the light. Black bars like those found in jails secured the windows. He felt more secure knowing the bars were there. The doctor turned on the lights as he walked down the dingy, brown hall to his office. These few minutes alone in the morning were important to him. He needed time to think, to move into his doctor mode without interruption. A new issue of the American Medical Association Journal lay on a table in the hallway. Mildred always left the newest issue there for a few days, removing it, usually untouched by the doctor, before she left for the weekend. This morning though, the cover, a handsome young doctor and the word "chemistry" in large print caught Dr. Kirby's eye. He picked the magazine up and pulled it close to his face, staring. A flashback to another day and time; a memory. A cold grin made its way across his face and the pupils of his eyes narrowed to reptile-like points as he recalled the chemistry course he'd made a D in at Louisiana State University. He thought about the final exam that would decide his fate, the exam he knew for sure he'd failed; a failure that would dismiss him from medical school. The grin left his face, replaced with a look of cold satisfaction as he remembered the fire in the chemistry department office that had destroyed the semester's grades for all 150 medical students. Then, the dean's decision that there was not time to create another final, that all students who had a passing grade in the professor's grade book, even if it was a D, would earn the chemistry credits needed to go on with their medical degree.

Galen came back to the moment feeling pleased with him self, and laid the medical journal back on the table.

Galen slipped off his jacket and put on a light blue doctor's smock, the costume he wore when he was at the office, and looking down at his feet, inspected the black, Wal-Mart tennis shoes that should have been thrown out long ago. In his mid sixties now, it took him longer to organize his morning activities, to think through his location, to think through the series of behaviors that would be expected of him this day. Dr. Galen Kirby was the perfect textbook case of a psychopath, but in this small, mostly illiterate Louisiana parish, no one had read the textbook. Those who could have and should have known avoided knowing any more about him than necessary since, after all, he was the only doctor left in town. Now, Dr. Kirby took a deep breath, his face tilted toward the ceiling, and then breathed out, dropping his chin to his chest, ignoring the musty, rank smell of the building that came partially from its age, partially from the Louisiana humidity that never seemed to go away, and partially from the fact that he wouldn't allow fragrant cleansers or even a candle to freshen the place. He liked it cool and damp and earthy, and he didn't worry about whether or not the office's atmosphere would affect his business since there was no place else for his clientele, mostly welfare patients and prisoners, to go. Dr. Kirby looked in the oval mirror in the bathroom to be sure his brown hair, splotched here and there with touches of gray, was in place, but avoided looking into his own dark eyes.

At the front desk where appointments were made, Dr. Kirby opened the appointment book to the day's date. It was a few minutes after nine; the staff would be arriving by 9:30. The first appointment was due in at 10:00. He scanned the book:

Jerry Smith (remove stitches in arm)

Margaret Fairchild (ingrown toenail)

Cecilia Adams (prenatal checkup – two month pregnancy)

"Cecilia Adams," he thought out loud. "One of the few professional families left in town. Father's a lawyer, mother plays tennis. Husband's studying to be a dentist," he smiled, pleased that she was coming to see him instead of driving into Monroe to a larger clinic. "Should be a nice baby. Good genes."

James Johnson (physical for high school athletics)

Consuella Morales (possible pregnancy).

He stopped. "Fifth child," he mumbled. "All born in Mexico. Can't take care of the ones they have. She sells homemade tamales. He's a migrant farm laborer. Live in an RV park outside of town. Don't even speak English. Weak, dead-end genes." Anger, the only emotion he felt on a regular basis, smoldered just below the surface. "How dare these people pro-create." He was livid as he pulled Consuella Morale's chart. No allergies to medications, no previous stillbirths. He'd have to think carefully before planning the loss of this one.He took a deep breath and exhaled slowly to try to calm himself. Looking again at the appointment book, he saw there were six prisoners from the detention center scheduled for the afternoon. They'd be escorted by the Sheriff, Johnny Johnson, and his deputy, Harold, a man who could barely read and write, so ignorant the sheriff's office was the only place he could get a job. The prisoners' appointments would mean looking at swollen joints and sore muscles, listening to complaints about headaches and sore throats and upset stomachs…and writing prescriptions. If it were up to the doctor, he'd give them all one final, fatal shot. There were lots of ways to do it; an overdose of caffeine in one giant shot was the easiest. A massive heart attack within minutes. If anyone ever did question the doctor's reports, they'd be looking for drugs, not caffeine.

And there were many other drugs that no one in this area of Louisiana would know anything about or be able to identify in any way. Like the Haitian Zombie powder made from a toxin in puffer fish created by a kind of bacteria Dr. Kirby had himself been carefully experimenting with over the last few years. A powder so deadly that even a milligram mixed in the right solution could cause death within hours. There was a fine line between using the powder as a pain killer that works by blocking the flow of sodium into and out of most nerves creating a sense of euphoria and well-being and eliminating pain, and stepping across the line so that the same toxin, mixed a little differently, would very slowly cause the person to become completely paralyzed and unable to communicate in any way. A condition that is deathlike, but not quite. One more step across the line, a pinhead more of the powder, and death within hours. Haitian Zombie powder. He liked the sound of it. As a matter of fact, he liked it so much he kept a few puffer fish in his aquarium at home. Pain killer and deadly poison contained within a little fish. The most potent poison known to mankind, a poison that throughout the literature and even in the penal code of Haiti was called the poison that can bring on "near death," and he owned six of the creatures. They were under his control. Life or death, it was up to him. These strange fish, each one containing enough of the toxin to create some six hundred deadly doses, or a couple of thousand zombies.

Galen hated to touch the prisoners, to be in the same room with them, to breathe the same air. He washed his hands until they were nearly raw once the prisoners left. But he and Sheriff Johnson had a good thing going; the prescriptions were a major source of income for them both.

"The doctor must tolerate the situation," he said out loud. He looked up as Toni, the head nurse, unlocked the front door and came in, followed by Iris, the receptionist, and Mildred, the second nurse.

"Good morning, Doctor," they chimed.

Nodding his head, Galen Kirby turned away and walked back to his office, looking at his feet as he shuffled along. The first of today's appointments would be arriving soon. He must focus. He must focus.

Chapter Five

Adrienne drove toward home, wondering what kind of mood Andrew would be in when she got there. Her morning meeting with Catriona Kirby had left her with much research to do. She'd spent the entire afternoon at the main library on 18th street in Monroe looking at microchips of old newspapers from all over the state, starting with two days ago and the obituary on Susanne Jasper. The short, two-paragraph article, as Adrienne had hoped, showed a picture of the young woman. Dark hair, overweight, dark eyes, a crooked face, a woman so unusually plain it was hard to imagine her attracting attention from any man. She wasn't smiling. The article confirmed what Catriona told her. Susanne Jasper had been found dead by police when her only neighbor, an elderly woman, reported that she hadn't seen her for a couple of days even though her car was outside in the driveway. The lady had knocked on the door and got no response. The police reported no signs of foul play associated with the 39-year old woman's death. No one knew where Susanne Jasper came from, and no one had been seen coming and going, not friends, not family. She had not lived there long. It seemed Susanne Jasper just kept to herself. The coroner's report declared the death to be of natural causes. No sign of drugs or alcohol. No signs of foul play.

Adrienne cringed as she thought about who the coroner was that had done the autopsy and signed the death certificate. Susanne's ex-lover, the doctor, a family practitioner, possibly the father of her child. What kind of man could do an autopsy on a woman who was the mother of his child? A woman with whom he'd had a lengthy affair? She answered her own question.

"Only a psychopath," she thought out loud. "Is it possible to live with a psychopath for ten years and not know?" She thought about all the betrayals Catriona Kirby had been willing to live with while pretending to be blind, pushing them aside like they didn't matter. A life so shallow, so surface, so empty. It just didn't fit. Trying to get her mind off the case, she called Andrew on one of the four phones she kept for different purposes in her car.

"What do you want for supper? I'll pick something up on my way home. I have to go back out tonight to finish some details on a case."

Andrew sighed and said it didn't matter.

"I'll bring chicken," she hung up the phone.

There was an emptiness in Andrew's voice, a kind of resignation Adrienne didn't want to think about. He'd put himself in this position; there was nothing she could do about it, nothing she wanted to do about it. Still, she was very aware that the worst kind of loneliness is the kind you feel when someone who refuses to know you is there. She thought about her own life, her own loneliness. She and Andrew had planned a life together; they'd molded a future, or at least she'd believed they had. She thought about the complete, whole companionship she'd dreamed of all her adult life. All had become a nightmare. Now, she chose to live in the silence of the dark, both on the job and at home, staying away from Andrew as much as possible. She rarely slept well even on good nights, hating to give in to sleep. Sleep brought disturbed messages to the fore, the old reoccurring dreams, the remorse and old regrets, the overpowering sense of dread and futility. The fierce, desperate void in her life. The flashbacks in her dreams that went from adult to child, back to adult again. The little girl afraid to fall asleep for fear her stepfather would enter her room; the adult afraid to sleep for fear of violence from an abusive husband, the man who killed her only child. The terrifying coldness of the empty crib. The burning dread with Andrew, knowing he was seeing another woman. Back and forth, back and forth. Too many night tortures to sleep as long as it could be avoided. Now, she allowed her mind to roam back to the gentleness and comfort in Mel's voice and the invitation to join him at Cottonport this evening, one of the popular coffeehouses in Antique Alley, just a few blocks from Reward Yourself, where she'd met with Catriona.

"No reason not to go. Just finishing up a few details on his case." She tried to shut all other thoughts out of her mind, but a vision of Mel's twinkling, blue eyes and infectious, childlike smile tore at the enormous hole in her heart. It seemed like a long time until nine o'clock.

Chapter Six

Cottonport Coffeehouse was an old friend, a familiar place to the city of Monroe's literary crowd. Fiction writers, performing art lovers, poets, musicians were regular participants in the weekly open-mics held there. It was a comfortably casual place with its chipped, green paint and windows outlined with white Christmas lights. A neon guitar, blue and red, hung in the center of one of the two windows and gave out a lightening flash from time to time. The waiter and waitress both wore blue jeans with holes in the knees, and displayed body piercing in an array of places, nose, eyebrows, tongues, who knows where else. The owner, a man now in his forties, had never quite made it in the college scene or the literary field, so he brought what he thought of as the best of both worlds to him.

It was not unusual for Professor Mel Brighton to be found at Cottonport. A professor of literature at The University of Louisiana at Monroe, he loved the sound of congas accompanying the poetry of new, young writers, some of them his own students. He took pleasure in watching, and in hearing them come alive with their own creations, eaten up with an excitement they'd never before experienced, an excitement that Professor Mel knew could be found only in the power of the spoken word. On other nights, different bands or small groups of musicians played while the crowd talked, often about the hypocrisy of world governments and the idiocy of various organized religions, and as they debated the solutions to everything from war to taxes. Smoking was allowed, and some smoked openly more than just cigarettes.

Professor Mel had always loved what he thought of as the perfect climate for the cultural exchange of ideas, but the last few years, Cottonport had become more than a pass-time or a deviation from the routine, or a cultural release. It had become his home away from home. What used to be a once a week thing had become an almost nightly escape. It was much more comfortable and accommodating than evenings at home with his wife who was often working on a third or fourth bourbon and coke by the time he arrived. Sitting now at one of the small sidewalk tables just outside the door where the fresh night air was free of the thick cigarette smoke, he pushed his slightly long, dark hair with its traces of silver back from his forehead, and ran his hand down the back of his neck, resting it there for a moment. He could feel the tension in the muscles, and he began to roll his head from side to side, massaging away the day's stiffness. Lifting a glass of Merlot, he caught sight of his middle-aged reflection in the glass, and paused.

How did I get to this point in life so quickly? He thought. *And why am I, after success in so many areas, so disillusioned now?* The brightness of his enormous blue eyes dulled with confusion. Professor Mel had always been a passionate man. Passionate about art in every form. Passionate about life. But somehow, the passion had drifted away. He looked at the chilly, night sky, alive with stars and pulled at his charcoal gray, tweed, sports jacket with its black, leather patches on the elbows. He thought back to a time when each constellation held a special, sacred meaning for him. And the circle of the moon, too, shone down tonight, but even it had lost its magic. He sighed and checked his watch, eight forty-five, and wondered if Adrienne would come. He felt a silent dread that she wouldn't. If not, he'd never be able to call her again. His invitation this evening would have overstepped the bounds of their friendship and would force their relationship to be held at bay in that limbo state that can go no where, not forward or backward, but must just hang uncomfortable in the air. He worried, too, about the course of the evening if she did come. What could he say that wouldn't sound planned? He didn't know how he'd explain his need to see her without seeming to assume too much. After all, she was a married woman. She'd told him enough about Andrew to know that the marriage was a dismal failure, but that didn't change the fact that she still lived with him, still had a commitment to him. Mel wasn't sure of his own motive for asking Adrienne to come tonight, but he couldn't get her turquoise eyes, her laugh, her tender, comforting words and the unconditional emotional support she'd given him through this personal nightmare out of his mind. He did know that after all these weeks of working together to uncover his wife's adultery, a very special bond had been created, and, whatever games his heart and mind might be playing with one another, he couldn't stand the idea of not seeing Adrienne again. It felt like letting her go, and a force he didn't understand somewhere deep within him was pulling at him, telling him not to let that happen.

Feeling the weight of his thoughts deepening, his mind shifted to the wife he'd hired Adrienne to follow. During the first few years of his marriage he'd believed that being a "good" husband would in time eliminate Camille's drinking problem. He studied all the research on alcoholism and convinced her to get counseling, and to go to meetings that he attended with her. While she'd had extended periods of sobriety, she had never completely quit drinking. Two attempts at pregnancy had ended in miscarriage, and through the years, respect and communication had been drastically reduced, almost to the point of non-existence. He'd hidden the truth from himself with his studies, with doctorate school. He'd kept all friends at a comfortable distance with his charm and intellect, and his desire to protect his wife's reputation, or at least that's what he'd told himself all those years. His dedication to the relationship had become numb, had turned to duty, but he'd never considered divorce. In his circle of friends, you just didn't do that. Now, it was just a matter of time until her promiscuity would be common knowledge. He lived with the fear that it might already be, that maybe his colleagues had known all along. Mel sighed and motioned to the waiter for another glass of wine.

Adrienne turned south at the foot of the Lea Joyner Bridge and onto Trenton Street. Two blocks down on her left was the giant bell that signaled the entrance to Antique Alley. She drove slowly past Trenton Street Café and its confusion of cars pulling in and out, one of the only busy places other than the coffeehouses in Antique Alley this time of evening. Delia Borden's Art Gallery and Yoga Studio, a place Adrienne had spent many evenings trying to learn to relax back in the days immediately following Andrew's accident, was on her right. She stopped the car for a moment and looked at the giant ferns hanging above the studio's doorway, and the smoke of the incense burning on holders beneath the window.

"Breathe deeply," she whispered to herself. "Hold. Exhale slowly."

She turned the corner to the right. One more turn and she'd be on Natchitoches Street. Cottonport sat in the middle of that block. Deciding to drive around the block to get her courage up, Adrienne wondered if she'd be able to see Mel through the window. Most likely he wouldn't be looking out, but even if he was, she had several vehicles, a necessary thing in her line of work, and Mel had never seen the car she was driving tonight. She wondered if somehow her subconscious had arranged that intentionally so that she could check things out and still run if she decided to do so. It dawned on her that she and Mel had met dozens of times while she was working on his case.

This time should feel no different. But it was different. The whole context of their relationship had changed. She felt a surge of emotion as she drove around the corner.

"Oh, God," the words jumped from Adrienne's mouth. There he was, Mel, sitting outside at a sidewalk table. "What now?" She dare not speed up too quickly or he might see her. He was only a few feet away. She'd just keep moving along in the line of cars and ease her way down the street. She turned the corner onto Wood Street, and pulled into a parking space, out of sight of Cottonport and Mel. She put the car in park and lay her head on the steering wheel, her heart pounding. The radio purred the words to a song, "Crashing into love. How high can you go before it all comes crashing down?" Adrienne slammed her palm into the button, silencing the music. *What am I doing?* She asked herself. *These feelings I have, these feelings I'm hoping he has, are all wrong. Nothing good can come from something wrong.* She looked into her own eyes in the rearview mirror. *Maybe he feels nothing at all. Maybe it is just a gesture of appreciation for all my hard work. He's like that.* "A gentleman and a scholar," she smirked. "What a fool I am if that's the case." Adrienne didn't know which would be more confusing, Mel's invitation turning out to be merely an act of kindness and appreciation, or discovering that he, too, had feelings beyond their working relationship. Was he simply trying to find that comfort zone between love and friendship? She looked at her watch. Nine fifteen. If she was going to do it, it'd have to be now. She backed out of the parking lot and made her way around the block and over to Natchitoches Street. She edged down the road toward Cottonport…. The sidewalk table was empty; Mel was gone.

"Shit!" Adrienne yelled. "What kind of crazy am I?" She sighed, shaking her head, disgusted with her own lack of courage. "Private investigator with no guts." She turned into a parking space a few cars down, turned off the engine, and sat in the dark. Now, whatever his reason, it was all over. Even the possibility of friendship, anything more than the working relationship of the past, was over. *If his invitation was to romance, I've slammed the door in his face. If it was to thank me, he'll know I thought it to be more, and will think I didn't come because I'm not interested, that he was just another job.* She was overwhelmed with her own childish behavior that led her to drive around the block instead of just meeting Mel and having a glass of wine with a friend, seeing from their meeting where he intended for it to go. There she was, running again from the ghosts that haunt her.

I'm so stupid. Now, nothing can remain. Mel's just another job that's ended. She sat silently in the dark, staring out the window. Lighting a cigarette and rolling the window part way down for a little air, Adrienne could hear the sound of jazz coming from Cottonport. She felt herself being pulled into a deep, hopeless pit of quicksand. *Doomed to sorrow,* she thought, as she blew the cigarette smoke into the night air. *Oh well. Can't go home this early. Might as well go in and have a glass of wine. No hurry to be anywhere for anyone* now. She locked her car and wove her way down the sidewalk and in through the crowd while all around her, fireflies flashed their warning signals in the cool night air. She just wanted to find a small, out of the way table, but instead, bumped into something solid and unyielding.

"Mel," she gasped. "I thought you were gone."

"Thought, or were hoping?" Mel questioned, looking hard into her eyes.

"I was late. I thought…"

"Forget it," Mel said, wrapping his arm around her and guiding her back through the crowd. "Let's get out of here."

On the sidewalk outside, in the shadow of the building next door, Mel stopped again and turned toward Adrienne. Placing his hands on both her shoulders, he looked into her eyes again, those eyes that could not lie, that had never been able to lie to him even through all the months of working on his case. "Adrienne," he said, and nothing more. Adrienne felt her heart crashing with no way to escape, no desire to escape, no matter what the rest of the words to the song had warned. "Let's get out of here," Mel said again, wrapping his arm around her and hurriedly escorting her to his car.

Chapter Seven

Azalea bushes and Myrtle trees lined the sidewalk that curved around to the front of the gray, concrete Bayou Parish courthouse building in Destiny, their sweet aroma distracting attention from the building's ugliness. Adrienne walked up the steps to the lobby and pushed the button to the third floor. As the elevator door closed behind her, she tried to focus on her new client, Catriona Kirby, and the beginning of the investigation into Dr. Galen Kirby's past, but Mel kept monopolizing her thoughts.

"We don't choose who we fall in love with, Adrienne. Some things just happen," he'd whispered as he looked ever so carefully into her eyes.

After leaving Cottonport, they'd driven a few blocks to Harvey's Smokeless Dance Hall on Wood Street. Adrienne hadn't had a cigarette the whole night, something she thought she'd never be able to do in a lifetime, and it hadn't even bothered her. Her every thought had been caught up in Mel. They drank wine and talked, and he held her close while overhead fans with wooden blades stirred the air, and sawdust-covered hardwood floors comforted their feet as they waltzed to the music of Celine Dion, " Have you ever touched the sky?" The words floated through the air. Adrienne's heart feasted on the excitement until she'd felt like it would burst. She'd been totally captured in the grip of the intensity she'd seen accumulating in Mel's eyes, in the magnitude of the emotion. That conflict of her heart and her intellect at odds with one another had created the sense of unease she'd felt before, but now it had all shifted as she gave her emotions over to the flames burning in her heart. The moment was electric. There could no longer be any doubt about what was between them. The unease now came from the simple realization that they were both married to others, that they had no right to the emotions that were rapidly escalating. And in Adrienne's mind was another fleeting thought about those obstacles within her that caused her to doubt her ability to accept the affection of a man, a doubt that had never been resolved. Within the depths of her she knew that she had kept any strong feelings for Andrew at a distance, an arm's length away, even before the accident. She wondered now if it was possible, if she was capable of depth and true intimacy in a relationship. A flame of pain flashed through her mind. Deep and true love had always seemed just outside her reach. Could Mel bring reality to the word love? Was he its literal definition for her? How could she possibly define him when she couldn't even begin to define herself?

Last night's regular nightmare of abuse and distrust had transformed itself this time into a warning from the mythical tale of Daedalus and Icarus that she was playing with fire. In the dream, she was made of wax and was flying closer and closer to the sun, laying the ground work for her own melt-down, her own emotional destruction. She could hear Daedalus yelling the warning, but she flew faster and faster, shutting him out.

This morning, Adrienne's thoughts were disjointed, the world shifting and wavering around her. She needed to concentrate on her new case, the healer-murder suspect, but she could literally feel Mel's crisp, blue eyes staring into hers with unrelenting determination. The elevator creaked open. Adrienne took a deep breath and headed for the front desk at the Public Records Office.

"Good morning," the records clerk, Mary, smiled. "What brings you to Destiny so early this morning" Or should I say, who brings you?"

"Working on a case, Mary," Adrienne chided. "You know I can't give you names."

"I know." Mary opened the half-door, allowing Adrienne to enter. "But it's fun to try to guess. Help yourself." She smiled and went back to her desk.

Adrienne headed for the tables where enormous 2' x 2' books of alphabetized public records lay chained to the tables holding them. Marriage records, divorce records, birth records, death certificates, tax liens, mortgages showing what property a person owned or had ever owned, and warrants for arrests as well as any charges ever filed against a person in this parish. All were a matter of public record. A person's personal and business life, all summarized on a few pages of paper in these enormous books available for all the world to see if they chose to do so.

"K - - Kirby," she mumbled to herself. "Should be about book four or five. " She lifted book four and rolled it over to its back. It ended with the I's. "K's, about the middle of book five." She rolled book four back over to its original position and pulled up a chair. Opening book five to its approximate middle, she located the K's. "Kirby, Galen, M.D." Adrienne glanced down, then turned the page. She turned another, then another and another.

"Warrant for arrest - destruction of property. Malicious mischief. Twelve forty-five A.M. Neighbor witnessed Dr. Kirby slitting tires on car of ex-girlfriend, Sheila Martin, as it sat in her driveway. Warrant served. Plea of guilty. Fine: $250. Restraining order signed by judge on behalf of plaintiff."

"Divorce petition filed. Defendant, Dr. Galen Kirby; Plaintiff, Natalie J. Kirby. Petition sites adultery and emotional abuse."

So the little wife found out when the warrant was served on behalf of the ex-girlfriend. I'll bet that was an interesting evening at the Kirby household. Adrienne wrote down the dates, the charges, and the outcomes. The divorce was granted on behalf of the plaintiff, Natalie Kirby, and a court date was set to settle community property and child support arrangements and alimony. *Catriona was right about him being a womanizer all his life,* Adrienne reminded herself. She looked further down the page.

"Subpoena to appear in court. Charge, cruelty to animals. Cynthia Stanton states that Dr. Kirby captured pet cats of at least two neighbors, including hers, and performed surgery on them to practice surgery he would be performing on patients the following week. Both cats died. Additional charges filed by owner of the second cat." Adrienne's mouth fell open. *What kind of sick is this?* She thought. "Defendant states he believed the cats to be strays. Ethics charges filed with the state board of medical examiners, as ordered by the judge."

"Connie Hanover, assault and battery. Plaintiff states that about eleven p.m. the night of June 14, she had pulled up to a four-way stop sign. Dr. Kirby pulled up beside her, left his vehicle running, opened her door and forced her out of her car. Plaintiff claims that Dr. Kirby struck her in the face with his hand, pulled her to the shoulder of the road and shoved her into the ditch, stating that he was taking her car. An unidentified short, heavy-set black man remained in Dr. Kirby's vehicle. Plaintiff states that she had been dating Dr. Kirby for over a year, and that the car was a gift from him. Defendant states that he had loaned the vehicle in question to Connie Hanover to use during the time they were dating, and had requested its return repeatedly since the break up of the relationship so that he could give it to his new girl friend. No injuries to the plaintiff were found, and there were no eye-witnesses. The man in Dr. Kirby's car remains unidentified. The vehicle is registered in the name of the defendant. Charges dismissed."

Adrienne read on, taking notes as fast as she could write.

"Lane Hall, on behalf of his minor son, plaintiff, Joseph Hall, alleges that Dr. Galen Kirby performed an illegal abortion on his own daughter, Megan Kirby, a minor, and that said minor plaintiff, Joseph Hall, is the father of the unborn child. Lane Hall declares that he and his wife have suffered emotional harm at the loss of their grandchild, and that their minor son has suffered great emotional duress due to the loss of his child, and has been deprived the opportunity to participate in making a decision about the life of the fetus. Said minor plaintiff states that the abortion was performed without his previous knowledge and against the will of the mother, Dr. Kirby's daughter, Megan Kirby.

"Defendant, Galen Kirby, testifies that his daughter suffered from health problems at the time of the pregnancy, and that the pregnancy was a threat to her life. The court finds that under Louisiana law, the life of the mother takes priority. While the performing of an abortion on his own daughter is unethical, it is not illegal. Charges dismissed. Court ordered letter explaining unethical behavior of Dr. Galen Kirby to the State Medical Board. Court asks board to require mental evaluation of Dr. Kirby.

"State psychiatrist/psychologist and M.D., Dr. Linn Robins, appeared before the Board with the outcome of Dr. Galen Kirby's mental evaluation. Report concludes that Dr. Kirby suffers from a mental condition called, "anti-social personality disorder," better known as psychopathic or sociopathic disorder, and that due to this condition, Dr. Kirby will continue to act out in an unacceptable fashion, including violence and other destructive behaviors, when he feels he is not in full control of any given situation. Dr. Robins stated that the psychopathic mind is not governed by conscience, and since it feels no guilt, it experiences no remorse, and therefore does not learn from past mistakes. Action taken: State Board of Medical Examiners explains to Dr. Kirby in official letter that further action against him is not being taken at this time due to the fact that he is the only doctor remaining in the parish."

"My God," Adrienne gulped. *He killed his own unborn grandchild. He performed an abortion on his own daughter. If he could do that, the question of how he could perform an autopsy on an ex-girlfriend becomes moot. I thought I'd heard it all, but this guy is a real psycho.* She turned the page.

"Lane Hall on behalf of his minor son, plaintiff, Joseph Hall, alleges that Dr. Galen Kirby, an adult, attacked Joseph Hall, a minor, in the parking lot of said plaintiff's school as he was leaving for the day, and that Dr. Kirby choked the plaintiff until he was unconscious. Ambulance was called; Joseph Hall was hospitalized overnight. Warrant issued and served for Dr. Kirby. Bond set at $25,000. Defendant bonded out two hours after arrest."

Adrienne finished her notes and tossed her pen down on the table. Sitting back in her chair, she rubbed her eyes with both hands. She dared not even whisper what she was thinking.

They've known he's a psychopath for the last 25 years, and they've done nothing to stop him, she thought. *All they've done is cover up his behavior. Sheriff Johnny Johnson knows all this stuff. The paperwork, every bit of it, goes through his office.* Adrienne flipped through more pages, adding to her notes. Ethics charges

--- allowing children in the operating room creating unsafe and unsanitary conditions

--- wrong medications given to pregnant woman resulting in stillborn fetus; father
threatens Dr.'s life.

--- tubes of at least two women patients tied without patients' previous knowledge and/or
permission

--- prescribed penicillin to an allergic patient, resulting in hemorrage.

--- refusal to respond to medical emergency at nursing home when called by nurse on
duty concerning one of his patients. Patient dies.

--- report filed by prisoner that he did not receive medication from prescription written by
Dr. Kirby. Same prisoner beaten by guard. Guard says prisoner attempted escape.

--- Prisoner suffers broken ankle; taken back to Dr. Kirby. Dr. Kirby sends prisoner away with crutches. Refuses to write prescription for painkiller. After
release, prisoner goes to doctor in Monroe. Physician states that ankle should have
been set. Will now require surgery and steel pins.

--- Dr. Galen Kirby's office ransacked. Large amounts of prescription drugs stolen,
prisoners, patients records destroyed—windows broken out, attempt to start office fire—Dr. Kirby out of town.

Adrienne slammed the giant book shut and sat in silence. She realized that she was witnessing the outcome of the workings of a true psychopathic mind. *Catriona Kirby is too intelligent to be this ignorant,* she thought. Adrienne wondered what she'd gotten herself into. How much of all this did Catriona know, and why was she hiding the truth? If there was this much general mess about the man, Adrienne couldn't help but wonder what wasn't on the records. Was this some kind of scam, and if so, what was Catriona really hoping to accomplish by hiring her? Did she really think Adrienne wouldn't find out?

Chapter Eight

Sheriff Johnson stood, flashlight in hand, looking down while his deputy, Harold, ran yellow "do not cross" tape around a fifty foot area where the bodies had been found. The old, black man who'd found them still looked pale and shaken.

"Hard to believe a blue gum that dark could turn that white," the sheriff mumbled to himself with some amusement. The old man had come up the levee to check his trout lines. He'd put them out right at dusk, so the killings had taken place sometime after dark. He hadn't seen any signs of anyone around, no car or truck, no one. He'd stumbled across the bodies and run as fast as he could to call the sheriff.

The sheriff was a hard man. Running a maximum- security prison for the last fifteen years, he'd seen violent death before. This one wasn't that much different, except that it appeared to be an execution. Not a robbery or a fight that got out of control. He understood how those things happened. He'd even killed two men himself when he'd walked right into the middle of a liquor store robbery. The guy at the counter held a 38. The guy at the beer cooler was packing a nine- millimeter. He'd seen the gun in the man's hand as he started to turn at the sound of the old cowbell over the door. The sheriff hadn't even bothered to identify himself as he drew his own gun and fired two shots into the man's chest. The colt 45 he carried wasn't as accurate as the nine millimeter, but the hollow point slugs he used were devastating, and at such close range, he couldn't miss. Those two slugs had lifted the robber clean over the counter, spattering blood all over the cigarettes and Playboy magazine rack as they exited the man's back. The robber at the beer cooler fired as he bolted for the back door. The nine millimeter rounds had gone wide, shattering the glass in the door, the store front window, and the windshield in the clerk's car. Sheriff Johnson had calmly dropped his giant frame into a crouched firing stance like he'd been taught at the academy, and returned fire. His first round took the man low in the right side of his back, spinning him around. The second hit him in the pit of the stomach, taking out four vertebrae as it exited his back. The third shot had taken most of the left side of the robber's face before embedding itself in the metal door of the cooler. The whole town – all two thousand people – had called him a hero, a man's man. Right at the moment, he was a very worried man.

Sheriff Johnson looked more carefully at the two bodies. Their hands were tied behind their backs with plastic ties. They'd been forced to their knees and each one methodically shot once in the back of the head. They'd been hit by a pro all right. But for what reasons, and who did the pro work for? The two convicts Sheriff Johnson kept around for deals like this had called him earlier in the night to report that the sheriff's deal had gone off without a hitch. Both of the men were hard and experienced. Jimmy, the older and the bigger of the two at 6'3" and 270lbs, blonde hair, empty blue eyes had gotten his ass in a ringer when the sheriff busted him with three kilos of uncut coke a few years ago. The sheriff had quickly come to realize that he needed a man like Jimmy. Tyrone's luck had run out a few months later when the sheriff found what had turned out to be a half ounce of rocked up crack stashed in three or four places around his house. Sheriff Johnson made both men the same deal. Work for him and the charges would be dropped. A nice place to live and a large paycheck every so often for any services rendered. Jimmy had jumped at the offer. Tyrone, a black man a little over 6 feet tall, with long, ropy muscles and the lean build and natural suspicion of the black born and raised in the south, had taken a little longer to accept the sheriff's offer. But now, twelve years later, both men had proven they could be trusted to handle the job. They'd even grown to like the idea that they were "in" with the sheriff. It gave them a feeling of power both were too ignorant and too dangerous to gain any other way. Tonight they'd met their connection at a truck stop south of town just before the I-20 highway intercepts with highway 167. Cops watched for crap like this once you got on I-20, but Jimmy and Tyrone had never seen them set up at the tuck stop. They sold the drugs for fifty grand and split. No big deal. They called in on time with no problem. No, the sheriff knew they hadn't done the killings. They liked the status quo. He'd take his deputy, Harold, and go have a talk with him after he left here; see what he thought might of happened, see if he'd heard any rumors around town that he needed to know about. See if he recognized the two dead men as easily as he did, but for now, that would have to wait.

Sheriff Johnson looked at Harold who had the I.Q. of a brick. Even stupidity had its uses. Harold never questioned orders. He was as strong as an ox, and was more loyal than even old Bo, his blue tick hound. Sheriff Johnson knew he'd need that as he watched the brand new Ford truck with the show bumper and the shiny, thousand dollar winch come to a sliding stop.

"The doctor has arrived," he mumbled as a lanky, sixty-two year old man got out of the truck. The sheriff didn't kid himself. He knew that if people ever found out half the stuff he'd been involved in, even been in charge of getting done over the years, they'd call him an evil man and lock his ass up so fast even Dale Ernhart would be stunned. He was also aware that if people new half the things he knew about the doctor, the real stuff, not the petty things they put down on public record, the stuff no one knew but him, they'd hang the slimy son of a bitch and call him a fallen angel, which brought him back to his current problem. How much did the doctor know? Was it him who hired the pro to kill the two guys? The sheriff wouldn't put it past him, if he'd found out how he'd changed their little arrangement over the last year. There'd been no direct indications from the doctor that he knew anything, but the sheriff had noticed that he was hanging around more, showing up at some rather inconvenient times.

Sheriff Johnson smiled as he thought about how the doctor had approached him with his offer so long ago. It had seemed so simple then. It was simple, and he needed the money. He'd actually made it easy for the doc. All the sheriff had to do was arrange for the doctor to get the medical contract for the prisoners, and he'd do the rest for a nice little slice of the pie. The sheriff had been more than happy to agree. After all, at the time, he wasn't doing anything wrong himself outside of pocketing a few funds on the side once in a while, or beating up a mouthy prisoner just for the hell of it. It had all been done by the doctor. He was the one who picked the inmates. He was the one who changed their medical files and wrote the prescriptions for medicine the prisoners never got, and added the extra medical care that he billed the federal government for. A white collar crime. A fine, maybe a little jail time in some minimum security Hotel Hilton even if they got a conviction, which he doubted would ever have a chance of happening. Not in this corrupt little town. Too many people had secrets to hide, and the sheriff knew most of them.

But that all changed one afternoon when one of the inmates who'd been taken to the doc's office tried to get the doctor to give him painkillers. He'd refused. The inmate accused him of letting the prisoners suffer, using them to milk the system by writing prescriptions, collecting the drugs and selling them illegally at a higher price. The prisoner was dangerously close to the truth. That particular dumb-ass inmate hadn't known it then, but he'd sealed his own fate. The sheriff had been at home working on his deer rifle when the doctor called.

"That junkie you brought me today knows the game," the doctor warned.

"There ain't no way, Doc. He's just guessing. Trying to get you mad to see what you'll say. No way he knows anything."

"We can't take a chance. He talks around the prison, gets enough people upset. Too much talk's not a good thing."

"I'll handle it." The sheriff needed Dr. Kirby to stay calm. He knew firsthand the doctor's tendency to lose control if he got agitated, to do things he didn't even remember doing later. "I'll come by in an hour for a dose. Don't want you seen at the prison on off hours. I'll call you later to come out and confirm the cause of death." He hung up the phone. Sometimes babysitting the doctor was the hardest part of all, but he needed him for a couple more years. By next election year, the way he'd rearranged things behind the scene, he'd have enough money put back to just slide on out of town and disappear over the horizon to a nice, quiet beach somewhere. That is as long as the doctor didn't find out about the sheriff's new, accelerated cut. Dr. Kirby's mental abilities were sliding fast. No telling when he'd slip and end them both up in prison. But the sheriff was making more than double the profit now, and five times the cut the doctor thought he was getting. He'd had to go outside the community to work out the details, but that was all right. Until now. Somebody had found out about the sheriff's new help, and now they were dead.

Chapter Nine

Adrienne was sitting in a back booth at Reward Yourself a few minutes after 10 o'clock a.m. She wanted to be there before Catriona Kirby arrived at 10:30. Wanted to observe her as she entered the dimly lit coffeehouse; to consider her from a whole different perspective. Catriona had lied to her, and Adrienne wasn't sure why, but she intended to find out. She watched now as Catriona stood in the doorway, her featureless silhouette pursued by the bright sun which fought to invade the security of their rendezvous. It took a moment for Catriona's eyes to adjust to the change of the light, and so she stood looking around the room until she finally focused on Adrienne in the booth near the back. Adrienne watched the woman make her way toward her. Catriona Kirby was too attractive, too intelligent, too organized to live the way she claimed to have lived all these years for the reasons she'd given Adrienne. She even had her own money. Adrienne's private investigator nose smelled something out of line. She didn't know what Catriona Kirby was up to yet, but it was only a matter of time. She'd work the puzzle for awhile, but she needed more of the pieces to fit.

"Hello, Adrienne," Catriona said as she smoothed her linen skirt and sat down.

"You're sure you weren't followed?" Adrienne asked.

"Yes. I told Galen I was driving to Shreveport to shop. That's something I do often; there's no reason for him to suspect anything. I brought your money. Cash." She handed an envelope filled with $100 bills to Adrienne. Adrienne put the envelope in her purse without opening it, alongside the handgun she'd decided not to take out just yet.

"Did you bring pictures of Dr. Kirby?"

"Yes. A close up of his face, and one of him standing in the yard." She handed the photographs to Adrienne.

45

"I want you to take this phone and keep it in your purse," Adrienne explained. "Have it with you at all times. Use it when you call me. There's no way for scanners to intercept on this line. Write down the phone number I'm giving you and use it when you want to get in touch with me, not my office phone. Do you understand?"

"Yes, of course." Catriona put the number in a safe place in her purse.

"Why did you lie to me?" Adrienne looked directly into Catriona's eyes.

"Lie?" Catriona questioned.

"Yes, lie. Dr Kirby has a twenty year long record of violence and unethical behavior in your town and you've been married to him for ten of those years. You have to know some of this stuff. Why didn't you just tell me and save me a day of trashing through court house records on my time and your dollar?"

Catriona looked serious, but not surprised. "I was afraid you'd think I was a gold-digger and that you wouldn't take my case. Some of the things he's done are so bazaar, I was afraid you wouldn't believe me."

"You were probably right," Adrienne snapped. "So what's to stop me from walking away from your case right now?"

"I thought if you met me, got to know me a little, you'd see that I need help, that you'd believe me when I tell you my life's in danger. That my husband may be a killer. I believe he killed those two women, but there's something else too. I'm not sure what. There are just too many bits and pieces that don't fit. And besides," she smiled, "you put the money in your purse."

"Well you'd better start telling me some of those bits and pieces, and this time, tell the truth." Adrienne was in no mood for any more games, especially ones that put her on the heels of a possible killer.

"I believe Galen's tied into some kind of a drug scam. A couple of weeks ago, I got a phone call from a prisoner. He had to talk quietly. He was on someone's stolen cell phone, and the prisoner who'd stolen it had only given him two minutes to talk. He told me he thought my husband was going to have him killed. That he'd found out about a scam to cheat the federal government out of funds for medications, that he's selling them on the illegal market. He said Galen and the sheriff are both in on it, and probably others too. He said I'm the only person he could take a chance on trusting, that if anyone finds out what he knows, he's a dead man. All this about the same time I heard of Susanne Jasper's death. I didn't know which way to turn. The prisoner wanted me to try to get the Attorney General's Office to investigate. He thought they'd believe it, coming from me instead of an inmate. Three days after the phone call, that prisoner was found dead, supposedly of natural causes. I was afraid if I told you all of this at the beginning you'd not want to get involved. I checked up on you, Adrienne. You're the best in the state. You're not tied in with anyone in Bayou Parish. You're the only one I could possibly turn to. Please Adrienne, I need your help There's no telling who else may die, maybe even me."

"Did you call the Attorney General's Office?"

"Yes, but I didn't tell them who I was. I was afraid they'd think it was just a marital vendetta of some sort if they knew I was his wife, or worse case scenario, that someone in that office might possibly be involved. They told me there'd been suspicions about Dr. Kirby for years, ones they had never been able to substantiate. That invariably, the information given to them would just be some little bit of gossip or circumstantial evidence based on nothing that could be proven. They even told me he'd been named as the person who'd hired the kidnapping and disappearance of another doctor in town before I married him, but the man showed up later in Florida and refused to name anyone or press any charges in his sudden out of state move. The Attorney General's Office said that until someone has concrete evidence against Galen, there's nothing they can do. We've got to find that concrete evidence, Adrienne, before he can do any more damage, or take any more lives. And I can't leave him until we find it. I'd never again be safe."

"We? Adrienne questioned.

"I want to help. I need to be in on things, to know what's going on. My life may be at stake here too. I can't just sit idly by and watch. I can help you know who to talk to and where to look for information. Then, someday, when he's behind bars, I can get my life back."

Adrienne listened and was impressed with the determination in Catriona's voice. "Just for the record, why did you marry Galen Kirby? I'm assuming you didn't know some of the garbage about him at that time, including the fact that the court had already declared him a psychopath, but you must have known some of it. That much crap can't be kept a total secret in a town that size."

"You're right, I had heard some of it, but I wasn't from Bayou Parish. I didn't know anyone well, and people aren't going to just come up to you and tell you that the man you're engaged to marry, a doctor in the community, is a psychopath. Looking back now, it seems as foolish to me as I'm sure it must to you. It's all the same old clichés. I thought I could make him happy. I thought I could be happy. I didn't need his money, my family has its own money. His other wife had been dependent and needy, totally different from me. People like me are expected to marry within a certain class, Adrienne, and he's a doctor. My family had chosen for me a successful attorney who I found disgusting. I was thirty five years old. Galen was the better choice of the two. Time and youth were passing me by. He was wonderful to me when we were dating. He took me dancing and for moonlit walks and on evening boat rides. He had explanations for the failure of his marriage. Long hours away from home night after night, working in the emergency room while he was establishing his career and building a practice. How do you explain matters of the heart, Adrienne? All the lies we're willing to tell ourselves in the name of love? How do you make something rational out of an emotion that's totally irrational? Love has nothing to do with common sense. Perfectly intelligent people make fools of themselves on a regular basis when they think they're in love. They do things they wouldn't even consider under any other circumstances. I rationalized his past completely away, believed what I wanted to believe, until the shadows began to creep in one at a time, and I could no longer ignore them."

Adrienne listened and understood more than she wanted to admit exactly what Catriona was saying. She thought about the distance between common sense and impulse, the poison that slowly drips into ones' character a drop at a time, making their whole life a contradiction in terms. She wondered how it's possible that humans can be so foreign to themselves. But she knew Catriona had given all the explanation that could be given, that human beings create their own emotional fiction.

"We've got to begin with what we're pretty sure to be true, and fill in the picture from there," Adrienne broke the mood. "The stuff I found on record at the court house is horrible. We could use it in the courtroom to destroy his character if this was just a divorce case, but there's no evidence there that could be used in a court of law to prove anything beyond that. You're sure he was having an affair with Susanne Jasper?"

"Yes, I'm positive."

"And now she's dead. We'll start with that. You said he sent her gifts. How do you know?"

"There was a teenage girl working at the flower shop when I went in one day to pick out a potted plant for a friend. The girl recognized me as Galen's wife and asked me how I had enjoyed the "rose a day for 30 days," a special promotion they were running. She'd been there the day Galen placed the order, but evidently only overheard that part of it. I was shocked, but kept my calm. I told her it was wonderful, but that I was pretty sure I'd only received

29, and I needed to look at the date on the order. She got it for me. I memorized the date and address where the flowers had been sent."

"Why wouldn't he be afraid to place an order like that from a local flower shop if it wasn't going to you?"

"In his profession things like that happen all the time. Doctors send flowers and gifts to other doctors' offices, or to representatives of drug companies. They send special presents to patients who've been with them for long periods of time. No one would question him anyway. I told you, adultery is laughed at. My husband has the reputation of being a womanizer."

"Where would he keep his personal records that might have receipts for things like the flowers?"

"I'm not sure. He has a safe in our bedroom closet, but I have the combination. I don't think he'd keep anything like that at home."

"Not likely. What about at his clinic?"

"Maybe. I have a key to the clinic itself, but I don't have a key to his personal office within the clinic."

"Is there a second key anywhere that you know of?"

"No. Not even the nurses have keys to his private office."

"Would you recognize the key from the others on his key ring?"

"Maybe. I think so."

Adrienne thought for a moment. "I want you to find a time when you can take the key to his office without him missing it and get another one made. Then put the original back exactly where it was. Don't forget to pay attention to which keys are beside it on his key ring. Some people have the order of their keys memorized, and that wouldn't surprise me coming from him. Psychopaths are very good at memorizing detail. That's how they get through life, often without being discovered."

"His office is closed on Thursdays," Catriona said. "He usually plays golf."

"This is Wednesday. Is there any reason he might go to his office tomorrow instead of to the golf course."

"None that I know of. He looks forward to golf on Thursdays. He's good at it. It gives him an opportunity to be the center of attention."

"So it should be safe to take his key tonight and return it tomorrow night?"

"Probably as safe as it will ever be." Catriona didn't sound too sure of herself.

"You said you want to help. Are you up to it?"

"I do want to help. What do I do if I get caught?"

"Don't get caught."

Catriona shivered. Splashes of color appeared on her face. Adrienne wondered what personal storms she might already have weathered through her marriage to this man.

"A lot of my cases involve child custody," Adrienne started again. "Proving a parent unfit in some way, or negligent. Social Services in Monroe likes me. They supervise all the smaller offices in the outlying parishes including where Susanne Jasper's body and her baby were found. I have a few connections. While you're taking care of the key tomorrow, I'll pay them a visit. See what I can find out about the child. Whether or not any relatives ever showed up to claim him." Adrienne looked at Catriona with concern. "Just be calm," she encouraged. "Don't act any different in any way. Keep it simple. Get the key tonight while he's showering. Send him off with a smile to the golf course tomorrow. Get the duplicate key made someplace where the people won't recognize you, even if that means driving to another town. Put the new key on your key ring. When he gets in the shower Thursday night, put his key back exactly where it came from. Can you do that?"

"Yes. I can." Catriona looked at Adrienne. "When shall we meet again?"

"Let's shoot for tomorrow afternoon after you've got the key made. You call me when you've got it done and we'll decide on when and where. Don't won't to develop a pattern. That's how investigators find answers. They look for patterns." She left Catriona sitting silently by herself at the table.

Chapter Ten

Galen Kirby stood up from the recliner where he'd been sitting reading the evening newspaper and started turning out lights. That was Catriona's cue to make ready for bed. He never asked her if she was ready to end the day, or if she was staying up to read, or if she was tired. He just turned off lights and expected her to follow. It had always been that way. He was not comfortable with anything out of his routine, and so he needed total control of everything that went on around him. Even Catriona's bedtime. She lay down the book she was reading and headed for the bedroom.

"You seem out of sorts this evening, Catriona," he commented. "Antsy. Is something wrong?"

"No, she smiled. Probably just too much caffeine today." She told herself she had to be calm. She turned down the covers on the king size bed and turned on the bedroom television while Galen began to empty his pockets on the dresser. She forced herself not to look. She heard the rattle of keys as he laid them down next to pocket change and chapstick. He pulled pajamas out of a drawer and went into the bathroom. Catriona heard the water start and the shower door close. She turned the volume on the television up just a tiny bit, and looked at the dresser top. The keys were there. She looked into the bathroom and saw Galen's shadow through the steamy shower door. It had to be now. Carefully, her shaking hands picked up the keys while she prayed they'd make no noise. She eliminated in her mind the ones she knew belonged to other things. His truck, her car, the house, the storage shed, the clinic. There were three keys left. Two were small and gold. She didn't think it could be either of them. The other one looked only slightly different from the clinic key. She prayed it was the one. She removed it and lay the others back down, just as he turned the water off. Catriona stuffed the key in the side pocket of her purse and opened the drawer to pull out her pajamas just as the shower door opened. Galen stood drying himself as she went into the bathroom and turned the water on to fill the tub.

Catriona wished she could just go under water and hide. There was no reason for Galen to look at his keys tonight, no need whatsoever. Still, she was not used to this kind of thing. She knew that taking the key was the right thing to do, that it had to be done, but she was afraid, nonetheless. She wondered how Adrienne could live each day this way. Wondered what it was that drove her? There must be some nightmare hidden deep inside her that made all the drama worthwhile. Catriona wondered, too, why some small part of her own conscience was trying to convince her now that she'd done something wrong? Everything inside her seemed somehow off center. Not just this night. From the very beginning of her relationship with Galen she'd had to close off parts of herself, had to section off pieces of her own need and pretend they didn't exist. Through the years, she had mastered the fine art of carefully controlled response when he was around. She'd been silently aware of his potential for wrath that lay just below the surface almost from the beginning. Her existence with him had always been like walking on egg-shells. She'd been alone with her thoughts, confused, like an insecure child, but recognizing that her attempt at love was a dismal failure. Suddenly now, she realized Galen was talking to someone. She'd been so caught up in her thoughts she hadn't heard the phone ring.

"I'm on my way," she heard him say.

The sudden pounding in her head and heart was so loud she was afraid he could hear it.

"I have to go," he said to her as he picked his keys up from the dresser. "They've found two bodies on the levee south of town."

Chapter Eleven

"Hello, Doc," Sheriff Johnson said as Galen Kirby got out of his truck and walked toward him and Deputy Harold. The sheriff tried to read something in the walk of the doctor since he knew there'd be nothing but ice in his eyes, to feel out whether the doctor recognized the dead men, and whether or not he might know anything about their deaths.

"Sheriff." Dr. Kirby replied. "What've we got here?"

"Both shot once in the back of the head, execution style. Both tied up. No sign of a struggle. Might have been meeting someone here, but there's no vehicle. Only found one set of tire tracks. Ground's still soft from last week's rain. Grass is tall enough to see the tracks pretty clear. Drove right on up to the levee. Guess they might have been tied up somewhere else and brought here, but the shooting definitely took place here. Shells are still on the ground. Need you to give me the approximate time of death. There'll have to be autopsies." The sheriff looked at the doctor for a sign of any kind of recognition. There was none.

Dr. Galen Kirby stood over the two bodies and stared, expressionless, but inside he was very pleased. The two dead men were dealers who'd picked up a lot of money's worth of stash that should have belonged to him. The killings had gone well. Little Frankie Dalton, named so appropriately by his father after one of the historical Dalton brother criminals, had made it look like a professional job, and the timing was just right. The doctor was at home with his wife when it took place.

"Take the crime scene pictures and call the ambulance sheriff," Dr. Kirby said. "Have them take the bodies to the morgue. I'll begin the autopsies first thing in the morning."

"There goes your golf game," the sheriff smiled.

Dr. Kirby got in his truck and drove back down the levee and into town to his clinic. He pulled into the small parking lot in back and shut off the engine. The parking lot was always dark at night with the shadows of giant tree branches hanging low, but it was a cloudy night, and so it was extra dark without even a hint of moonlight. He sat waiting. Out of the shadows, a figure made its way toward him. It was Little Frankie Dalton. Only a little over five feet tall and weighing in at a hundred pounds, Frankie had the chip on his shoulder often seen on small men, the kind of chip that makes them think they have to fist-fight the world to prove they're men. But Frankie didn't mind swaying the fight a little more in his favor by using a baseball bat or a club, or a gun if necessary to prove his point. As a matter of fact, he'd only been out of prison for a couple of years on a manslaughter charge. Everyone knew he'd run over the guy in cold blood, but his brothers and the barkeeper were the only eye witnesses, and the barkeeper sure didn't want to get on the wrong side of the Dalton brothers. He had a family to think about. Add to that the fact that Frankie's father raised all three of his sons to think that the criminal mind was something to be proud of, and the fact that all four men had violent tempers, and Frankie Dalton added up to be one cocky and dangerous son of a bitch.

The doctor got out of his truck and unlocked the back door to the clinic so they could go inside. He didn't want to take a chance they might be seen together.

"Any problems?" he asked the man standing before him who seemed dangerously edgy.

"None," Frankie replied. "What took you so long to get here?"

"You got the stash?" The doctor asked him.

"Right here." He reached inside his oversized coat and pulled out two large plastic bags filled with several thousand pills, a drug supplier's dream come true, but he didn't hand the bags to the doctor. "Where's my money?"

"In the safe in my office," Dr. Kirby said as he walked toward the door to his office. "It's bagged up and waiting for you."

"Then let's get this thing over with," Frankie was squirming with nerves, "and get out of here." Suddenly, headlights flashed through the glass on the clinic's back door.

"Who's that?" Frankie whispered.

"I don't know, but you've got to get out of here before anyone sees you with me," Dr. Kirby replied. "Give me the drugs and go. Call me tomorrow."

"Not a chance, Doc. These bags aren't leaving my hands until I get my money."

"Just go. Hurry up. It looks like it's the sheriff." Dr. Kirby shuffled Frankie Dalton out the front door just as the sheriff came up the back hall.

"Sheriff?" the doctor said walking toward him.

"Everything all right in here, Doc? Sheriff Johnson eyed him suspiciously.

"Just leaving a note for my staff that I'll be performing the autopsies tomorrow and Friday mornings. They'll have to reschedule my Friday appointments.... I'm through. Let's get some rest. Tomorrow's going to be a busy day." Dr. Kirby led the way to the back and out the door, locking it behind him. He took a quick glance around to be sure there was no sign of Little Frankie Dalton.

Chapter Twelve

"Adrienne Hargrove," Adrienne said as she reached for her secure phone that lay ringing on the night stand beside the bed. She'd been on the edge of sleep, but nothing she'd miss. Andrew shifted beside her.

"Adrienne, this is Catriona Kirby."

Adrienne shook the fuzziness from her head. "Did you get the key?" She was puzzled that Catriona could talk this time of night.

"Yes," Catriona answered. "But right after I put it in my purse, Galen got a phone call. Two bodies were found on the levee south of town. He's the coroner. He had to go. Of course he took his key ring. If he needs anything out of his personal office! Adrienne, what am I going to do?" Catriona Kirby sounded scared to death.

"Listen to me, Catriona. Don't panic. The levee outside of town is a long way from his office. Does he keep a doctor's bag at home?"

"Yes. He took it with him."

"Then chances are he won't go to his office tonight. No matter what, you can't act like there's anything wrong. Do what you usually do when he's called out on this kind of thing. What will he expect you to be doing when he gets back home?"

"I go to bed. He doesn't like to talk about his work. I'm usually asleep when he gets home."

"Good. Do exactly that. It's better that he not see you in the light anyway, or talk to you. If he looks at you, he'll be able to read you. Psychopaths are gifted at that, and your voice is shaking like a leaf. Go to bed. Go to sleep, or at least pretend to be asleep. There's nothing you can do tonight. Tomorrow, go on with the plan exactly the way we discussed it. Get the key made, then call me so we can meet and figure out what to do next. Tomorrow evening you'll put the original key back on his key ring.

"Adrienne, I'm so frightened."

"Catriona, you've got to stay calm. You can do this. He's not going to go to the clinic. Even if he does, even if he tries to open his private office door, there's no reason he would connect the missing key with you. You are calling me on the secure phone I gave you?"

"Yes."

"All right. Get hold of yourself. Since he's gone, I want you to do one more thing tonight. Get a couple of hairs from his brush and bring them to me tomorrow. Put them in a plastic bag. I can get his DNA run from them. We'll need that if we're going to find out more about his link to the child of the dead woman. Can you do that?"

"Yes." Catriona seemed calmer.

"Do it, then go to bed. All these years, you've been telling yourself it will be alright. Tell yourself one more time, Catriona. You've been scared before. You've been confused before. You made it through those times all by yourself. This time, you have me. You can do it."

"I can do it. I will do it....Adrienne?"

"Yes?"

"You really are there for me. I've never had that before, not even as a child. Thank you."

"Tomorrow." Adrienne hung up the phone and lay staring at the ceiling. Something inside of her told her to relax, that it really would be alright, but she knew there were no guarantees. She'd have to take the same advice she'd given to Catriona and wait to see what tomorrow would bring. A chill went down her spine as she thought of Catriona lying there in bed pretending to be asleep, waiting for her psychopathic husband to come home and lay down beside her, a man capable of all sorts of horrendous things, maybe even cold-blooded murder. A part of Adrienne's mind fought to help her understand what it is in a woman's heart that can keep her so off-center. At the same time, another part of her fought to pry her loose from any kind of reasoning. After, all, Andrew lay next to her sleeping just like they were a couple who still had a dream left.

Chapter Thirteen

Adrienne lit her second cigarette of the morning as she drove toward the Child Protective Service office in Monroe. She hadn't heard from Catriona yet this morning, but since there was no way of knowing for sure where Dr. Kirby would be spending his day, Adrienne was afraid to try to reach her. The phone plugged into the dashboard, not the secure phone she'd told Catriona to use, rang, and she reached for it.

"Hello," she said without identifying herself, since the traffic was too thick to take her eyes off the road long enough to check the number on the caller I.D.

"Good morning," said Mel's deep and inviting voice, bringing an instant smile to Adrienne's face. "Where are you?"

"I'm almost to Monroe," Adrienne replied. "Working on a case."

"That's my girl. Doing her part to rid the world of evil," he chuckled. "Meet me for lunch? I have something to tell you."

"I'm not sure how long it will take me on this job," she said, knowing there wasn't any way she was going to say no to the invitation.

"I can make it anytime between eleven and two," Mel replied. "I'll be in my office working on a poetry unit. Call me there when you're freed up. Enoch's on Louisville OK?"

"Sure," Adrienne said. "I'll call you." She hung up the phone, settled in her mind that she didn't want to listen to that little nagging in her conscience. Not when it came to Mel. She pulled into the Child Protective Service parking lot and put her cigarette out as she walked in the front door.

"May I help you?" A stuffy looking receptionist wearing a flowery, cotton house-dress asked.

"I'm here to see Julia Anderson," Adrienne answered.

"You're name please."

"Adrienne Hargrove."

"One moment." Adrienne glanced around the office. The walls were covered with bright-colored pictures of animals and playgrounds, things children would like, and she thought about the last time she was here, a couple of years ago, in the middle of the night. She'd been a part of an investigation to break up a drug trafficking ring. The police officers had returned fire on a car, killing its passengers, all but one, an eight month old infant huddled up on a blanket on the floor of the back seat, screaming. They'd asked Adrienne to deliver the child to Julia at this same office. Adrienne held and comforted the child while Julia located baby bottles and went for formula, then returned and spent the next four hours, until three in the morning, trying to find a foster home that had room for one more neglected and endangered child. The child had been about the same age and size as Adrienne's own little boy when he died at the hands of his father. Adrienne and Julia had worked together before, but not on anything quite so horrifying. It was a miracle the child hadn't been killed. Adrienne brought herself back to the moment before her heart had a chance to get too heavy.

Julia Anderson came up the hallway. "Adrienne Hargrove! How are you?" She smiled as she gave Adrienne a friendly hug. "What brings you here?"

"I need to talk to you about a case, privately." She glanced toward the receptionist who seemed to be concentrating on everything except her own business.

"Sure. Let's go in my office. Long time, no see." She led Adrienne down the hall. "Would you like a cup of coffee?"

"Black," Adrienne smiled.

"Two black coffees, please," Julia called over her shoulder to the receptionist.

Adrienne looked around the small but comfortable office while they waited for the coffee. Julia's framed credentials, Dr. Julia Anderson, Ph.D, Sociology, Louisiana State University hung on the wall behind her desk along with several awards. Adrienne seated herself in the leather chair across from Julia, who sat behind her desk.

"A young woman was found dead in her home a couple of weeks ago in Bayou Parish," Adrienne started. "Neighbors got worried and called the police."

"Yes, a sad case," Julia shook her head. "A young mother, all alone." She remembered the case.

"I need to know what became of the child. Your office supervises all the smaller parishes. I was pretty sure you'd know," Adrienne told her as the receptionist entered with two steaming mugs of coffee on a yellow porcelain tray. They waited for her to leave.

"Is this a police investigation? You know I can't release that information, Adrienne, unless it's an official police investigation."

"Not yet, but it will become one if what I expect is true. Look. There's a chance the baby's mother was murdered by someone in a powerful position. I'm not sure about the motive yet. All I need to know from you is whether the child's father has come forward to claim him."

"No, he has not. I can tell you that much," Julia volunteered.

"What about grandparents on either side?"

"No. No one. It's my understanding that no one even claimed the woman's body. The child is in a foster home. I know how personally involved you get when there's a child involved, Adrienne, but I can't tell you anymore than that. Actually, I don't know anymore than that. It's not my case."

"But you know where the child is?"

"I can't tell you that."

"I know, I know," Andrienne answered. "I need you to visit the foster home and bring me a hair from the baby's head."

"A hair! What forever for?" Julia was surprised.

"I may know who the father is. The hair will help me prove it. I just need you to think of a reason to visit the baby and bring me a hair you know for sure is his. If I find out the man I'm investigating is the father. Well, it's possible the death may have been a murder. It's even possible that the child could be in danger."

Julia looked hard at Adrienne. "She died of natural causes. There was an autopsy."

Adrienne held her composure. She didn't feel comfortable telling Julia the rest of the story, at least not yet. "There may have been foul play. If so, either eliminating the man or proving him to be the father will clear up a few things."

"Who hired you?"

Adrienne hesitated. "The man's wife. That's all I can say. You know, client confidentiality and all."

Julia Anderson took a deep breath. "You have reason to believe the child's in danger?"

"It's possible."

"I'll see what I can do." Julia was concerned. "I'll call you tomorrow."

"Thanks Julia," Adrienne said as she gave the woman a quick hug and left.

In her car, Adrienne wasn't sure what to do next. She was beginning to worry about Catriona and why she hadn't called. She was going to need that key to Galen's office, probably more than once, and Adrienne sure hoped nothing had gone wrong. She looked at her watch. It was only 9:30, but she felt sure Catriona would have called by now if Dr. Kirby had gone to the golf course. On the other hand, it was entirely possible that Catriona was waiting to call until she got the key made and returned home. Adrienne wondered, too, about the two dead men on the levee, and whether or not Dr. Kirby would be performing autopsies. After all, he was the coroner. Maybe he wouldn't go to the golf course at all today. She would just have to wait for Catriona to call. In the meantime, she'd try to find out who owned the house Susanne Jasper was living in when she died, and start checking out the circumstances around the death of the first woman five years ago, Drusilla Gifford.

* * *

It was eleven o'clock. Adrienne decided to call Mel for lunch. Still no word from Catriona, but Adrienne had found some interesting information in the public records. The house Susanne Jasper was living in when she died was being handled by a small property management company, but was privately owned. They'd refused to tell her who owned the house, but there was dead silence at the other end of the phone when she asked them if it was owned by Dr. Galen Kirby. They replied that they were not free to divulge that information. Adrienne decided not to push it, and knew she needed to cover her tracks. She didn't want them calling Dr. Kirby, so she gave them a false name and told them she was interested in living in the area where the house was located, and she wasn't aware of any other vacancies like that one, not in town, but not too far out in the country either. She didn't know Dr. Kirby, but someone had told her he owned the house. They seemed satisfied with the lie, but one never knew about these things for sure. None of this was exactly new information, but it was information that confirmed again Dr. Kirby's personal connection to the dead woman, Susanne Jasper.

"Dr. Mel Brighton," a very professorly voice said.

"Well hello, Dr. Brighton," Adrienne teased. "I'm hungry. How about you?"

Mel's eyes lit up. "It'll take me fifteen minutes to get to Enoch's. Where are you?" he asked.

"I'm coming from down town. Just turned onto Desiard heading toward Louisville. I'll get us a table."

"I'm on my way," he hung up the phone.

How nice it was to hear a voice that was glad to be talking to her. How easy it was for them to be together, to talk and be comfortable with one another, just like they had a history together. Adrienne guessed that in a way they did. She certainly knew more about his personal life than she'd ever known about either of her husbands before she married them. It'd been so very long since she'd experienced a man looking forward to just sitting with her and talking, someone who greeted her with a smile. Had it ever been that way with Andrew? She couldn't remember. A phone was ringing. Adrienne shook loose from her thoughts and reached for the secure phone lying on the passenger seat.

"Adrienne Hargrove," she answered.

"Adrienne, it's Catriona," an excited voice replied.

"Is everything alright?" Adrienne asked. "I've been worried. What's going on?"

"I'm sorry I couldn't call sooner. I did as you suggested last night. Galen was gone several hours. I pretended to be asleep when he got home. He came to bed without a word and stuffed the usual line of pillows between us. He doesn't like to be touched when he's sleeping."

Cold like a snake, Adrienne thought.

"He didn't go to the golf course today. He has to start the autopsies on the two men they found dead last night. He didn't leave for the Medical Examiners Office until ten o'clock. I just finished getting the key made. So far, everything seems alright."

"That's good news," Adrienne reassured. "What happens at his office on Thursday's while he's gone?" she asked.

"The nurses come in at the regular time and takes care of patients who don't need to be seen by the doctor, but they close for the day at noon."

"So there'll be no one there this afternoon?"

"No."

"Where exactly will Dr. Kirby be this afternoon? Do you know?"

"He started the autopsies this morning. He expects them to last two days, maybe longer."

"So he'll be at the hospital?"

"Yes. They take bodies to the parish morgue at the Medical Examiner's Office, and that's a part of our community hospital."

"OK. That's good. I want you to meet me at Wendy's at two o'clock. We'll leave your car there, and drive back to the clinic. We don't want your car to be seen. I'll drop you off in the back, and park across the street so I can watch while you're inside." Adrienne explained.

"Me inside?" Catriona gasped.

"It's legal for you to be in his office, Catriona. It's not for me. Be sure you have your cell phone with you when you go in so I can call you if there should be any kind of activity on the street, anyone who even looks like they're interested in Dr. Kirby's office. We'll talk about what you need to look for while we're driving there. Right now, I have to meet another client. I'll see you at two o'clock at Wendy's." Adrienne hung up the phone and pulled into the parking lot at Enoch's Irish Pub. *Meeting a client.* She smiled as Mel pulled up beside her. *Just a little white lie.*

Adrienne didn't usually drink alcohol during the middle of the day, and never beer at all, but she loved the thick, dark Guinness they served at Enoch's. Mel ordered sweet tea and laughed as Adrienne wiped the creamy Guinness foam from her top lip. The beer was bitter and rich, and she loved the way it felt going down. The owner's wife, Teri, handed them both a menu. Mel opened his. Adrienne handed hers back unopened. She always ordered the same thing when she came to Enoch's.

"I'll have the best sandwich in the world," she said, her mouth already watering. "The Park Avenue, please." She wondered at her own lighthearted mood.

The Park Avenue was made with giant Portobello mushrooms on rye bread, Swiss cheese, avocado, sprouts, tomato, and some kind of special sauce that Adrienne had never quite been able to figure out when she tried to make the sandwich at home. The only place to get a perfect Park Avenue was at Enoch's, and the only way to eat it was with a Guinness.

"It's our most popular sandwich," Teri smiled.

Adrienne watched Mel as he ordered a roast beef po'boy with extra gravy, and realized how good she felt sitting here across the table from him. Even with all the rottenness that came into her daily life as an investigator, just being in the same room with Mel, well, it made a lot of things seem worthwhile. Mel seemed excited. Adrienne remembered he had something important to tell her.

"What's up?" She questioned him as Teri walked away from the table.

"I did it," he answered with a sound of satisfaction in his voice.

"Did what?"

"Signed the divorce papers. My lawyer is filing them as we speak. Camille will be served sometime next week."

Adrienne stared into Mel's eyes. "Are you absolutely sure that's what you really want, Mel, after all the years you've invested in your marriage?"

"That's exactly why I am sure, Adrienne. After all these years, it still feels like an uphill battle. Until you came along, I'd resigned myself to the idea that's all it would ever be, all it ever could be. When I hired you, I wanted to know the truth, but I didn't really believe there was any way out. Now, for the first time in my life there's someone on my side, someone who sees my strengths and weaknesses and still cares."

Adrienne thought, *what weaknesses? He's as perfect as any human being could ever be.*

"Someone who accepts me as I am. When I'm with you, Adrienne, I feel hopeful again. All these years with Camille, I've felt like a failure. She needs me to be made of iron, but no matter how hard I've tried, in her eyes I'm weak. I'm a failure because she's a failure. With you, well, we're strong for each other."

Adrienne listened while chaos began to plague her mind. Mel's divorce was supposed to be for the right reasons, adultery, alcohol abuse, failed attempts at reconciliation, not so he could be with her! Sure she thought about being with Mel, had dreamed about it, was probably in love with him, but she'd always known that she couldn't act on those feelings, that there was a line she couldn't cross, wouldn't cross.

"Mel, there's still Andrew," she reminded him now, "and he needs me."

"He uses you." Mel leaned close. "Exactly what Camille's always done. Used me for her own selfish purposes. Andrew doesn't love you. You don't smother the heart out of someone you love. You don't extinguish their very soul so they can't even find a piece of themselves. You don't scream and yell and order and demand. I've heard him in the background when you and I were talking on the phone. He's made you feel guilty for his accident like Camille's blamed me for her drinking and depression, and he's used that guilt to push out of your mind his adultery and emotional abuse. Answer one question." Mel's voice was serious and concerned, and it seemed as if he'd thought out how he would answer Adrienne's objections so well he almost sounded like he was reading from a script. "If there'd been no accident, would you still be married to Andrew? Do you really think he'd have straightened up and been faithful and loving to you?"

Adrienne stared in shock. Mel was right. She'd made the decision to get a divorce before the accident happened. That's why she'd been following Andrew, to catch him with his girlfriend and tell him to his face. It had been so long now, she'd locked away the idea that she could ever have a loving relationship. Even the possibility seemed remote. She'd resigned herself that this was her fate. Still in her heart, Adrienne knew Mel was right. If Andrew was well and they were still married, he'd still be cheating. The woman she'd caught him with hadn't been the first one. Nothing in his heart had changed. She looked at Mel, but couldn't speak.

"I'm going to tell Camille this evening that I'm moving into the Marriott by the Mall until I have time to look for an apartment. I want you to do what you were on your way to do before the accident, Adrienne. It's time to have a real life, to have a chance at real love. I want you to get a divorce."

Teri stood at the table holding plates heaped with giant sandwiches. "I sure hope you're really hungry," she teased. "More sweet tea? She asked Mel.

"Please.:

"Another Guinness?"

"Yes, and make it a pint this time," Adrienne stared at Mel. He was planning a future for the two of them. He had such a circle of confidence about him. *What a delicious dream*, she thought, *the two of us together, in love.*

Chapter Fourteen

Adrienne was waiting for Catriona at Wendy's when she pulled up.

"Are you ready?" she asked.

"This is so scary," Catriona replied.

"There will only be a few crucial moments, Catriona. You'll be in and out before you know it. In the meantime, if anyone should see you going in or coming out of the clinic, is there a legitimate reason you might be there, one that Dr. Kirby would understand if someone mentioned it to him?"

Catriona thought for a minute. "I take Celebrex for mild arthritis pain. He gives me samples. A couple of times when I've run out, I've stopped in when he wasn't there to pick them up, but the nurses were there both times."

"That's OK. If anyone should ever ask for any reason, that's why you were there. OK?"

"OK." Catriona realized why Adrienne was considered the best in the business. She paid attention to every detail.

"Now, let's talk about things to look for, and remember, the things we need won't be kept where the nurses or anyone else might have easy access to them. They'll be someplace out of the way. Look for receipts related to gifts. Any kind of papers connected to houses or rental property; there's reason to believe he owns the house Susanne Jasper was living in. Anything that even hints at Susanne Jasper or the other woman, Drusilla Gifford. Hospital documents of any kind for hospitals in Monroe or any place else that might seem suspicious. Car payments other than the ones you're familiar with. Any kind of documents that could possibly be connected to the child. Any and all information you find that deals with the prisoners in any way, illnesses, prescriptions, deaths, everything. Anything that mentions law enforcement agents, including the sheriff. Every suspicious document of any kind. Anything that just doesn't quite seem to fit with what you know about your husband and his work, and your life together. Where's the copy machine from his office?"

"It's in the room behind the nurses' station."

"Make copies quickly and put the originals back just as you found them. Don't make a mistake, Catriona. The proof is in the details; remember that."

They were almost to the clinic. Catriona's heart was racing. Adrienne apologized in advance as she cracked a window and lit a cigarette to calm her own nerves. She drove by the clinic once and circled the block. A flashback to the other evening when she met Mel at Cottonport. She'd circled the block to check things out. In that couple of minutes while she was out of sight, he'd disappeared inside. *Amazing what I almost missed by circling the block.*

"Nothing out of the ordinary," she said to Catriona. "Do you have your keys ready?"

"Yes."

"Your cell phone's in your pocket?"

"Yes."

"If I should see anyone coming anywhere near the clinic, I'll call you in plenty of time. Grab some Celebrex, go out the back door and over to the post office right behind the clinic just like nothing's wrong. Take a deep breath, Catriona, and remember why you're doing this. You want to be safe from Dr. Galen Kirby, and you want to be free of him. Got it?"

"Got it." Catriona got out at the back of the clinic. Adrienne pulled quickly away and started around the block one more time, and then to the back to position herself where she'd have a clear view.

On the street behind the clinic, from the Auto Parts store, Little Frankie Dalton watched as Catriona unlocked the back door to the clinic and slipped quickly inside. He and the good doctor hadn't finished their deal last night, and Frankie was anxious to collect his money. He also didn't care to be hanging around Destiny with a thousand illegal pills in his pockets. *A man could get himself killed.* He smiled thinking about the two dead men on the levee, the ones he'd stolen the pills back from. The pills Sheriff Johnson had been carefully skimming off the top of Dr. Kirby's prescriptions. Dr. Kirby was meeting Little Frankie sometime late this afternoon to pay him off. No exact time. He didn't know when he'd be able to get away from the autopsy. Frankie was to watch until he saw him arrive, then come to the back door of the clinic.

Wonder what the doctor's little woman's doing here, Frankie was puzzled, but keenly interested. *No way he'd want her here today, knowing what's about to go down. Why the hell's she going in the back door .Why's she not driving her own car? Who the hell was that woman that dropped her off?*

Inside the clinic, Catriona headed straight for the nurses' station and the Celebrex samples. She grabbed a dozen packets and shoved them in her pocket. Next, she went to the door of Galen's office, unlocked it and went inside. *Thank God the key works.* She turned on the desk lamp and headed for the file cabinet. She looked first under the J's for Jasper, but found nothing. She looked under R's for rental, and finding nothing there, looked under P for property. A copy of the deed for their home and papers for the clinic were the only things she found. She thumbed through file after file looking for anything that could possibly be connected in some way. Susanne Jasper, the child, or the house they'd been living in. She looked for any kind of medical records for prisoners that might have a connection to the illegal drug deals the prisoner had told her were going on when he asked for her help. Still nothing. Steadying her nerves, Catriona went back to the nurses' station and found the file for the prisoner who'd called her. Finally. At least it was something. She pulled his chart. It showed him as deceased. T*hey killed him.* Maybe it would say something about the cause of death. She made a Xerox copy, than returned the file to its place among the others. She went back to Galen's office and worked her way through his desk drawers. Nothing. Nothing.

It's all too organized, she thought. *There's something wrong with this picture.* Catriona stood facing the coat closet. *Maybe.* She opened the door. A couple of doctor's smocks hanging on one side, a change of clothes, a couple of pairs of shoes. Then, in the very back corner, a small, gray, two-drawer file cabinet. Hurriedly, Catriona tried each of the drawers. They were locked. There was no way her key was going to fit. She remembered the small, gold keys on his key ring. *Now what?* She went back to Galen's desk and found a sterling silver letter opener. She remembered seeing him unlock an old file cabinet at home where he'd stored some fishing lures with a similar letter opener. Down on her knees so she could see the lock better, she tried her luck, doing all she could to steady her hand. "Please, please," she whispered. POP. The lock sprung loose. Catriona pulled open the first drawer and found a gold mine. Receipts from the flower shop, deeds on several houses and property in other towns. Documents for the prisoners' medical care, and a handful of birth certificates. She looked quickly. She saw no birth certificates that belonged to Galen's children. Who did all these birth certificates belong to and why was he hiding them? Catriona ran to the copy machine and started to work as hurriedly as possible. She ran back to the closet and replaced the originals, she hoped, exactly as she had found them. She pulled open the second drawer. Money. A stack of papers, and a plastic bag full of money. The vibrator on Catriona's phone went off. She nearly jumped out of her skin.

"Now that's a pretty sight," a man's voice behind her taunted. Catriona screamed. "I don't think either one of us want to draw attention to the doctor's office, now do we?" Little Frankie Dalton asked, pointing his gun at Catriona's head. "Just hand me the money and I'll go on my way. The good doctor owes it to me, and by the way, he's meeting me here this afternoon. Could be here any minute now. Of course I'll have to pretend that I haven't been here and haven't seen anything, won't I. We wouldn't want him to know we've had this little meeting. Then he'll just have to pay me a second time, won't he? If he wants his drugs that is. I'm sure you're not going to mention to him that you ran into me while you were breaking into the file cabinet in his closet." Little Frankie smiled.

Catriona was frozen with fear. She stood motionless while Frankie Dalton gathered up the bag of money, never taking his eyes or the gun off of her, and made his way out the back door and out of sight. Catriona grabbed her phone that was still vibrating.

"Adrienne," she yelled into the receiver, remembering that Little Frankie said Dr. Kirby could be there any minute.

"Get out! Get out now!" Adrienne commanded.

Catriona looked back at the file cabinet drawers. Should she close them or leave them open? Hope it would take time for Galen to notice they'd been disturbed, or let it appear to have been a robbery? How could she possibly know? The whole world seemed to be holding its breath.

"GET OUT NOW! Adrienne yelled in her ear.

Catriona slammed the drawers shut and closed the closet door. She left the office door open behind her. Galen was coming after the money. He'd have to go in his office. If the door was closed, he'd look for his key, and she still had it. She turned out the light and quickly exited through the back door. Once outside, she lifted her head, and walked nonchalantly with the papers tucked under her arm across the street and over to the post office. She stood waiting in the lobby, trying not to tremble. Adrienne got out of the car and followed her into the post office foyer just as Frankie Dalton disappeared into his car sitting at the Auto Parts store, and Dr Kirby pulled up in the clinic parking lot behind the building, in plain view of them all.

Little Frankie gave the doctor a couple of minutes inside, then got out of his car again and put the bag of money in the trunk under the spare tire. He walked across the street and knocked on the back door of the clinic. The doctor opened the door and Little Frankie slid in beside him.

* * *

"What happened?" Catriona whispered as she and Adrienne stood in the post office lobby watching and waiting out the rest of the scenario. "You were supposed to warn me." She was trembling.

"Come on, let's get out of here," Adrienne answered, thankful that at least Catriona got out before Dr. Kirby arrived. She and Catriona got in her car and headed back to Wendy's.

"By the time I drove around the block and found a parking place where I could see, a man was going in the back door of the clinic. Who was he? What did he want? Thank God you're alright."

"I've never seen him before," Catriona shivered as she talked, "but he had a gun. He said Galen owed him money. Adrienne, I found a file drawer full of money in a plastic bag. That man took it. He knew Galen was coming here this afternoon; he was here to meet him. He took the money and said we'd both have to pretend we knew nothing about it. He said it wouldn't hurt Galen to pay him twice for the pills, especially if he didn't know he was doing so."

A tangle of disconnected thoughts did somersaults in Adrienne's mind. She had to go back. She had to get a picture of the man as he came out the back door. She had to find out who he was. She slammed on her breaks and turned the car around, pushing the accelerator to the floor.

"Get in the back seat and get down on the floor," Adrienne ordered. Catriona didn't hesitate even slightly as she climbed over the seat and wrapped herself into a fetal position on the floor. Adrienne slowed down as she neared the clinic. She pulled in to the Dollar General and parked between two trucks where it would be harder for the strange man and the doctor to see her when they came out. She kept the engine running, pulled her high powered camera out of the console, and focused it for a close up of the strange little man's face even from a hundred feet away, if he and the doctor hadn't already left. She was in luck. The stranger was coming out the back door. She started the camera rolling and followed him all the way to his car. Dr. Kirby was still inside the clinic. Adrienne slumped down in her seat as the man backed his car out and headed her direction. "Stay down," she warned Catriona, and waited until Little Frankie was a block past the Dollar General before she pulled out of the parking lot, keeping herself behind two cars that were behind him. All she needed was the right angle to get a clear picture of the license tag on his car. Then it was child's play to get his name and address. Snap. Snap. Adrienne shot the pictures just as Little Frankie Dalton turned the corner onto a dead end street where Adrienne would have been a fool to follow.

"All's clear. You can get up now," Adrienne told Catriona. She lit a cigarette, took a deep drag, and headed back down the highway to Catriona's SUV.

Chapter Fifteen

Catriona pulled into the driveway of her house, quivering with fear. Thank God Galen wasn't home yet. She parked and nearly ran to get inside. She took a deep breath only after the door was closed behind her and her purse put away. She checked the messages on the answering machine; nothing important, and pulled out the secure phone to call Adrienne.

"He's not home yet. Everything seems to be alright."

"Good." Adrienne breathed a breath of relief. "Stay calm. There's no way the guy who threatened you is going to tell your husband you were in his office. HE wasn't supposed to be there. He'll bilk him for the money he says the doctor owes him, and get paid twice. This evening, Catriona, you've got to be sure you do nothing to raise the doctor's suspicion, especially while you've still got that key. Don't change your routine in any way. Don't be over-attentive or under-attentive. As soon as it's possible, get the key back on his key ring. I'll let you know tomorrow what I find in the papers you were able to copy, and what we need to do next. You've got to do the best acting job of your life tonight. This needs to be an Academy Award performance."

Catriona hung up the phone and poured a glass of Merlot. She drank it down as fast as she could and poured another. She had to calm her nerves.

Dr. Galen Kirby opened the door behind her.

Chapter Sixteen

Mel's heart was filled with intangible thoughts and feelings that catapulted off one another as he pulled into his driveway. It had been a long day, especially since he and Adrienne parted after lunch. He wanted to stay floating on the cloud that moved him forward when he thought about a future with Adrienne, but first, he had to make his way through the dark cloud hanging over him. He had to tell Camille he was leaving her.

"It has to be now," he whispered as he unlocked the door to his house and went inside. Camille was in the den with a bourbon and coke in hand, as usual. She turned around to face Mel. He could see that she'd already had several drinks. Even standing still, she staggered.

"I'm going to a hotel," he said, and walked toward their bedroom. "We'll talk tomorrow when you're sober, about a divorce."

"Like hell you are," Camille answered, raising the gun she held in her hand and pointing it toward Mel. He stared for a moment, then turned and closed the bedroom door behind him. Even drunk, he knew she wouldn't shoot. She'd tried this desperate stunt before when he'd threatened to leave. That time it had worked. That time was before he met Adrienne. This time he pulled a large, black suitcase from the closet and threw in a handful of clothes, hangers and all. He grabbed underwear and socks from a drawer and tossed in a few grooming items, then zipped the bag. He took a deep breath as he opened the bedroom door....Camille was passed out on the floor, the gun still in her hand. It was a miracle it hadn't discharged when she'd fallen. Mel removed the gun and put it back in the cabinet Camille had taken it from. He stood over her figure, listening to the heavy breathing of this woman he'd sworn to love and protect forever, in good times and in bad. Their wedding day seemed like light years away, like a time from some ancient history. Now, today, he'd had all the bad he could handle. He was ready for some of the good, but it wouldn't be with Camille. He closed the door behind him.

Adrienne pulled into her drive wondering what kind of mood Andrew would be in this evening. There was no way to know. Sometimes it depended on how much of what medicines he'd taken that day. Sometimes it depended on how much pain he was in. Sometimes it depended on how much time he'd spent dwelling on the fact that Adrienne had been gone, leaving him alone. After all, being alone with one's self could have the affect of forcing a man to look at himself for what he really is

. The porch light was on, but the rocking chairs were empty. Adrienne stood on the long, back porch that wrapped its way around the house, and looked out toward the pond. She could see Andrew's silhouette sitting on the dock overlooking the water. He didn't turn around. Adrienne lit a cigarette and stood for a moment, watching. What could she say? What did she want to say? Even five years after his accident, she was still eaten up with guilt and bitterness, and Andrew focused all his attention on being sure she'd keep feeling that way. Even after doing everything it was possible for a human to do to feel something meaningful for him again, Adrienne was empty. She wondered now about the regions of darkness in her heart, and whether or not there really was a way back into the light.

Andrew was walking toward her, fishing pole in hand. He stopped on the porch and looked her in the eye, then without a word opened the door and went inside. The blades of the porch rocking chair creaked their pitiful sighs while Adrienne finished her cigarette alone in the cool night air.

Chapter Seventeen

Psychopath: An intra-species incapable of an emotional connection to the rest of humanity. They do not understand or appreciate the impact their behavior has on others, nor do they care, intellectually, about the negative impact their behavior has on others. Psychopaths are emotionally blind. While they may have high verbal intelligence, they are totally lacking in emotional intelligence. However, even the most severe and disabled psychopath presents a technical appearance of sanity, and often succeeds in business or professional activities. Psychopaths can feel fear, anger, sadness, in the moment, but not guilt. They have no physical sensation of guilt. When they discover their behavior is not tolerable by society, psychopaths react by hiding it, NEVER by SUPPRESSING or changing it.

Catriona jumped as Galen closed the door behind her. She sat the glass of wine on the kitchen cabinet and turned around.

"Hello, Dear," Dr. Kirby said, noticing the wine. "Isn't it a little early in the evening?"

"Galen," she said, walking toward him with a smile. "I was just wondering when you might be getting home. Are you hungry? I was about to fix myself a little supper." She hoped he couldn't hear her heart pounding.

"Not really; just tired. It's been a very long day." He walked calmly into the den and stood looking out the giant glass wall that made up its back side. He stared out over the lake, wanting to pick up the vase of flowers sitting a few feet from him and throw them. He'd love to hear the shattering of the glass. He clinched his fists and ground his teeth. Someone had manipulated him. His anger was matched only by the coldness in his eyes, but in the subtle light of the den, that would remain his secret. What to do? He needed to think this thing through. *How could the money be gone unless Little Frankie Dalton took it, and why would he risk that when the money was going to be given to him anyway? Unless he was double-dipping, like the sheriff. Take the money, keep the drugs and make his own separate deal. Double the money, maybe more. I hope not, Little Frankie, I really hope not* . His file cabinet had definitely been broken into, forced open, but how would Little Frankie have gotten into the clinic and then into his office? The door hadn't been forced, but it had been left standing wide open. *The sheriff is the only other person who has a key.* That had been necessary. The doctor and the sheriff never arrived at the same time when they had their secret meetings. *He wouldn't be fool enough to take the money even if he'd known somehow that it was there.* That part didn't make sense. Of course, there were a lot of things that hadn't made sense until very recently. To the best of Galen's knowledge, Sheriff Johnson still didn't know he'd found out the sheriff was scamming the scam, stealing from the profits off the top. He'd been taking pills after he'd filled the prescriptions the doctor had written for the prisoners, before he packaged them up, with the doctor's permission, to sell to the dealer. The two dead guys on the levee were the go-between for the sheriff and his own personal dealer on the side. It hadn't been that hard to figure out. But there was no way for the sheriff to know the doctor had hired Little Frankie Dalton to kill the two. Not yet anyway. Had Sheriff Johnson actually thought the doctor to be so stupid he wouldn't check from time to time on the drug supply? The pharmacist, Jerry Kreiger's, loyalty was to the doctor. He was getting his cut directly from him. Besides, Dr. Kirby hadn't hinted there was anything wrong when he asked Jerry to see the records on the filled prescriptions. He'd just told Jerry he wanted to be sure nothing would seem suspicious to the outside world if the Feds ever did ask any questions. "Just a safety check," Dr Kirby had said with a smile. The pharmacist gladly cooperated. After all, he was pocketing an extra $20,000 a year through the doctor's little "bonus" system, and no one would ever be able to prove he knew anything about the scam. All he did was fill the prescriptions written by the doctor for the prisoners and hand the bottles of medicine to Sheriff Johnson when he came in to pick them up. It was easy to slip in a few extra pills now and then, especially the painkillers and barbiturates. And it was easy to look the other way if the doctor wanted a particular prescription filled every two weeks instead of once a month. No problem. Of course the three of them always made it look like the prescriptions were for prisoners. Whether or not the prisoners got all or even any of the medicine didn't matter, and it certainly had nothing to do with the pharmacist. No way to point a finger his way if anyone official ever questioned.

The sheriff couldn't have found out that I hired Little Frankie Dalton to put those two creeps out of their misery, the doctor reasoned silently. *Not this soon. Even if he had, it wouldn't explain the missing money.* The whole thing looked like one giant, endless circle, but Dr. Kirby had no intentions of running around the circle. He'd find a way to catch an end. The only one who knew for sure the doctor had a significant amount of money in his office was Little Frankie Dalton. Dalton was meeting the doctor there to collect the $10,000 for killing the two men before they could make their delivery to the dealer, confiscating the drugs and returning them to Dr. Kirby, all without the sheriff suspecting it was connected to the doctor in any way. Little Frankie knew the money was in the office. The doctor was about to open the hidden file cabinet and pay him off the night of the murders just before the sheriff walked in on them. But that scenario still didn't explain how Little Frankie could have gotten into the office without breaking in. Little Frankie Dalton knew where the money was and how much there should be. The sheriff had a key to the office. Was the sheriff pulling a double scam again? Had he gotten to Little Frankie somehow? *Bottom line. They'll both have to go.* It wasn't that the doctor was fearful of what they might do, it was that his anger was overpowering his reasoning. They'd created a loop and he wasn't in the center, wasn't in control of it. Not yet anyway. Yes, they'd both have to go. He just needed to decide how and in what order. His own special potion would do the trick. No mess, no fuss, but surefire deadly.

Another turn of events was eating away at the doctor as he thought through the day's events. The stack of birth certificates in his file cabinet so carefully organized by sex and year of birth had been tampered with. They were in the top drawer, not the drawer with the money, but it was obvious they'd been shuffled through. Dr. Kirby had examined each and every infant meticulously as soon as it was born, and had numbered them according to his personal preferences. Each birth certificate had that special, tiny number penciled in on the bottom left corner, and he knew the order by heart. The ones who looked the most like him with dark hair and ivory skin, the largest birth weights, the ones he considered to have the most perfect features, they were his specialties. Even the sheriff didn't know about the business of selling babies, and how much delight Galen took in the personal creation of each one and the placing of them in his "approved" homes where the talents and abilities they'd inherited from him would be carefully nurtured and his blood spread throughout all of Louisiana, Texas, and Mississippi. They'd not grow up in poverty like he had, not have their gifts limited by lack of opportunity. Each one had been placed in a home of distinction where it would be easy for him to check on its progress.

The birth certificate dilemma put another little twist on the doctor's state of mind.

* * *

Galen laid down the newspaper he'd been pretending to read, turned off the television and walked over to the two hundred gallon saltwater aquarium that stood against the wall. An eel squirmed its way into a back corner as he approached, and a hawk fish perched on an artificial rock waited, motionless, for its prey to wander by. Galen took special delight in owning the half dozen puffer fish he'd raised himself, an interest ever since he'd read about the "Haitian Zombies" created by Voodoo doctors in Haiti using the potentially deadly puffer fish neurotoxin, tetrodotoxin. Given exactly the right, miniscule dose of a powder made partially from the toxin, a person could be totally paralyzed and his body functions slowed to the point that he would appear to be dead. The Voodoo doctors would then have the victim publicly buried, wait for the poison to pass its peek but before the oxygen in the casket ran out, and perform magic over the grave. Ordering the grave to be dug up and the casket opened, the superstitious villagers would believe the Voodoo doctor had the power to resurrect the dead. Dr. Kirby loved the intricacy of the plot, and the control the Voodoo doctors had over entire villages. Recently, too, Galen had read about the careful use of the deadly poison as a pain killer for terminal cancer patients. Pain killers were a highly sought out commodity on the illegal drug market. Maybe this one would play a part in his future. He watched as the puffers ate the food he'd sprinkled over them and then turned toward the glass and looked straight at him as though they were asking for more. Catriona remarked from time to time that she loved the way the round, spiny puffer fish seemed to look you right in the eye like a playful puppy. Galen hated that part of their personality

Without a word, Galen walked slowly to the bedroom, his eyes watching the floor. Catriona laid down her book and followed. She turned on the TV in the bedroom and began turning down the covers on the bed while Galen emptied his pockets on the dresser and got ready for his shower. She heard the clinking of change, and finally the metallic clank of the keys. Catriona held her breath, her back turned to him, and waited for him to walk away. Moments later, she heard the sound of the water in the shower. Only then did she turn around. Catriona shrieked! Galen stood, naked, only inches from her.

"Galen, you scared me to death," she literally shook.

"Why so nervous tonight? His face was serious. "I neglected to tell you that I finished the first autopsy today. It was rather uncomplicated. I'll begin the second in the morning. I'll be leaving early. No need for you to get up." He walked back to the shower and closed its door behind him. Catriona shivered thinking about this man, her husband, someone she had once loved, spending his day cutting open the body of another human being and dismantling it piece by piece. She composed herself and took the original key from her pocket. With quivering hands she worked it back on to his key ring right beside the key to the clinic, exactly where she'd found it.

Chapter Eighteen

Adrienne checked the messages on the answering machine in her study. Nothing particularly important. A message from the parents of a teenager wanting her to check out a couple of their daughter's friends. She'd call them in the morning and recommend another P.I. She was just too busy with this healer case right now to take on anything else.

Andrew paced the floor for awhile like an impatient animal, stopping momentarily a couple of times to make eye contact with Adrienne, but not saying a word. Like a vicious dog, his eyes were daring, even threatening, and she knew that the chance for attack was great if she showed strength by staring back. The only way to defuse the attack was to look down at the ground and back slowly away, not giving his eyes a chance to scour her face. She moved to safety behind her desk and turned on her computer, afraid Andrew would want to talk, but he finally went to bed, dragging the air tank that made it possible for him to breathe on its stiff and angry stand along side him. At least the evening hadn't ended in the screaming match that was often the case.

Adrienne clicked on internet and typed in her private investigator's registered code number for the State Department of Motor Vehicles, then typed the license tag number of the car she and Catriona had followed from Dr. Kirby's office. In seconds the information she needed was in front of her. She grabbed a pen to write it down. Frankie Dalton, Winnsboro, Louisiana. She hadn't been to Winnsboro on a case in a while. Tomorrow would be as good a day as any to find out more about Frankie Dalton.

She poured a glass of wine and drank it down fast. She needed the first one to help her unwind, to begin counteracting the enormous amount of caffeine she'd consumed during the day in the form of coffee, and on the days when the coffee didn't do the trick, the Yellow Jackets she took to help keep her awake and alert. Just enough wine and she'd be relaxed in time to sleep for three or four hours before she got up and put on another pot of coffee and started the routine all over again. She poured a second glass and sat down at her desk again to begin looking over the papers Catriona'd copied today. Needing to think without interruption, the late night quiet was just right. But daytime and night time, Adrienne's thoughts and feelings were confused. She had decided long ago that she'd probably always be confused. She tried to concentrate on the case, but was hit by a surge of loneliness. There's something about the night that gives substance to loneliness, that breathes life into it and gives it the opportunity to take shape and to overwhelm. Her awareness of the thousand lies that made up her life and the lives of the people who hire her made Adrienne even colder than the crisp autumn night. She was glad to have her work and people like Catriona Kirby and her healer husband to think about. She didn't want to take a chance on missing anything that might be important, so she started by sorting the papers by topic: receipts, titles, deeds, medical records, birth certificates.

"Birth certificates? What are all these birth certificates? What's he doing with," Adrienne counted, "twenty-seven birth certificates? According to the records at the court house, since the medical malpractice suit about too many questionable stillborns, Dr. Kirby hadn't been allowed to deliver babies. Even if he had been, why would he have twenty-seven birth certificates hidden with all this other crap?"

She spread the birth certificates out in front of her. The dates of birth covered a span of approximately fifteen years. Adrienne started to make a list of birth dates and names of parents. As she wrote, the blood began to rush to her head. A sudden knowing. Each original birth certificate had a second birth certificate for the same child with a different set of parents attached to the back. The original for each child listed the mother as unmarried. Adrienne's mind raced. These babies had been given up for adoption. The second copy listed a second mother as married and also named the father. They had to be the adoptive parents. Drusilla Gifford and Susanne Jasper were among the unmarried mothers who had produced the babies. There were two birth certificates naming Susanne Jasper as the unmarried mother. She'd given birth to two different children in three years. But there was only one birth certificate for the second child. Adrienne looked at the date. That had to be the child that was with Susanne when she died, an infant boy a few months old. He had not been placed for adoption. Why?

"Not one single mother named a father," Adrienne thought out loud.

"Maybe they just didn't want the fathers involved in the decision to give the infants up for adoption. But still, there's something terribly wrong with this picture. My God," she felt like she'd been hit in the chest with a sledge hammer. "Dr Kirby's in some kind of baby selling racket." She tried to piece together the things she knew to be true about the man. What was it the literature had said? He couldn't feel deep emotion or make permanent connections to other humans. Psychopaths, mentally, turn humans into objects, making it easy to dispense of them. *But Galen Kirby would think of these women as genetically inferior,* Adrienne's mind raced. *Psychopaths are always in it for themselves. Whatever's going on here, it's not to improve the quality of life for the babies or their mothers, and it's definitely not to make a difference to the couples adopting them or "for the sake of society,"* she ridiculed. Her mind strained to make sense of it all. *The psychopathic mind is focused on self, ego. Psychiatrists called them self-centered and self-important. They value people in terms of their material value or to in some way feel self-fulfilled. They have no appreciation or understanding for the negative impact their behavior has on others. Nor do they care about the impact their behavior has on others. They're emotionally blind.* Adrienne remembered reading that psychopaths' brains are actually different, that the frontal lobe is abnormal. One of the articles she'd read explained that all social primates, including humans, have highly developed frontal lobes, and that human beings have the largest of all. This frontal lobe is responsible for self-control, planning, judgment, and balance of individual versus social needs. The right orbital frontal cortex is involved in fear conditioning, and the Limbic System is the center of emotions. The article explained that psychopaths have lowered neural activity in these areas, resulting in the fact that they have a remarkable lack of social and ethical judgment, and a deficiency in their reactions to fear-evoking stimuli. They live a double-life, often effectively hiding their "black side," but always on the verge of some kind of trouble. Adrienne locked her hands behind her head and sat back to think for a moment.

"So Dr Kirby would have no conscience whatsoever about any pain he might cause these mothers. They and their babies would just be objects to him, as easy to own and control, and even to sell, as a litter of puppies. And the really creepy thing is, he'd not experience any kind of fear or anxiety about doing something that horrendous."

Adrienne finished her notes about the birth certificates and sat back again. *I've got to find these mothers who gave their babies up and find out exactly how it all went down and* what part *Dr. Kirby played*. She froze momentarily wondering why Susanne Jasper and Drusilla Gifford had ended up dead, and cringing to think that some of the other mothers might possibly be dead, too. She wondered why Susanne Jasper's second baby had not been given up for adoption, and whether that fact had anything to do with Susanne's death. *There's still a giant piece missing. I've got to get the DNA run on that baby. I've got to know whether the doctor is in or out on the genetic scene.* She had a connection in the police department in Baton Rouge, a detective who'd once been a private investigator in Monroe. He and Adrienne had overlapped on a few cases back in the early days right after Andrew's accident. She hadn't seen Mike Morris in awhile, but they'd learned to trust each other back then, and she knew he'd tried to help her get established in the business at a time in her life when she'd come close to losing everything. She was pretty sure he'd help her now. Mike would know the right forensic people. Maybe he could convince them to run the DNA samples on the baby and the doctor. Getting a hold of Mike would be top priority in the morning.

Next, Adrienne looked at the deeds. Houses in Winnsboro, Delhi, Rayville, Epps, Oak Grove, Ruston, Arcadia, several in Monroe, and the one outside of Destiny where Susanne Jasper had been found dead. Catriona found the deeds in a file folder labeled "rental property," and the property management company Adrienne had spoken with concerning the house Susanne Jasper had been living in was listed as the management company for all of the properties. *What's going on with all that?* Adrienne was puzzled. She'd hoped to find information that would help her prove the drug scam the doctor was involved in with the sheriff, and since the surfacing of Little Frankie Dalton, she'd begun to suspect the doctor or sheriff or both, might be involved in the murders of the two men on the levee as well. She'd hoped the deaths of Susanne Jasper and Drusilla Gifford had been tied in someway with information they had to the drug scam. That would make figuring the whole thing out much simpler. Adrienne also expected to find information that would help her prove Susanne Jasper's baby was Dr. Kirby's, providing Adrienne with a plausible double motive for the doctor's involvement in the woman's death to present to the district attorney, and a fool-proof reason why he shouldn't have been allowed to perform the autopsy determining the cause of death. From there, Adrienne believed any judge would consider exhuming Susanne Jasper's body and having a forensic expert not connected with Dr. Kirby look for the cause of death with the idea of foul play in mind. Adrienne had been pretty sure all along that she'd find out Dr. Kirby was the father of

Susanne's baby, but now she wasn't sure. Could it be the reason Susanne's baby was still with her when she died was because it was Dr. Kirby's child? Never in her wildest imagination had she expected to discover he was selling babies. And where were the fathers of all those babies? Had not one of them questioned what was going to happen to his child? Second priority on Adrienne's list was to start locating the adoptive parents and see if she could learn anything from them. If she could get any of them to talk to her that is. Some of them would most likely still live at the same addresses, but adoption's considered a very private affair by most people, and Adrienne had no authority to make them talk to her. If the parents knew what was going on, they'd most likely slam the door in her face. She'd have to think up some kind of lie to get them to talk. She thought for a moment, again, about her own double-life.

Suddenly something Adrienne had read at the courthouse in Bayou Parish when she'd first taken the case came to mind. Dr. Kirby had been accused of causing the stillbirths of infants he thought to come from genetically inferior parents. There had been no real evidence, just hearsay, but still. He didn't sell those infants, he killed them. Drusilla Gifford was an unemployed high school dropout when she died, and Susanne Jasper a Vo-tech nurse's aid. Neither of them had even a relative to claim their body. They would be total losers in the Dr. Kirby's eyes. Adrienne was pretty sure that if she checked the backgrounds of the other unmarried mothers, she'd find out they were about the same, people Dr. Kirby would consider inferior. *What's missing here?* A light went on in Adrienne's head just as though someone had flipped a switch. She went to the table where she kept her old Psychology Today magazines and found the one with the article she'd read before. She needed to see the information again, in print.

"The psychopath has a history of behavior where he does not learn from his mistakes. He must be in total control, and will do his best to create situations where others are totally dependent on him. The psychopath makes his own social rules and creates his own expectations of others. He uses people for excitement, entertainment, to build self-esteem. He values people only in terms of their material value."

Adrenalin raged through Adrienne. Thousands of stinging ants crawled just below the surface of her skin. "My God, my God," she stood up. "There's only one way it makes any sense. There's only one scenario that fits the sick bastard's reasoning, his total rearrangement of reality. He's producing and selling his own offspring. That fits exactly his self-centered, self-important view of the world. But how can I prove it? These may be women he thinks of as inferior, but they're easy to control, totally dependent. It's his sperm, his seed. He just considers the women incubators. His narcissistic mind would allow him to believe his DNA would elevate the produce! An alien," she said. "Some kind of bottom feeder. A monster. There are a probable twenty-seven families out there unknowingly raising the seed of a psychopath?" The overwhelming need not to know these things hit Adrienne like a fist in the stomach. She thought she would vomit. She reached for the trash can just in case she did.

"This can't wait for morning," Adrienne picked up the phone. "Information? Baton Rouge, Louisiana. Baton Rouge Police Department. I'll hold." *What am I going to tell Mike?* She asked herself while she waited for the operator to give her the number. *This is all so insane, it even sounds impossible to me.* She wrote down the number, hung up the phone, and went outside on the back porch to smoke a cigarette. Adrienne sat in the dark in a wooden rocker and waited for the steam to clear from her mind. The full moon reflected in the pond, giving it a silvery glow. Somewhere in the distance she could hear a hoot owl calling, and bull frogs hidden in the pampas grass croaked their heavy songs. There were thunderstorms in the distance. Even in October the Louisiana humidity was thick and sultry, and Adrienne could see the outline of giant black clouds as the lightening flashed in the distance. Thunder storms. She felt sick again.

"Let's weather life's storms together," Mel had said. "Let's live like all we have is this very moment."

Adrienne felt tears well up in her eyes. She felt so totally alone right now, and her new suspicions about this case sure weren't helping. She longed for Mel's little boy smile to soothe and comfort her, to tell her that everything would be all right. *How can this world be so rotten?* A tear ran down her cheek. She needed Mel to be right, to have the answers to all her emotional tortures, but almost instantly she was aware that she was looking at his love and having expectations of how it would fill her needs. *How could I ever fill his needs? This honest and trustworthy, almost naive man. So cultured and dignified. So handsome. So truly good.* She felt so damaged by life's games. How could private detective Adrienne Hargrove possibly ever be what Professor Mel Brighton needed? Maybe, for her, it would have to be enough just to know that truly good people do exist. She might never be able to be sure she was one of them. Adrienne took a deep breath. She had to call Mike Morris now.

* * *

Professor Mel Brighton tossed and turned in his bed at the Marriott Hotel. Sleep was out of the question. He knew he should feel sad, and maybe even guilty, for leaving Camille passed out drunk on the floor of their home, but he didn't. He told himself there'd been too many years of sorrow and guilt, and that he wanted those feelings to be things of the past with no chance of becoming a part of the future. He sat up and pushed his disheveled hair back out of his eyes. His sleeplessness was Adrienne's fault. He wanted to feel joyful and hopeful inside and he did when he thought about her. How could that be wrong? For the first time in his life, he didn't care if it was wrong. He was fifty-five years old! He wanted a chance at love before it was too late. He'd never even come close to feeling like this before. Nothing was going to keep him from finding the happiness he knew he could have with Adrienne. Nothing. He poured a glass of Merlot and went to the window. City lights dotting the view seemed like bright signals, omens, telling him it's now or never. *I don't want to wait for my life to be behind me and look back in sorrow understanding what it might have been.* He was reminded of Henry David Thoreau's words, ones he had quoted to his own students so many, many times. "I shall not looking back on my life discover that I never really lived at all." No matter what it took, he and Adrienne had to be together.

Chapter Nineteen

Mike Morris agreed to meet with Adrienne and listen to the whole story. There wasn't much that shocked him anymore, he'd been in the business at some level for a long time, but he was finding what she was telling him to be pretty farfetched. He was a kind man in his sixties with a silver handlebar mustache and thick eyeglasses with round, black rims. He'd listened attentively as Adrienne explained her theory to him over the phone.

Mike had gained a few pounds over the years, and he wore suspenders now instead of a belt, but other than that, he hadn't changed much since the last time he'd seen Adrienne. He wondered if she had. You'd usually catch him with a cigar hanging out of his mouth, but he rarely lit it. It was just a nervous habit, something to do with his mouth when he wasn't talking. Next to Adrienne, Mike Morris had probably been the best PI the state of Louisiana ever had, and an honest one, too, unlike some he and Adrienne both knew that gave private investigators the stereotype of being scumbags.

Mike had met Adrienne at a moment in time when he didn't know how he would have the courage to keep his own life going. His wife of thirty years had been killed in her sleep by an intruder while he was out on an investigation. One of the hundreds of adulteries that had paid his salary over the years. His wife had wanted him to retire. There was no reason not to. They'd managed their money well, raised their kids right. Mike knew the answer, and it haunted him. He enjoyed his work. He loved looking at the dark side of people's nature. As a result, he was sitting in a car in the dark on a quiet neighborhood street in Baton Rouge watching a man sneak out of his lover's house at two o'clock in the morning then go home to his wife letting her think his plane had been delayed, while his own wife was being murdered in their bedroom at home. A robbery gone bad. No one knew for sure why the burglar had killed her. The jewelry on her dresser was gone along with a few other thing around the house. Maybe she'd turned over or made a noise in her sleep and he thought she was awake. They'd never know. The killer had never been found. Every single clue hit a dead end. Mike shut down his private investigator's business and took a position as a detective with the police department hoping that somewhere along the way he'd catch a break and run into the son of a bitch that killed his wife. He knew for sure what he was going to do if it ever happened. With a master's degree in criminal justice and his years of experience as a PI, the police department had been glad to get him. Adrienne had shown him back then the kind of strength it took to rise above the total collapse of your personal world. Mike knew her to be a person with a lot of common sense, when it came to her work at least. He'd never understood why she stayed with Andrew.

Now, this stuff on the case she called, "The Healer," would have to come a long way before he could justify ordering a DNA test, even for Adrienne, especially when it wasn't part of a police investigation. He sure hoped she wasn't planning to get him in the big middle of something. His life was simpler now, and he wanted to keep it that way, but he'd look at what she was bringing him later today. That was the least he could do for an old friend.

Adrienne headed to Child Protective Services to pick up the baby's hairs from Julia Anderson. She left the agency with a plastic zip lock bag with several of the soft, shiny fibers inside and a piece of information from Julia that she wasn't sure exactly what to do with. It appeared the baby might be Down Syndrome. Mentally defective. This was the first time Julia had seen the infant. Now, Adrienne didn't know how to put her finger on it, but she knew the child's defect had something to do with the fact that he hadn't been adopted, and probably the murder of its mother as well. *Innocence,* she thought, as she placed the bag carefully in her briefcase alongside the birth certificates. *Totally stripped away just like these hairs from a baby's head.* A quarter after nine she called Catriona to see if she'd gotten hairs from Galen's brush. She needed them today. She was meeting Mike Morris at Moulotte's Cajun Restaurant in Alexandria, about halfway between Monroe and Baton Rouge. He'd agreed to hear her out and help her if he could. Adrienne was taking the birth certificates with her to convince Mike of what she suspected. If she was wrong, she wanted to know his theory. She'd need his ties to the police department, too, to put a case together that a prosecuting attorney would be willing to listen to.

"Did you get the key back on Dr. Kirby's key ring without any problems?" she asked Catriona now.

"Yes, and I never want to have to do it again. You'll never know how close he came to catching me."

"That parts over, Catriona, but there's a lot more to do. I warned you from the beginning that there might be things turn up in this investigation you wouldn't want to know. The evidence is leading me places even I don't want to go, but it's too late to turn back now."

"What is it, Adrienne? What have you found? I need to know who this man is I've lived with, I'm still living with, for ten years?"

"If what I think is true, he's a monster. Sub-human. There's no other way to put it. But you can't back out now, Catriona. I've got to have your help. If I can pull this thing together, we'll be able to put him away for the rest of his life either in prison, or more likely a mental institute. I'm meeting with a detective from Baton Rouge later today to see if he can get these hairs DNA'd for me. Then we'll know whether or not Susanne Jasper's little boy is Dr. Kirby's child. It'll take a few days to get the results, but they will eliminate any doubt. After that, you and I need to sit down and talk, and I'll discuss the evidence with you, and what we've got to do to get a conviction. I don't think there's much doubt the man's a murderer, I just haven't figured out yet how he did it without any outward signs on the bodies." She stopped short of telling Catriona that she suspected he'd killed more than just these two women, possibly many more.

"I have a degree in biology, Adrienne, with a minor in chemistry. There are many ways to kill a person with no outward signs of violence. There are chemicals in every household that are deadly when used incorrectly. Something as simple as caffeine in massive doses can cause a heart attack. And besides, Galen's a physician. He has access to any kind of chemicals or medicines he wants. No questions asked. There are all sorts of ways to poison a person without it being obvious to anyone. "

Adrienne thought about the amount of caffeine she fed her own body everyday. She'd start cutting down, right after this case was over. "Those are possibilities we'll need to discuss, but not now. After we get the DNA results back," she told Catriona. "In the meantime, how long will it take you to get to Love's Truck Stop?"

"I can be there in thirty minutes."

"It'll take me about forty-five. Meet me at the Arby's at Love's Truck Stop. Don't forget to bring the hair." Adrienne hung up the phone, rummaged around through the papers scattered on the car seat for her Zippo, and lit a cigarette. She took a few drags and pulled into a Kangaroo for a bathroom stop. She bought a large, black coffee and a package of Yellow Jackets, just in case she needed them later. She couldn't worry about the dangers of caffeine right now. This was already looking like it'd be at least a twenty-hour work day. She couldn't take a chance on getting sleepy and having a wreck coming home tonight.

Andrew was still asleep when she left this morning. She pulled out of the truck stop and onto I-20 and called him now.

"Yeah," Andrew answered the phone.

"Just thought I'd say hello and see what you have planned for your day," Adrienne replied.

"Oh I thought I'd take a nice, leisurely horseback ride and then meet my friends at the country club for a picnic lunch," he said sarcastically. "What'd you think I have planned?"

"I was just trying to get today off to a better start, Andrew. I didn't mean to stir things up. Sarah's coming to take you to your doctor's appointment. I called her before I left. You have a breathing therapy session after that. I wasn't sure if you'd remember. I have to drive to south Louisiana today and I'm not sure when I'll be back."

"So what's new?" Andrew hung up the phone.

Adrienne lit another cigarette and took a drink of her coffee. She'd had a little too much wine last night, but at least there'd been no nightmares. It was taking her longer to get her energy level up today though. The caffeine would kick in pretty soon, and she'd feel like herself again, whatever that meant. If not, she'd take a Yellow Jacket after lunch. She turned into Love's parking lot and saw Catriona's mint-green SUV in front of Arby's. She pulled up alongside it and put her cigarette out in the ashtray, noticing the sign "This is a smoke-free environment" posted irritatingly on the front door. Catriona was drinking diet Sprite and eating a Market Fresh sandwich.

"Would you like something?" she asked Adrienne. "I was starving. My nerves are so on edge when Galen's there all I can do is pick at my food."

"Too early for me," Adrienne answered. "Besides, I've got some people to track down before I leave for Alexandria. You brought the hair samples?"

"Yes," Catriona answered, wiping her mouth with a napkin and reaching inside her purse. She handed Adrienne the plastic bag.

"There's no doubt they're Galen's hair?" Adrienne asked.

"There's no one else there but me and the maid." Catriona explained.

"And Galen doesn't allow anyone to touch his personal items. He puts his brush and comb in an exact spot turned an exact way. Even the maid's not allowed to touch it. He cleans his own sink."

Just one more piece of a psychopathic mind, Adrienne thought. *Total control.* But in this case, she was glad. There could be no doubt the hairs were Galen's.

"Call me tomorrow morning as early as you safely can," Adrienne told her. "I'll let you know then what our next move will be. In the meantime, just keep doing what you're doing." She smiled at Catriona. "You should have been an actress. You're definitely working on an Academy Award performance. Catriona returned the smile, thankful for a momentary release from all the tension.

"I'll talk to you tomorrow." Adrienne left hair samples in hand, paying for a Hershey's with a little more caffeine as she left, and headed back to Monroe to start looking for the six families listed on the birth certificates who had lived there when they adopted their babies. She wanted to try to talk to as many of them as possible before she left to meet with Mike.

Adrienne thought as she drove. She hadn't been able to come up with any lies that seemed believable to try to explain to the adoptive parents of these children why she was investigating the circumstances around their adoption without causing them to panic. She'd decided to try giving as little information as possible to the first family she talked to, and yet telling them bits and pieces of the truth. She'd also decided to start with the oldest child to be adopted in Monroe, a fourteen year old boy, thinking that maybe the parents would feel less intimidated than the parents of an infant or very young child. She could only hope her strategy would work. If it didn't? Well, she'd cross that road when she came to it. She turned onto Forsythe and into the driveway of an upscale house with a BMW and an SUV sitting in the driveway. Her identification in hand, she rang the doorbell. Sometimes, if she flashed her I.D. quickly and people didn't look too carefully, they'd assume she was the police and would feel obligated to talk to her. Of course they were not, but she sure wasn't going to tell them. A man in his mid-forties opened the door.

"Mr. Stevens?" Adrienne asked.

"Yes?"

"My name is Adrienne Hargrove," she flashed the I.D. in his face, then quickly dropped the hand it was in to her side. "I'd like to talk to you about your son, Jason. Is he here?"

"No. He I let him drive to the store. He'll be right back." He paused. "What's wrong?" His voice raised in pitch. "Has he been in an accident?"

"No, no," Adrienne answered quickly, wondering how a parent could be talked into letting a fourteen year old drive. But she didn't want to get on the wrong side of the man right off the bat. "Nothing like that. As a matter of fact, it'd be better if we talked while he's gone. Is Mrs. Stevens home?"

"Yes. Come in." It had worked. He thought Adrienne was someone official. "This is my wife, Margaret. I'm sorry, what did you say your name was?"

"Investigator Adrienne Hargrove," Adrienne greeted the woman with a handshake, purposely leaving off the word "private" from her introduction.

"Please sit down. What's wrong?" Margaret Stevens asked.

"Maybe nothing Mrs. Stevens, but I need to ask you a few questions about the adoption of your son, Jason."

Mr. and Mrs. Stevens looked at one another in shock.

"What do you mean? What kind of questions?" Mr. Stevens asked. "Who wants to know about our son's adoption?"

"First of all, does Jason know he's adopted? I don't want to say or do anything in his presence should he come in that could possibly cause any kind of alarm." Adrienne hoped this would put the parents somewhat at ease.

"Yes, he knows. But it's not something we make a habit of talking about. It's not an issue in this household," Mrs. Stevens replied. "He's our son. We've had him since birth. That we're not his biological parents has nothing to do with the way we live our lives. Why are you asking us these things?"

"I just have a few simple questions. There's no reason for alarm. The information I need doesn't affect the adoption itself in any way, I assure you," Adrienne stretched the truth, hoping she was right. "There's reason to believe a certain person involved in a number of adoptions that were handled in the Northeast Louisiana area, including the adoption of your son, may be involved in some legal problems. Your son is your son. It has nothing to do with him specifically. We're just trying to tie some loose ends together." She slipped in the word "we," hoping to give the impression there was a united front involved in the investigation.

"There's no way the adoption of our son is connected with any legal problems," Mr. Stevens added. "We were extremely careful. We'd read about people adopting children only to find out years later that the adoptions weren't legal. We adopted our son privately through a physician. He took care of all the legal work and fees. He guaranteed the health of the mother and the infant. The mother was an unmarried woman who wanted her baby to have a good life. As you can see, we've given him that. He has everything a child could ever want or need. He's our only child."

Adrienne could feel her blood pressure rising as Mr. Stevens described the private adoption through a physician. She tried not to show her excitement.

"What were you told about your son's biological father?" she asked calmly, looking Mr. Stevens directly in the eye.

"That he was a teenaged boy, like the mother. Young and irresponsible. Of course we weren't given their names. We didn't care to know anyway. What does this have to do with the biological father?"

"As I said, Mr. Stevens. A man involved in some adoptions that were handled in Northeast Louisiana is possibly in some legal trouble. Maybe if you give me the name of the doctor who arranged the adoption we can let it go at that."

"Are you going to question the doctor?" Mrs. Stevens was anxious.

"No, I assure you I am not," Adrienne waited, afraid to push.

"His name is Dr. Galen Kirby. His office is in Bayou Parish. He was recommended to us by friends who had adopted a baby through him."

Adrienne could hardly contain herself, writing down the name like she'd never heard it before. Was she deceiving these people? Sure. Was it for their own good? She couldn't answer that. She only knew she had to do it, and it appeared her suspicions had been right. Dr. Galen Kirby was selling babies, and there was a very good chance they were his own flesh and blood. She had to ask one more question. Her curiosity would not let it rest.

"What kind of boy is Jason?" she smiled. "Any problems to speak of? I know young boys can be a handful."

"They surely can," Mrs. Stevens replied, seemingly more at ease. "He's had his share of ups and downs. But he's been in therapy. He's doing fine now."

"What kind of problems was he having?" Adrienne urged.

"Just normal boy stuff carried a little overboard," Mr. Stevens inserted with a bit of a defensive note in his voice. "Neighbors accused him of killing their cat a few years ago when he was about nine or ten. I assure you, it was all a misunderstanding. Jason's very intelligent. Interested in chemistry. Made some kind of chemical combination at school that had the potential to be explosive. He was suspended for awhile and removed permanently from the chemistry class. He was just curious. He didn't plan to do anything harmful with it. All that was a long time ago. Everything's been fine since we started therapy last year."

Last year, Adrienne thought. *About the time puberty sets in, things are so out of control they decide therapy is necessary. The literature says therapy often makes a psychopath worse Gives him the sense he's losing control.*

The front door opened and fourteen year old Jason Stevens walked in. The parents looked at each other and then at Adrienne.

"Jason, this is Ms. Hargrove," Mr. Stevens made the introduction.

The boy, a dead ringer for Galen Kirby looked at her with cold, empty eyes.

Chapter Twenty

It had been a long time since Adrienne had seen her detective friend, Mike Morris. As she drove, she thought about his friendly face with the twinkling green eyes and the unlit cigar that was usually hanging between his teeth. He was a real character, fairly light-hearted for a person whose career put him in touch with the slime of the earth on a daily basis. Adrienne suspected Mike had been a fun person to be around before his wife's death, but she'd known him only briefly then. She met him right about the time she was murdered.

I wonder what shape his life has taken, Adrienne thought. *How do you ever get over losing someone you've loved to violence?* She wondered if he'd remarried, or was dating someone. He was sort of a father figure person, not particularly good looking, just an average Joe kind of guy. Pleasant and settled and comfortable to be around, wise, but still with a gruff side that didn't believe in playing games with the important stuff. *By the time you're in your sixties, a person should be able to have a little security and sense of peace.* Adrienne hoped he had found his way back to some kind of happiness. She pulled into the parking lot at Mulotte's Cajun Restaurant....

"It's good to see you," Mike took the cigar out of his mouth and gave Adrienne a big hug. "How's life been treating you? You still living with that dumb-ass jerk you married?"

"Still living with him," Adrienne smiled.

"You get enough of his crap, you can always move in with me. It's an open invitation," Mike pulled a seat out for Adrienne, then sat down across the table from her just as the waitress arrived and laid menus on the table. Adrienne assumed Mike's playful invitation to move in with him answered her question as to whether or not he was still single.

"What can I get you folks to drink?" the dark-skinned, Cajun woman asked in her south Louisiana Cajun French accent.

"Bud-Lite," Mike answered.

"Sweet tea for me." Adrienne opened her menu and waited for the waitress to leave.

"What's this all about?" Mike started the conversation. "You think some local doctor's involved in a black market baby racket?"

"Yeah, a doctor in Destiny, and I'm pretty sure the baby-selling has led to at least a couple of murders, mothers of two of the infants he's sold." She explained the whole scenario, beginning with Catriona Kirby hiring her to look into the suspicious deaths of two women she knew for sure her doctor/husband had had affairs with. Catriona also had reason to believe Dr. Kirby was involved in some kind of drug scam, possibly with the sheriff, and during the course of Adrienne's investigation to this point, there'd been two shootings and the theft of a large amount of money from the doctor's office that seemed to be tied in some way or another. Adrienne's view, as she explained it to Mike, was that the doctor's a certified psychopath, and that he's involved in all sorts of illegal activities in a small community where he's the only physician and where nobody talks. Except one prisoner. She told Mike about the desperate phone call from a parish prisoner who believed his life was in danger because he knew too much about the doctor and the sheriff's drug scam, and how that prisoner has since turned up dead, supposedly of natural causes. That particular fact seemed to get Mike's attention.

"What can I get you folks?" the waitress returned.

"I'll have the all-you-can-eat fried catfish," Mike answered. "Hush puppies, cole slaw and fries. Be sure to bring plenty of red sauce." Adrienne smiled as he ordered and couldn't help but think that Mike sure wasn't worried about having a he-man figure to help him attract the ladies.

"Seafood gumbo," Adrienne looked at the menu. "Heavy on the crab legs. Small bowl of dirty rice. Side salad with Creole French dressing." She handed the menu to the waitress. "Look," she said to Mike. "Let's do this one crime at a time. The bottom line is I've located the infant of the last woman he murdered."

"Maybe he murdered," Mike corrected her. "You've seen the child?"

"No. But I went to see Julia Anderson at Child Protective Services in Monroe, and she knows where the little boy is. You remember Julia?"

"Sure. Worked together a number of times when I was still in Monroe."

"She was able to get hairs from the baby's head. I think it's even worse than a black market baby racket, Mike. I think the man's fathering the babies himself." She waited to see Mike's reaction. "I have hair samples from the baby's head, and my client was able to get hairs from the doctor's brush. I've got to know if the little boy is the doctor's child."

"Come on now, Adrienne. That's pretty sick. Besides, even if you prove the baby was fathered by the doctor, it doesn't prove anything else. If I'm understanding you right, this baby wasn't sold. So proof of paternity gets you nowhere in a baby selling racket."

"I agree, but remember, the baby's mother died under very strange circumstances. Thirty years old and supposedly had a massive heart attack Another one of those 'natural' deaths that somehow seem to keep taking place all around the Healer."

"So? It happens."

The waitress arrived with Adrienne's salad and Mike's cole slaw.

"We know the doctor dated her in the recent past. And Mike, he's the same doctor that did the autopsy. He's the coroner."

Mike looked up from his food. "You gotta be kidding me."

"Fraid not. If we can prove the baby of this woman is his, I think we can get the D.A.'s office to look into the case. Maybe exhume the body, but I've got to get help from outside the parish, like you. The whole parish knows the Healer's a psycho. They just look the other way, pretend they don't know nothing, but I don't think they'll look the other way if this comes out. They won't be able to. The first step is testing the hair samples and seeing if we've got a match. What do you say?"

Mike picked up a catfish fillet. "I'll see what I can do," he said, dipping it in the red sauce.

Chapter Twenty-One

Adrienne headed north on highway 165 back toward Monroe. A feeling of success along with a twinge of "I told you so," spread through her as she blew cigarette smoke in the air and thought about her conversation with Mike. He'd had to agree that there's more to the case than meets the eye. He'd agreed, also, to get the DNA run provided Adrienne promised to keep him updated on the case. It would take three to five days, but he'd try to hurry it along if he could. This was the most bazaar case he had come across in a long time, and Mike Morris wasn't one to put much stock in being bored. Also, spending a couple of hours with Adrienne made him remember why it was he'd always liked her so much. She was genuine, the real thing. No pretense with Adrienne Hargrove. As honest as the day is long, and even with that temper of hers, as fair as they come. *Awful pretty, too,* he chewed on his cigar and grinned.

"No problem," Adrienne told him. "If things really get moving, it may end up in the State Attorney General's Office anyway, and that means bringing it to Baton Rouge, your neck of the woods," she smiled. "I'm not sure Bayou Parish has the professionals to handle it, ones that don't have some kind of tie to the Dr. Kirby anyway."

It was getting close to three o'clock in the afternoon, and it was almost two hours back to Monroe from Alexandria. Adrienne really wanted to visit one more of the adoptive families if she could before calling it quits for the day, so she lit a cigarette and put her foot to the accelerator. She was never in a hurry to get home, and she hadn't heard from Mel today, so her emotions were hanging heavy. She wondered if Mel had gone to the Marriott like he'd said, or if Camille had been able to convince him to stay. After all, she hadn't been served the divorce papers yet. Adrienne wished he would call, but she realized she had no right to wish for anything from Mel Brighton. He was still a married man. Here she was, feeling a connection to him. As much as she didn't want to admit it, already there would be a hole in her heart if he was no longer a part of her life.

Adrienne put the car on cruise setting it exactly five miles above the speed limit so she could fumble around through her notes on the adopted children without slowing down. She wanted to find the closest address as she came into Monroe. She'd have to go through the whole Investigator Adrienne Hargrove thing again. She had lucked out on the first family. Even got to see the boy. She hoped her luck would hold out this time.

"Oliver Road. That's off Louisville just east of 18th. Might as well try that one." Adrienne opened a can of diet coke as she drove and set it in the cup-holder, then lit another cigarette from the one she'd just finished, controlling the steering wheel with her knee while she accomplished the feat. She propped her notes up on the steering wheel and read as she drove, holding her cigarette in the hand that also held the steering wheel. This was another fourteen-year old, a girl. Adrienne wondered if psychopaths came in the female variety. All of the ones she'd read about had been male. She hoped she'd get a chance to see this girl, too. There was nothing in the literature to suggest that there was an absolute genetic link passing on the psychopathic condition, but there was evidence that it, like many other birth defects, was found more often in some families than others. Birth defect. Yes. An actual abnormality of the brain. Adrienne thought about the implications of that piece of information. If some people were actually born psychopaths like others were born diabetics, was there any way to change them, under any circumstances or conditions? And if a person like Dr. Kirby was born with a physical abnormality of the brain that tied directly to his behavior, shouldn't they be trying to help him instead of trying to lock him up? She thought back again to the research article she'd read about the psychopathic mind and the author's advice: "Abandon your efforts to help him. Protect yourself physically, emotionally, financially." *Besides*, she reminded herself. *Top priority is keeping other people safe from him, including Catriona Kirby, and very possibly Susanne Jasper's child. Most psychopaths don't become serial killers, but I'm pretty sure this one has.* Adrienne was even more worried about the safety of Susanne Jasper's little boy now that she knew he was Down Syndrome. Dr. Kirby had a penchant against human deficiencies in any way, and this one was very obvious. But if he was going to kill the baby, wouldn't he have done it when he killed the mother? Another piece to try to make fit. Adrienne wondered exactly where in the house the police had found the baby, and whether that could possibly have something to do with his survival. *One step at a time*, she thought. *Don't get too far ahead of yourself until the DNA results get back. Then you'll have something concrete to base the rest of your ideas on. Until then, it's all just speculation.*

Adrienne turned onto Oliver Road and began looking at house numbers. *There it is.* She turned into the drive. No vehicles visible. Adrienne played with the I.D. badge she held in her hand while she waited for someone to answer the doorbell. Nothing. She rang the bell again. Still nothing. No sounds coming from the house. She hesitated a moment, then walked down the porch steps and back to her car.

"Well, this one will have to wait." She looked at her watch. Five-thirty. "But it's not been a bad day's work." She thought back over the day's activities. She'd gotten the baby's hair samples from Julia Anderson and learned that Julia suspected the baby boy was afflicted with Down Syndrome. That could be a very important fact. She met with Catriona who had hair samples from Dr. Kirby, and Catriona would call her sometime tomorrow morning. She'd talked to one of the adoptive families and gotten plenty of circumstantial evidence that the doctor was black marketing babies. She'd also convinced herself beyond any doubt that the babies the doctor was selling were his own offspring. Any doubts she had left had quickly vanished after meeting Jason Stevens. She'd driven to Alexandria and met with Detective Mike Morris who would get the DNA testing started first thing tomorrow. Yes, a good day's work.

Adrienne had to admit she was exhausted, but there was no way she wanted to go home, not for several hours yet. She pulled into a Sonic and turned off the car. She wasn't really hungry, but this was a place she could sit quietly without being bothered and just think. She rolled down the car window and pushed the service button on the menu on the pole beside her car.

"Welcome to Sonic. May I help you?"

"Yeah, I'll have a Route 44 cherry lime aid," Adrienne answered. *Time to start laying off the caffeine for the day.*

"Would you like an order of onion rings or French fries with that," the voice behind the speaker asked.

If I wanted onion rings I'd of ordered onion rings, Adrienne wanted to answer. "No thank you," she smiled instead.

Adrienne laid her head back on the headrest and tried to relax. *I'm less than a mile from the Marriott. I wonder if Mel's there…There's no way it would be alright to just drop by a man's hotel room.*

A young black girl on skates rolled up to the car window. "Route 44 cherry lime aid. That'll be a $1.78." Adrienne handed the bubbly teenager $2.

"Keep the change." Adrienne took a giant drink of the cherry lime aid. It was a nice change from the coffee and cokes she'd been drinking all day. She headed toward the Marriott, even though home was forty-five minutes in the opposite direction. "I'll just drive through the parking lot and see if his car's there," she mumbled. "That can't hurt anything." She turned into the Marriott entrance. Nothing in the front parking lot. Nothing on either side. Nothing in the back parking lot. "Maybe he didn't leave Camille," she whispered. Confused by the thought, she headed back toward the highway and home. She came to a red light and stopped. Directly across from her, pointed toward the Marriott, Mel sat waiting for the light to change. They saw each other and smiled at just about the same time. *Seconds away from missing each other again,* she thought. *It's like a special hand is holding onto us, not letting us lose each other in the shadows.* Oh how she wanted to believe that could be true. Mel honked and pointed toward the hotel.

Adrienne laughed in spite of herself. "What the hell," she said and turned the car around as she pulled through the intersection to follow Mel. *To the ends of the earth.*

"You came by to see me," Mel was beaming as Adrienne got out of her car.

"I wouldn't exactly say that," Adrienne grinned.

"What exactly would you say?" he wrapped his arms around her and gave her a giant hug. "Let's go inside."

Adrienne knew she should say no, but she didn't. Mel took her hand and she followed as he led her to the elevator and up to the fourth floor. He unlocked the door and pushed it wide open.

"Da-da," he said with a wide sweep of his arms. "This is my current mansion. Won't you come in?" His blue eyes were aglow and Adrienne realized again how agonizingly beautiful they were. She walked in and he closed the door behind her. "A glass of wine, my fine lady?" he asked.

"I really shouldn't," Adrienne replied.

"And why not? Exactly what is it you think you shouldn't be doing, Adrienne?"

"Shouldn't." She stopped.

"Shouldn't be here with me," he answered for her, the former playfulness gone. "Even when we both know you do everything possible to avoid going home to Andrew? Even though we both know my marriage is over, has been over, really, for years now. That's no life, Adrienne. We both deserve more.

I'm not just another case you've worked on, and we're way past friendship. There's no way to go back even if we wanted to." He looked ever so seriously into her eyes. Adrienne was deeply aware that in every relationship there was a defining moment, and that once the moment was gone, it was gone forever. Was this that moment for her and Mel? His manliness took her breath away. He pulled her to him and put his mouth on hers. Warmth welled up inside her. The moment was electric. Mel was right. They could never go back to being just friends. This was that one special moment in their lifetime. She melted into the kiss and he guided her slowly to his bed.

Chapter Twenty-Two

Sheriff Johnny Johnson told the female officer at the front desk that he didn't want to be disturbed for the rest of the day and made his way back to his office. He closed the door behind him and sat down at the desk, his head swimming. Something weird was going on and he was afraid Dr. Galen Kirby had something to do with it. How much did Dr .Kirby know, and how'd he find out? Those questions had all the sheriff's nerves on edge. He'd replayed the whole scenario in his mind over and over again without coming to any conclusions. He had to get a grip on things. Something was terribly wrong.

Number one, the deal was carefully laid out far enough in advance to be sure there'd be no mess ups, and the sheriff had hired Dale and Walter to run the scam through his friend, Tony, in New Orleans who had no other ties to Bayou Parish. Tony had his own prostitution ring going He used Dale and Walter to rough up Johns when they got out of hand. They were both ignorant as the day was long, all muscle and no brain, but in his line of work, Tony needed guys like that. A regular paycheck and an extra prostitute on the side once in awhile, and the two ignorant sons of bitches did whatever Tony asked. All they had to do for the sheriff was get the drugs from the storage building out on the highway where he'd been accumulating them for over a year now, and meet the front man, Wilson, on the dock of the port just across the levee, less than a mile from the storage building, right after dark. Wilson would bring the money from the dealer whose name would remain anonymous, and exchange it for the two bags of drugs the sheriff had been skimming off the top of the prescription scam he and the doctor had been involved in for nearly fifteen years. The drugs in those two bags were worth a quarter of a million dollars, and the dealer was paying cash.

Wilson had no reason to kill Dale and Walter. He was getting his cut from the dealer as soon as he delivered the drugs to him. Wilson told the sheriff that

Dale and Walter were already dead when he got to their meeting place. He'd fled the scene and called the sheriff from a pay phone at a gas station. Wilson was shaking like a leaf when the sheriff talked to him. No, Sheriff Johnson was convinced. Wilson had nothing to gain from the murders. As a matter of fact, he lost all his pay when the deal was blown.

The dealer wasn't about to place himself in harms way by getting personally involved in a murder, so he could be ruled out. Dealers weren't much different from pimps, letting everybody else do the dirty work while they collect the profits. Sheriff Johnson knew Dr. Kirby had no qualms about murder. As a matter of fact, over the years he'd helped the sheriff put a few scum bags from the detention center out of their misery without even a hint of fowl play. Prisoners who'd gotten too close to figuring out how their prescriptions were being filled. But those deaths were accomplished with chemicals and special powders the doctor knew how to handle. He wasn't about to go shoot two guys on the levee. Too messy. The doctor didn't like blood. Might get his precious hands dirty. No, Dr. Kirby didn't shoot Dale and Walter. Didn't mean he didn't hire it done.

Second. big mystery. What was Little Frankie Dalton doing in Destiny? There was no mistaking the pit-faced little runt. Sheriff Johnson had seen him in the parking lot of the Auto Part store beside the post office and Dr. Kirby's clinic. He'd even seen him go in the back door of the clinic right in the middle of the afternoon, in broad daylight, while the doctor was at the hospital cutting Dale and Walter open. Little Frankie had opened the back door and walked right in! And the really spooky thing? He stayed no more than a couple of minutes and came right back out, followed a couple of minutes later by the doctor's wife who made her way over to the post office with a stack of papers under her arm!

"What the hell?" Sheriff Johnson said to himself now. "How'd Catriona Kirby, the country club queen, get tied in with someone as slimy as Little Frankie Dalton?" That had sure aroused the sheriff's curiosity. So much so he'd decided to hang around in the alleyway and see if the doctor had any other company while he was out of his office. Sure enough, Dr. Kirby himself followed just a few minutes later by Little Frankie Dalton creeping in the back door again. "What the hell?" The sheriff said again. A few minutes later, Little Frankie Dalton leaves, and thirty minutes after that Dr. Kirby. The doctor's office seemed to be a mighty busy place on the doctor's afternoon off. Sheriff Johnson took his hat off and scratched his head, ran his hand through his hair and put the hat back on.

"There's no way Catriona Kirby's going up on that levee in the dark and shoot two dope dealers, even if somehow she knew. That leaves Little Frankie Dalton. He's one mean son-of-a-bitch. Just as soon shoot you as look at you, but he's not been seen in Bayou Parish for at least a couple of years now. Looks like he's made friends with the doctor, maybe even got himself employed by him." Sheriff Johnson was thinking out loud. "Yeah, Little Frankie Dalton wouldn't think twice about shooting Dale and Walter. He'd do it for the fun of it, for target practice, especially if someone offered him a little money and protection from the law."

Sheriff Johnson tinkered a bit with the knowledge, than formed a rudimentary course of action. Number one in the plan, find out what Little Frankie Dalton was doing in town. Number two, find out what Catriona Kirby's doing hanging out with him. Sheriff Johnson would start by heading to Winnsboro, Little Frankie's old stomping grounds, first thing tomorrow morning and having a heart-to-heart with the little cockroach.

Chapter Twenty-Three

It was nearly midnight when Adrienne unlocked the door to her house and went as quietly as possible into her office. She had told Andrew she didn't know what time she'd be home, but still, she didn't want to take a chance on waking him up and having to face him tonight. She sat back in her swivel chair to think. The whole evening with Mel had been so unbelievably wonderful, so real, she didn't want anything to spoil it. In time, there'd be issues to discuss and decisions to make, decisions that would hurt someone, no matter how the dice fell, but not tonight. She just wanted to relish the moment. This was what it was like to be in love. She poured a glass of Cabernet and went to the back porch to smoke a cigarette. As much as she hated to, she needed to get her mind off of Mel and back on the Healer case. In the morning she'd drive to Winnsboro and see what she could find out about Frankie Dalton.

Chapter Twenty-Four

The orange sun crept over the horizon and spread its tentacles, bringing in the dawn. From every direction the warming chards touched the dew, and for a brief moment, the morning was aglow. Adrienne tossed and turned on the sofa as the remover of darkness made its way through the thin lace curtains and across the room. She laid in a cold sweat, afraid to open her eyes, afraid that it had all been just a dream. Panic hit as she sat up, then the realization. It had not been a dream. Mel's words rang in her ears. She could feel the touch of his hands on her skin. Smell the scent of him on her clothes. She wanted to drink the whole evening in again, relive it in her heart and mind one second, one word, one touch at a time…. The squeaking wheels of Andrew's air tank made it clear he was headed her direction. Adrienne wrapped the blanket around her and went to the kitchen to make coffee.

"What time did you finally get in last night?"

"It was nearly midnight. I didn't want to wake you."

"I tried to call you about ten. Why didn't you answer your phone?"

"I was on a stake out. All the ringers were turned off."

"And I guess you don't check for voice messages or caller I.D. anymore when you're on a stakeout."

"This is a very serious case, Andrew. Maybe the most important, and possibly the most dangerous one I've ever had. Sometimes I can't stop to do anything else. Can't look away for even a minute. I know it's hard for you to believe, but sometimes what I do is really important." She didn't want to argue this morning. She poured coffee in two dark brown mugs and handed one to him. "How did your doctor's appointment go?" She took a long drink of the strong coffee.

"About like always. Took a breathing treatment after my checkup. Got my prescriptions filled. Offered to take Sarah to lunch but she had someplace she had to be. Watched soap operas all afternoon. Real exciting day. You oughta try it sometime." He took his coffee and went to the back porch. Adrienne went for a shower.

Chapter Twenty-Five

Adrienne took her time driving to Winnsboro. It was really too early for anything to be open or much going on, but she didn't want to stay home with Andrew any longer than absolutely necessary. Their discussion this morning had not turned into an argument, but it was quickly heading that way. No doubt an argument would have erupted if she'd stayed around. Her conscience was keeping her from feeling what she really wanted to feel this morning. Not only over what had happened between her and Mel the evening before, but also over what she knew was a kind of pleading coming from Andrew. He'd never been good at soft words, or at apologies of any kind, but Adrienne was sensing that loneliness was overwhelming him to the point that he could find no joy in anything anymore. She knew that was a horrible way to feel, and she didn't want to be the cause of any human being feeling that way. But was it her fault? She wanted so much to believe it was not, that it was a result of the life choices he'd made for himself when he was healthy and should have been spending his time with her and committed to their marriage. He hadn't considered Adrienne's feelings whatsoever when he was off with his girlfriend back in the days before the accident. Adrienne had been so lonely and afraid back then. Had he cared?. Why should she care now? Andrew seemed to be aging faster now, too. His thinning, brown hair had much more gray. His skin was dry and tired, his eyes a dull, cloudy brown. *That's his problem too*, she told herself. *He ought to slow down on the anti-depressants. Nobody needs that much mood control.* Her own caffeine and nicotine highs popped into a corner of her mind, but she decided that was a different thing. *He created his own monster. He'll just have to live with it.*

The sign read, "Welcome to Winnsboro." Adrienne pulled into the Shell station and asked for directions to Ashberry Road. The boy behind the counter told her to go to the second light and turn right. The third parish road on her left would be Ashberry. She paid him for a package of Yellow Jackets and a pack of Virginia Slims, then headed toward the road the DMV record showed Frankie Dalton lived on. She needed to find an out of the way place to park where she'd have a clear view if he came out of the house, but where Frankie wouldn't see her car. Her camera would show him up close even from a hundred yards away, but she wasn't especially worried about that. Frankie Dalton was so short it'd be hard to confuse him with any other man.

Second light, turn right. She drove a little further. *Third road on the left.* "That's it." She made the turn onto Ashberry Road. On both sides of the road were deep drainage ditches filled two thirds with water and with leaves shed from the scattered trees. Weeds were waist high in the fields as far as Adrienne could see, and there were no houses. It didn't look like anyone lived on this road. She kept driving. *Could have been a false address,* she thought, *but the DMV's pretty good about sniffing out those kinds of things.* A little further down was an old, abandoned barn, so dilapidated on one side she didn't see how it was still standing. The road curved to the right and Adrienne saw a cluster of trees up ahead. An old house trailer sat in the middle of the trees, shaded by the overhanging branches. Adrienne slowed down and took a good look but didn't stop and turn around until she was far enough up the road that she could barely see the trailer. She opened the spiral notebook lying on the seat beside her and made a few notes.

"Brown and white house trailer. Attached front porch looks like it's about to fall down. Roofing tin propped up for skirting. Stack of old tires on the left end of the trailer. Pit bull chained to a tree in the front. 1980 Ford Mustang in dirt driveway."

It was for sure the car Adrienne and Catriona had followed from Dr. Kirby's office. *Charcoal gray primer, no hubcaps, same license number.* There was no mistaking it. She'd drive by again without slowing down to see if she saw any other signs of life in the trailer, then turn around in the intersection and make her way back to the other end of the road again to try to find a place to position herself. It would be more difficult than she'd expected. When she was on a stakeout in a neighborhood she could always park on the street between other cars, or a lot of times, she had a clear view simply by parking around the corner, or occasionally in a store parking lot. The busier the street or neighborhood the better. It made her less obvious. She could just blend in. But out here on this old country road there were very few places to hide, and she couldn't do much more driving around to look for one.

There wouldn't be much traffic out here. It would be real easy for someone in the trailer to notice her if she wasn't careful. The little Ford Probe she was driving was low to the ground, and dark green in color. She passed the trailer again and saw a small entrance road to a corn field a few yards away. She stopped and got out. The gate wasn't locked. She'd park just inside, shielded by the six foot high corn stalks on both sides. Unless someone passed up the trailer and came further down the road, they wouldn't see her. The nose of the Probe was just far enough out to give her a clear shot of anyone going in or coming out of the trailer. She set the camera on the dashboard and lined out its direction, then leveled its inch-long legs. Adrienne poured a hot cup of coffee from the thermos she'd brought with her and hunkered down to wait and see what the morning would bring. A few minutes later, her secure phone rang. It was Catriona.

"Good morning, Adrienne. I wanted to see how things went yesterday with the hair samples."

"Good morning, Catriona. Everything went fine. We'll know the results in a few days. Where are you?"

"I'm home. Galen left early. He said he had some business to take care of, so he postponed the second autopsy until this afternoon. I know he's going by the clinic though. He took one of the puffer fish from our aquarium with him. He said the one in his office had died and he wanted to replace it."

"He doesn't seem like a man who'd have pets."

"I don't think he considers them pets. He's very interested in science, and exotic tropical fish are interesting to explore. He has several varieties, but I think the puffer fish are his favorite. In some parts of the world they're a delicacy that must be prepared by a very specialized chef because they have a toxin that is the strongest poison known to science."

Why would anyone want to eat that? Adrienne wondered silently.

"There's research going on right now about how to safely use the toxin as a powerful painkiller for terminally ill patients. Galen's intrigued with the research. He has several articles about the Haitian Zombies created by Voodoo doctors using puffer fish."

"Look, Catriona. I'm on a stakeout. Trying to see what I can find out about a man named Frankie Dalton. Have you ever heard of him?"

"The name sounds vaguely familiar, but I can't place him. Why?"

"I think he's the man that cornered you in Dr. Kirby's office and took the money he said the doctor owed him. He lives in Winnsboro. Have you ever heard your husband talk about anyone in Winnsboro?"

"No. But then, Galen's very careful what he talks about at home. Are you in Winnsboro now?"

"Yes, and I've got to hang up. A car's coming up the road. I'll talk to you later." She hung up the phone and crouched down in the seat. A few moments later, she took a peek. The white car with shaded windows and antennae protruding from several places on its top pulled into the dirt drive and up to the trailer. Sheriff Johnson stepped out.

"What the hell?" Adrienne said as she quickly put her eye to the camera, focused it in and pushed the button to turn it on. "Let her roll."

The pit bull chained to the tree barreled toward the sheriff, snatched back suddenly when it reached the end of its chain a few inches short of the sheriff's leg. Sheriff Johnson raised his giant, fleshy leg and mashed his boot into the dogs face. Stunned, the dog shook its head, then lunged again, his fangs glaring. The door of the trailer opened to the disturbance outside and a barefoot Frankie Dalton, dressed in blue jeans and a black Harley Davidson tee-shirt with a hole ripped in the side, stepped out onto the porch. He stood, arms crossed in front of him, feet spread apart, and said something to Sheriff Johnson. Adrienne was much too far away for any audio, but from the look on Frankie's face, he appeared surprised to have a visit from the sheriff. Adrienne kept the camera rolling.

"Morning, Little Frankie. Why don't you call your dog back so I don't have to put my foot through his face again."

"Morning, Sheriff. Killer don't take too well to obedience training. Kind of has a mind of his own. But I don't think he can break his chain. He hasn't for a couple of weeks now anyway, since I bought that new heavy duty one."

Sheriff Johnson walked a couple of inches toward the dog, and waited for him to come close again. The dog lunged just as the sheriff pulled his night stick out of its holster and raised his arm back behind him to gain momentum. With all his force, he brought the club down on the dog's head. One yelp, and the pit bull lay lifeless on the ground.

"What the hell'd ya kill my dog for?" Little Frankie screamed at the sheriff as he made his way down the steps and toward the giant man.

"Didn't like the way he welcomed me," the sheriff answered, looking Little Frankie dead in the eye. "You and me need to have a little talk."

"We ain't got nothing to talk about, and you ain't got no authority in this parish," Little Frankie answered without coming any closer. "Get off my property."

Adrienne wished she could hear what they were saying. She hadn't been prepared though for the sight of the dog's slaughter and blood spewing everywhere, especially so early in the morning.

Sheriff Johnson walked toward the porch and Little Frankie Dalton, night stick still in hand. Little Frankie stood his ground.

"You and me need to have a talk," the sheriff repeated. "What'd ya say we go inside."

"Damn it," Adrienne pushed the button to turn off the camera, then sat back on the seat to try to figure out what the hell was going on, and to wait for Sheriff Johnson and maybe Frankie Dalton to come back outside. *What's the sheriff doing here? Maybe he's come to collect part of the money Mr. Dalton took from the file cabinet Catriona had open. Wait a minute. Frankie Dalton and the sheriff working a drug deal together using the doctor's money. No way. The prisoner told Catriona that the sheriff and the doctor were running the scam. Sheriff Johnson and Dr. Kirby together.* That made sense, and it would be an easy scam to run since the doctor and the sheriff both had a hand in controlling every move the prisoners made especially when it came to their prescription medications, the sheriff through his badge, the doctor through medicine and the fact that he had no conscience. No question, together they had all the power they'd need. But she still hadn't a clue how Frankie Dalton was caught up in all this. The sheriff's visit this morning didn't fit in to Adrienne's theory.

"I've got to hear what's going on in that house." The dog was dead; she'd just have to hope there weren't anymore around to warn them. She took the palm-size camcorder out of the console and pushed it down in her jacket pocket. The morning air was cool and still covered with dew. She pulled her collar up to protect the back of her neck and got out of the car, pushing the door gently shut. Even slight noises echoed in open country. There was no way of knowing how long the men would be in the trailer, and Adrienne sure didn't want to be seen walking down the road if they came out, so she crouched low and walked as close to the line of corn rows as she possibly could, hoping that if the trailer door opened, she could duck behind the corn in time. Then the most dangerous part. There was a good fifty feet of open ground between the last row of corn and the side of the trailer. No scrub brush, not even a single tree. She'd have to run across it. If Sheriff Johnson or Frankie Dalton came out during that time, she'd be in plain view with no place to hide. She hesitated, then took a deep breath and made a run for it….Adrienne mashed herself into the side of the trailer and tried to catch her breath. She pulled the camcorder out of her pocket and made her way around to a window in the back, then stopped to listen. Voices came from the back room. Adrienne got close and took a quick peek in the window. The men stood just a few feet away from her. Two men, both criminals, possibly murderers, separated from her by a few sheets of tin and a little sheetrock, on a country road without a house or another human being in sight. Even her cell phone was in the car. She was totally on her own with no way to get help. One wrong move and she could be looking just like that poor dog laying dead in the front yard. She wouldn't be the first person to disappear under Sheriff Johnson's watch. Her heart was pounding, but she had to stay. Whatever she'd found herself in the big middle of, it was too late to turn back now. She remembered saying those very words to Catriona Kirby. "Yeah, I think you're husband is a murderer, but I want you to go right on living with him, sitting at the table with him, sleeping in the same bed with him. It's too late to turn back now." *Oh God,* she thought. *Sometimes I say the stupidest things* .She turned the camera on and took twenty seconds of footage. Frankie Dalton looked like a little kid who'd aged too quickly standing there in front of the sheriff who was 6'3". She put the camera back in her pocket and positioned herself to listen, her ear as close to the window as she could get it.

"I like to know when visitors are coming to town," the sheriff grinned at Little Frankie.

"What makes you think I was in town?"

"Saw you myself. I'm surprised to see you associating with some of the professional people in the parish now."

"I don't know what you're talking about."

"Not only spending time with the doctor, but getting to know his wife a little better, too, when the doctor's not around." Frankie turned his back to the big man, a very risky move.

Adrienne's heart stood still. *Where the hell was he hiding?* She felt sick. *If the sheriff saw Frankie Dalton and Catriona Kirby coming out of the clinic that afternoon, he sure the shit could have seen me. I must be slipping.*

"An ass-hole like you the size of a midget's pretty hard to mistake."

Little Frankie turned back toward the giant man and looked at him with eyes of steel. Rage welled up inside him at the one insult that made him madder than anything else ever could. His dad had seen to that, and he'd seen to it well. He taught him how to cripple a man for life with a few select punches. There was nothing Frankie would like better right now than to put the big man out of his misery. If he had his gun he'd put a bullet right between his eyes, then add a second one for what the sheriff had done to his dog.

"You jealous, big man? She's a good lookin woman. Want a little of the action yourself?" What little common sense the fool might have had left in him appeared to be gone. Sheriff Johnson's size alone made him capable of sending Little Frankie to the next world. But Little Frankie needed to know if the sheriff had any idea what was really going on. He'd see if he could side-track him by letting him think he might be sleeping with the doctor's wife.

"You want me to believe a high society chick like that would take a second look at a bastard like you?" He laughed out loud, then grabbed Little Frankie by the collar with his left hand and pulled him close to his face. With his right hand, he pulled a.38 caliber pistol out of its holster and put it under Frankie's chin. "We ain't playin any more games, Little Frankie. You killed the men on the levee, and the doctor hired you to do it. You think I'm some kind of fool?"

Frankie stood motionless and didn't say a word. Adrienne was afraid to breath. She needed this on audio. If the sheriff got Little Frankie Dalton to admit the doctor had hired him to kill the men on the levee, that's all the evidence she and Catriona would need to take to the district attorney. They'd have him on murder charges. They could get him on the black market baby selling scam after that. She just hoped the sheriff wasn't going to kill the doctor instead.

"Now just why do you think the doctor would do that?" Frankie stalled again, his heart beating a little faster now.

"He found out about my latest business interest that didn't include him. You took the drugs too, off the bodies. Two bags worth a quarter of a million dollars. Left me empty-handed, and a dealer with a lot of what should have been my money in his pocket."

"You've got a vivid imagination, sheriff."

"Yeah, well, I'm about to help you clear a few cob webs out of yours." Sheriff Johnson cocked the trigger. "You want to live you tell me what the doctor knows, and his fair-haired wife. I'm real anxious to hear how she got in on this. Only other option is I put you and both of them out of their misery. Choice is yours." He pushed the gun barrel hard into Little Frankie's flesh.

"He saw you leave the pharmacy with prescriptions and head south on the highway. He followed you to the storage building. Something didn't seem right. He told the pharmacist he wanted to check a few things out, be sure everything was recorded right. He figured out what you've been doing. That's all I know."

"That ain't shit. How'd you get in on the picture?"

"He came out here. Told me he had a job for me. Big money."

"What's big money for a shit-face like you?"

"He offered me $10,000. All I had to do was be at the levee before the guys working for you arrived. Puttem out of their misery and bring the drugs back to him. He knew you'd call him to come to the levee to verify the deaths. That's how he'd know I'd done my job. After he looked at the bodies and talked to you, he'd come to the clinic. I'd be waiting for him in the bushes there."

"That's what he was doing that night when I was coming home from the levee. I saw the lights on in the back of the clinic. I have a key. I came in the back door. He was acting mighty strange."

"Yeah. We heard you come in. I left out the front." Little Frankie stopped short of telling him that he hadn't collected the money or given the doctor the bags of drugs. He needed some kind of leverage to be sure the sheriff wanted to keep him alive.

"How'd Dr. Kirby find out when the deal was going down?"

"He was having you followed. Had someone tapping your phone line."

"No way. It'd have to be someone in my department, someone smart enough to know how to do it"

"Or someone smart enough to know you'd think he was too dumb to know how to do it."

The sheriff stared at the little man's murky eyes.

"You saying Harold? My deputy Harold? He doesn't have the brains to come in out of the rain."

"You'd be surprised how smart a man can get real fast when there's thousands of dollars in it for him."

The sheriff shoved Little Frankie against the wall. "What's Catriona Kirby got to do with it?"

Little Frankie knew he'd have to be very careful what he said now. He had to let the sheriff know he had access to the drugs without letting him know he had them right here on his property, buried in a hole under his dead dog's house.

"The doctor only had half the money the night we were in his office," Little Frankie lied. " He said he'd have the rest for me the next day. Something about having to fill out some kind of form at the bank if he took out $10,000 or more at a time." Little Frankie remembered seeing that fact about a tax law in a movie one time, and decided to incorporate it into his own lie. "I was supposed to meet him at the clinic after it closed at noon. He was going to do one of the autopsies and then meet me there. No exact time, just sometime between noon and four, whenever he could get away from the hospital. I waited in my car at the Auto Parts store so I could see when he got to the clinic."

"And?" Sheriff Johnson pulled a chair from the table and whipped it around backwards. He sat down still holding the gun aimed at Little Frankie's heart. Little Frankie knew he'd have to get as close to the truth as he could with the next part of the story since the sheriff had seen him and Catriona Kirby come out the back door of the clinic.

"I was eating sunflower seeds, waiting for the doctor when I saw a car circle round the block and stop behind the clinic long enough to let Catriona Kirby get out. Some woman I've never seen before was driving the car." Adrienne's heart jumped. "The car left. Catriona used a key and went in the back door. Seemed strange to me. The clinic being closed and such, and the doctor planning to meet me there any minute. I waited a few minutes and went in behind her. She'd left the door unlocked. She was in Dr. Kirby's closet going through a file. The rest of my money was in there too. I held my gun on her while she handed me the money. I told her there was no need to kill her since I knew she'd want to keep our little secret, too. Besides which, everyone knows who she is, but she didn't have a clue who I was. She doesn't exactly mingle with my crowd. She was making copies of papers in his file and then putting them back. I didn't figure she was going to want him to know that."

"What kind of papers?"

"I don't know, but she was in a big hurry to get out of there when I told her he was meeting me there any minute."

The sheriff thought quietly. Dr. Kirby had women all over northeast Louisiana. Cheap, needy, low maintenance women that had no lives of their own. That was no secret. Everybody knew. Maybe his wife had gotten fed up, was looking for divorce material. Maybe she had a boyfriend herself. Could be. That would make sense. That would mean Catriona Kirby didn't necessarily know about his and the doctor's drug scam. On the other hand, if she was getting ready to file for divorce, she'd be extremely interested in verifying his income, especially anything he was trying to keep out of official records. Little Frankie said she'd been making Xerox copies of papers and putting them back in a file when he surprised her. Surely the doctor wouldn't keep records of their drug money in his office, or in writing anywhere for that matter. If so and she'd found them, Catriona could black mail the sheriff, or put him in prison for life if she talked to the right people. He'd have to have a private talk with her kind of like the one he was having right now with Little Frankie, and he'd have to do it very soon. Sheriff Johnson stood up and walked toward Frankie Dalton.

"You shot the men on the levee in the back of the head and took the bags of drugs it's taken me over a year to get. I don't believe you gave the drugs back to the doctor."

"How else was I gonna get paid?" Frankie yelled.

The sheriff was falling for the lie. Little Frankie hoped he was home free. He had a quarter of a million dollars worth of drugs hidden in his yard. He just had to be sure the doctor would never talk, even if the barrel of the sheriff's gun was shoved down his throat. The sheriff wouldn't need to kill Little Frankie. There's no way he could talk to authorities without incriminating himself, and he wasn't about to do that.

"You even think about talking to the doctor about our little meeting and they'll have to seine the Mississippi River to find what's left of your body parts. You got it?" Sheriff Johnson stared at Little Frankie for a few seconds, then headed for the front door of the trailer. Little Frankie stood motionless and silent.

Adrienne wanted to break into a run back to her car and out of Winnsboro as fast as the Ford Probe could carry her, but she didn't dare move. Besides the fact that she had to wait until the sheriff was completely gone, she needed to watch and listen to see what Little Frankie Dalton's next move would be. Would he call Dr. Kirby? Would he leave to go warn him that the sheriff was onto them? She needed to know. She was also very worried about where Sheriff Johnson was heading right now. She decided it was unlikely he'd confront Dr. Kirby at this point in the game. It was more likely he'd head for the snitch that had informed the doctor. If it hadn't been for Deputy Harold the sheriff would be a rich man right now. He wouldn't have to worry about being re-elected or his ties to the psychopath doctor, or even his connections to any of the murders over the years. He could just make his way down through south Louisiana then follow the gulf over to Texas and quietly slide on over into Mexico to find himself a nice resort town to call home. If it hadn't been for Deputy Harold. But he'd have to be real careful how he handled his deputy. He'd have to think it through. More important right now was Catriona Kirby. She could really mess things up. He'd have a little talk with her and find out exactly what she knew, see how dangerous she was to his plans for the future. It'd be a shame to have to eliminate such a pretty woman, but he could see to it if necessary. It'd serve the doctor right. Make him squirm a little harder. The more Sheriff Johnson thought about it, the more he liked the idea. Maybe if he thought hard, he could make it look like the deaths of Catriona Kirby and Deputy Harold were connected. *Hell*, he thought. *Maybe*

I can find a way to pin them both on the doctor. Put him away too. But first, I've got to get my stash back. Sheriff Johnson was pleased with the idea.

Adrienne was trying to keep up with the Sheriff's sick kind of reasoning. She knew Deputy Harold's life was definitely in danger. *I've got to get out of here,* she thought. *I've got to get help before Sheriff Johnson kills Harold. Who in the hell can I talk to? Who'd believe me?* Then suddenly another thought hit her like a ton of bricks. *Holy shit. Catriona! Sheriff Johnson thinks she's involved. Thinks she may know about the drug scam. His he-man mentality might very well try to even the score with the doctor by harming the doctor's wife even if she didn't know anything. I've got to get to my phone! I've got to warn her! It's Catriona he's most likely to go after now. He'll have to take his time figuring out how to get ready of his deputy.* Adrienne took a quick peek in the window. Little Frankie had a fifth of Jack Daniels in his hand and was standing motionless, staring at the front door. Sheriff Johnson's car left dust flying behind him. Adrienne made a run back across the open space and to her car hidden in the cornfield. She sat winded, and tried to catch her breath while she dialed Catriona's house. No answer. "God help me reach her," she whispered as she tried her cell phone number. "Come on, come on." Five rings, six. The voice mail clicked on. "Catriona, this is Adrienne." She was still breathless. "Get out of Destiny. Don't stop anywhere until you get to Monroe. Meet me at Reward Yourself in Antique Alley. Don't leave there," she nearly yelled, "until I get there. No matter what." Adrienne started her car and looked up the road to be sure all was clear before she pulled out in the open. In the distance she could see the dark spot of a vehicle coming toward her. "What now?" she asked, grabbing her shoulder bag from the back seat. Her hands trembled as she opened the clasp and took hold of the handgun she'd tucked away the first day she went to meet Catriona Kirby. It had only been a matter of days, but so much had happened, it seemed like ages ago. She picked up her binoculars and focused on the dark spot. "Maybe it's just a car coming down the road, going somewhere beyond Frankie Dalton's and the cornfield. "Please," she prayed, "let them just cruise right on by." The idea that a normal person doing normal things could be in that vehicle seemed surreal to her. "Please," she prayed again as the vehicle increased in size and focus. "I've got to get out of here. People are going to die!" The dark spot was getting larger and larger. Adrienne scrunched down in the seat with her eyes level at the bottom of her car window, waiting to see what kind of vehicle it was and if it would just go on by. She knew if it was the sheriff returning, Little Frankie Dalton was a dead man. On the other hand, if the sheriff was still on his way back to Bayou Parish, Deputy Harold and Catriona Kirby were both in great danger. The vehicle slowed down as it approached Little Frankie's dirt driveway. It wasn't the sheriff's car. It was a steel-gray truck with a flashy show bumper. Dr. Galen Kirby turned into Little Frankie Dalton's drive.

Adrienne was paralyzed. It wasn't like her to come unstrung, but she was close to doing so now. "What the hell is he doing here? He's supposed to be doing autopsies today?" She had to get a hold of herself. The doctor wasn't here to kill Little Frankie, at least not yet. He was here to get the drugs Little Frankie was hiding. She needed to get back to the trailer window and get the scene on film. It could be all she'd need to put the Dr. Kirby away for a long, long time. Her mind deviated from the doctor for a moment. *I've got to get a hold of Catriona before I do anything else. The first place the sheriff would look for her would be at her home, and I know she's not there, or at least I'm pretty sure she's not there. She takes the secure cell phone with her wherever she goes, so most likely it won't be more than a few minutes before she'll get my message. Maybe she was in a check out line somewhere or the bathroom when I called. She'll get the message. It'll take her forty-five minutes to get to Reward Yourself if she's in Destiny, but only twenty minutes to get completely out of Bayou Parish. It'll take the sheriff forty-five minutes to get back to town from here.* "Please, Catriona," she said out loud, get that message and get out of Bayou Parish in the next few minutes."

If Adrienne was right and the sheriff went for Catriona first, where would he look for her when he discovered she wasn't home? *Where would she be? Where.... the Country Club. That's* where *the sheriff would look next.* Adrienne swallowed hard, that's where Catriona would most likely be. Adrienne had emphasized to Catriona from the moment she'd agreed to take the case that she was to keep her normal routine, to keep doing the things she'd always done as far as humanly possible so no unnecessary attention would be drawn to her. The advice she'd given to protect Catriona might very well be the thing that would cost her her life. Neither of the women had known for sure at the time who all might be involved with Dr. Kirby's activities. As far as that goes, they still weren't positive, and they weren't sure of the extent of the crimes and how they were tied together. All they knew for sure was that he's a very dangerous man.

Adrienne hadn't taken her eyes off Little Frankie Dalton's trailer for one second. The doctor got out of his truck, stood looking at the dead dog lying at the end of a chain, and was now standing on Little Frankie's front porch waiting for the door to open. As much as Adrienne wanted to take off in the opposite direction on Ashberry Road, she knew she had to get back to the window at the back of Frankie Dalton's trailer. She had to hear the conversation that would most likely make a lot of the missing pieces fit, at least as far as the drug scam and the murders on the levee were concerned. That would put Little Frankie Dalton, Sheriff Johnson and yes, Dr. Galen Kirby in prison where they belong. Then Adrienne would get Detective Mike Morris to help her figure out the rest of the black market baby racket. She wondered if it was possible the dead women had found out about the drug scam, or maybe were even involved in it. She sure wished Mike and his detective expertise was with her now. It hit her that she was really terrified for herself if she got caught sitting in this cornfield, and for Catriona who was in dire danger, especially if she didn't get Adrienne's message. There was a giant lump in her throat. She didn't like to think of herself as vulnerable in any way. She tried to come across as tough as possible for that very reason. Strong, independent, intelligent, no nonsense. But at this moment, she felt the other side of her surface. The insecure little girl that wanted to be held and comforted, cherished and protected was trying to assert herself. "No time to get all emotional," she told herself. "The doctor's in. I've got to get back to that trailer." She tried to muster up courage. "I've got to try to reach Catriona at the Country Club first."

Her intellect screamed at her, "Take action, Adrienne, move. Don't just sit here. *Definitely no time for a cigarette now.* She pulled the northeast Louisiana telephone directory out of the stack of phone directories in the back seat and looked up the number for the country club. With trembling hands she pushed the numbers on the phone. It was ringing. *Please, please. Please let her be there.*

"Destiny Country Club," a man's voice.

"Hi," Adrienne tried to sound calm and friendly. "Is Catriona Kirby there? I tried her cell phone but didn't get an answer."

"She was here earlier," the voice at the other end replied. "I'm not sure if she's still around."

"Would you mind checking, please?"

"Sure." The man put Adrienne on hold. Elevator music played its ridiculous calm in her ear. She looked back over at the trailer. Dr. Kirby was inside.

"Hello?" Catriona's voice.

"Catriona. Thank God. Listen to me. Don't show any alarm. You're in danger. Leave the Country Club now. Don't go home first. Meet me at Reward Yourself. Don't leave until I get there no matter how long it takes me. Sheriff Johnson may be looking for you right now. He'll be coming from Winnsboro. That means he'll take the Delhi highway over to I-20 and then into Destiny. You take the back way from the Country Club. Stay out of his way." She had no way of knowing if Catriona had ever traveled the back way. She didn't want to take a chance that she'd get on I-20, the easiest route, and possibly cross paths with the sheriff. "I'll get there as soon as I possibly can. Remember," Adrienne tried to encourage, realizing that Catriona must be terrified, "Academy Award performance. Gotta go." She clicked the button.

"Talk to you later, "Catriona said into the phone as she smiled at the Country Club bartender and hung up the phone. "Thank you." She turned away and walked slowly back outside where she'd been sitting at an umbrella'd table drinking lemonade with a couple of the other wives. She picked up her glass and took a sip through the long straw. "Gotta run," she smiled. "See you all at Canasta." She picked up her purse and walked nonchalantly out the gate and to her car.

Adrienne clicked off the camera and listened as carefully as possible. Little Frankie Dalton stood two feet from the window, whiskey bottle in hand, and Dr. Kirby stood a few feet away facing him. Dr. Kirby held his left hand like there was something in it, something small and completely concealed. Adrienne had no idea what it might be, but at least it wasn't a gun.

"Let's both have a drink," Dr. Kirby said to Little Frankie, "and talk about this. You've got the drugs, I've got the money. We can finish our deal today. You do have the drugs here, on your property?"

"I've got the drugs." Little Frankie answered.

"Fine, fine. I'll have some of that Jack Daniels you're holding, on the rocks. Pour yourself one. We'll toast a job well done."

Adrienne had a really bad feeling about what was going down. Little Frankie walked into the kitchen and pulled out two glasses. Adrienne could barely see his arm around the corner as he mixed the two drinks, then came back into the room and handed one to the doctor. The doctor took a sip, then sat down on the sofa and crossed his legs like he and Little Frankie were two old buddies having a friendly chat.

"Now," he started. "The $10,000 is in my truck. You get the drugs and we'll get this thing finished."

Little Frankie looked at the doctor. "Things've changed Doc. Had a little visit from the sheriff this morning. I'm gonna have to get a long ways from here fast and that's gonna take more than $10,000."

The doctor froze. He sat his drink on the end table and fumbled with whatever it was he was holding in his hand. He'd already lost $10,000 on this deal, the money someone had stolen from his office, and he didn't intend to lose anymore. "The sheriff was here?"

"I can get by on $100,000, for awhile at least."

"You discussed our arrangement with Sheriff Johnson?"

"I didn't discuss shit with anyone," Little Frankie was livid. "The bastard figured it out himself. He came here this morning telling me what he knew. Making threats. You must have passed him on the highway."

Dr. Kirby hadn't seen the sheriff, nor had the sheriff seen him, but that really didn't matter at the moment. What did matter was that the doctor get the drugs from Little Frankie and get out of Little Frankie's house and back to town. He needed to start the second autopsy right away. No one would ever know he'd been gone. The vial with the puffer fish toxin, just the right amount to kill Little Frankie slowly over the next couple of hours, was in his land. He just needed to get the bags of drugs, then he'd put the precious drops in his drink. It didn't matter if Little Frankie drank it now or later, within a few hours of ingesting it, he'd be dead. Dr. Kirby had thought about mixing the toxin so he could just keep Little Frankie in a zombie state for a few days, comatose, just in case he'd hidden the drugs, before he increased its strength and killed him. He'd been wanting to experiment on a human instead of cats ever since he'd read the literature about the Voodoo doctors in Haiti and how they had the worship of whole villages who believed they were bringing the dead back to life. "Haitian Zombies," the literature called them, created by the exact science of administering puffer fish toxin, the most potent toxin known to mankind. Easily deadly, but with tedious care, Dr. Kirby had perfected doses that could be used to create the zombie state from the Haitian recipe. Of course he'd had to practice on neighborhood cats, and that was different, but he'd been successful with them. If time permitted, if he had a few more days, Little Frankie Dalton would be the perfect candidate for the doctor's first attempt to create a human zombie. No one would ever miss Little Frankie Dalton except his two brothers, and they were both in prison. His dad was already dead, and his mother had abandoned them all years ago, in fear for her own life at their hands. He was a slime ball, a genetic defect. The world would be better off without him. But that was before the doctor discovered the sheriff had figured out the situation. The sheriff's new knowledge changed the whole course of action Dr. Kirby would need to take. One puffer fish provided up to six hundred deadly doses, a couple of thousand "zombie" doses. Oh well, he'd follow through with the experiment somewhere down the road when a safer opportunity presented itself. Today, he'd administer the deadly dose to Little Frankie. Tomorrow, to the sheriff. But first, he needed the bags of drugs Little Frankie had hidden somewhere on his property, most likely in this trailer. The quarter of a million dollars they were worth was part of it, but definitely not the most important part. The most important part of everything in life was that Dr. Kirby have control. The sheriff had deceived him and manipulated their arrangement so that he was in control. Now Little Frankie Dalton was doing the same. *They should have known better.*

"Show me the drugs first, then we'll talk money."

"I don't think so, Doc. I think you'll go to the bank and get the rest of the money and meet me at the bus depot in Monroe. Bring it in small denominations in a duffel bag. You hand me the money, I'll hand you the drugs. No other options."

The doctor was silent for a moment. *No other options.* The phrase infuriated him. He looked at Little Frankie with serpent eyes. "I'll have one more drink before I go," he said, handing Little Frankie his empty glass.

Little Frankie took the doctor's glass and went to the kitchen. Adrienne cringed as she watched Dr. Kirby open a small vial and pour something into Little Frankie's drink that sat on the coffee table. Little Frankie came back into the room and handed Dr. Kirby a second glass of Jack Daniels.

"Another toast, to the future," the doctor raised his glass.

"I don't think so," Little Frankie answered. "Just tell me how soon you can be at the bus depot."

"I'll call you."

"No phone calls, Doc. You meet me at the bus depot in Monroe at six o'clock this evening or I leave with the drugs." Little Frankie walked to the front door and opened it, an invitation for the doctor to leave. He raised the pistol in his hand, surprising the doctor. "See you at six."

"I'm supposed to be starting an autopsy at two o'clock."

"Cancel it."

"I can't. It's already been postponed once. It has to be done today or the sheriff will be asking questions."

Little Frankie looked at him with frustration, but he sure didn't want any more trouble out of the sheriff right now. "Tomorrow morning. I'll give you until eleven o'clock. I'll be at the bus depot. If you're one minute late, I'm leaving and the drugs are going with me. And I'm making a little anonymous phone call to the Feds on my way out, explaining you and the sheriff's little side business."

"I'll be there," Dr. Kirby said, not wanting to leave until he knew where the drugs were hidden, but not having any choice. It wouldn't be too hard to find them in this run down old trailer, and Frankie wasn't smart enough, in the doctor's view, to have hidden them anywhere else.

Adrienne watched in silence as Dr. Kirby went out the front door. At least he didn't know anything about Catriona's involvement yet. Nothing had been said to incriminate her. Evidently Little Frankie hadn't wanted to complicate matters any further, and Catriona was no direct threat to him. So Dr. Kirby would be looking to settle the score with the sheriff, not his wife. At least Catriona was safe from her husband for now.

Little Frankie locked the door behind the doctor and picked up his drink that was still sitting on the table. Adrienne pounded on the trailer window. "No," she yelled, but it was too late. He'd gulped it down, every last drop.

Little Frankie stood on the steps to the trailer's back door pointing his gun at Adrienne's chest. "Who the hell are you? What're you doing in my back yard?"

"Never mind who I am. Dr. Kirby put something in your drink. It may have been some kind of poison."

"What're you trying to pull? And I'm gonna ask you one more time, who are you?" He walked toward Adrienne, the gun steady in his hand.

"Adrienne Hargrove, I've been following Dr. Kirby." She had to tell him something.

"You a private eye?"

"Yes. Doing a job for the doctor's wife. Seems Dr. Kirby has a girlfriend or two on the side."

"You trying to catch the doc with a woman?" He chuckled. "Hey," he stopped for a moment. "That was you driving the car that dropped Mrs. Kirby off the day me and her had our little run in at the doctor's office. She was taking papers out of his file. What'd she tell you about me?"

"Nothing. She was looking for information on his girlfriends." She couldn't let Little Frankie know she knew about the drugs or the sheriff, but she really didn't want to stand here and watch him drop dead either. "Please listen to me." She had to get him back to the moment. "I was watching through the window. When you went in the kitchen Dr. Kirby put something in your drink."

"You sayin he tried to poison me?"

"Maybe. All I know is he put something in your drink."

"I don't think the doctor wants to see me dead right now. But I do think you better come inside. We need to have a little talk about what you overheard." He motioned with the gun for Adrienne to walk in front of him and go inside the trailer. "I don't feel nothing. I think you're trying to pull something. Let's have that little talk." He locked the back door and ordered Adrienne to sit down.

Adrienne looked around the shabby room. The faded, green shag carpet was matted and filthy. The sofa had once been orange plaid, now it was shades of sickening butterscotch and diluted lemon, interspersed with patches of dirt and stains. The front windows were covered with aluminum foil to keep the afternoon sun from shining in. Thank goodness for Adrienne Little Frankie hadn't seen it necessary to do the same with the back windows.

"What's on the camcorder," he said, walking toward her.

"Nothing. I was expecting to find the doctor with a woman. That would have made my case," she tried to fake a smile as she built the lie.

"Yeah, well, let's just take a look," he reached out for the camcorder, still pointing the gun.

"There's nothing you'd be interested in," Adrienne tried to stall until she could think of a way out of the situation.

"I'll decide how interesting...Little Frankie stopped in the middle of his sentence. He gasped once, dropped the gun and fell to the floor. Adrienne lunged forward and kicked the gun across the room. She fell to one knee and rolled Little Frankie over on his back. She put her head to his chest and listened. He was still breathing. She ran for the phone and dialed 911.

"Quick," she said to the operator. "A man's unconscious! He may have been poisoned." She gave the address on Ashberry Road.

"Helps on the way. Your name please."

Adrienne hung up the phone. There was no more she could do to help Little Frankie and she was pretty sure Sheriff Johnson was looking for Catriona, whose life might very well be next. Adrienne left out the back door and ran across the cornfield to her car. She locked the car doors and drove as fast as possible back up Ashberry Road and over to the Winnsboro highway. The 911 emergency vehicle passed her on its way to Little Frankie's house. She sure hoped he'd survive. He'd be going to prison for the murders of the two men on the levee. Maybe he'd want company bad enough to finger the doctor and the sheriff. *That would sure save a lot of problems*, Adrienne thought as she turned onto I-20 and headed for West Monroe and Reward Yourself.

Sheriff Johnson pulled through the parking lot of the Bayou Parish Hospital and around to the side entrance leading to the Medical Examiner's Office. Dr. Kirby's truck wasn't there, so he parked and went inside. "Where's Dr. Kirby?" he asked the nurse on duty. "I thought he was doing the second autopsy today."

"We expect him any time now," the nurse answered.

The sheriff went back to his car and pulled around behind the hospital where he'd be able to see the doctor when he arrived. Thirty minutes later the doctor pulled up and went inside. Sheriff Johnson, satisfied as to the doctor's whereabouts, left for the Kirby's house. He'd pay Mrs. Kirby a little visit.

"Shit," the sheriff said, seeing that Catriona Kirby's SUV was not home. "Dam women don't ever stay home anymore." He made a quick loop through the circular drive and went back to the stop light, then made his way to the country club. Checking out the cars in the parking lot, he was again disappointed. *Now what? I've got to get to her and find out what she knows. Where would she be? Those country club bitches spend most of their time playing cards at the country club or shopping in Shreveport. Hmm. Shreveport. Maybe I'll spend some time cruising I-20 between the intersection and Destiny. She has to come home sooner or later. There's nowhere else in town for her to go. If she's gone to Shreveport or Monroe, either one, she has to come I-20 to get back home. And there's twenty-five miles of lonely highway between that intersection and town.* Perfect place for the sheriff to pull her over in his official car, intended to intimidate. Spending the afternoon cruising and watching for Catriona Kirby would give him time to figure out what to do about Deputy Harold and Little Frankie Dalton. He still needed the doctor, at least a little while longer.

Chapter Twenty-Six

Adrienne came out of Winnsboro on the Rayville exit, reached I-20 and turned west. From there it would still take about thirty minutes to get to Reward Yourself in West Monroe. In a way she was glad for the time alone. It would give her a chance to think and put a period on a few things that up until now had question marks. Exactly what did she know? She knew the prisoner who'd called Catriona and who had later been found dead was right about Dr. Kirby and Sheriff Johnson's illegal drug scam. Sheriff Johnson contracted, legally, the prisoners' medical care to Dr. Kirby. The sheriff took prisoners who were sick or who had medical complaints to Dr. Kirby, and a few well ones too, for good measure. Dr. Kirby wrote legitimate prescriptions for the prisoners for antibiotics and other common medications that would be paid for by the state, but he also wrote prescriptions for painkillers and other narcotic drugs the state paid for under the prisoners' names, but the prisoners never got. Sheriff Johnson had the prescriptions filled and picked them up at the pharmacy. He gave the prisoners what he and the doctor had agreed on, and then stored the rest until they accumulated enough narcotics to make a large scale illegal sale. The doctor would profit in two ways. First, the state would be paying him for the prisoners' office calls and the drug companies paying him a percentage for prescribing their drugs, and second, narcotics were highly desirable on the illegal drug market, so he'd make major money by selling to traffickers. Dr. Kirby needed Sheriff Johnson to get the prisoners to him, to fill the prescriptions and skim the drugs they were going to sell. He had to be paying him a major part of the profit.

Sheriff Johnson's part in the scam, well that was obvious. He couldn't deal without the doctor. But evidently from the things Adrienne had overheard, Sheriff Johnson had gotten a bit greedy, was double-dipping. He was hiding more pills than the doctor knew about, and selling them to a different trafficker, keeping all the money. To do that, the sheriff needed someone between him and the second dealer to make the sale. The two dead men on the levee. Dr. Kirby'd found out what Sheriff Johnson was doing. How? An inside job, Sheriff Johnson's deputy, Harold, according to Little Frankie. The man the sheriff thought was too stupid to have a clue. But when a man's supporting a family on $800 a month, it doesn't take much to turn him into a traitor. Harold rode along on duty with Sheriff Johnson nearly every day. He'd seen and overheard enough to figure out what the sheriff was doing and offered the information to Dr. Kirby, for the right price. Dr. Kirby hired Little Frankie Dalton to kill the sheriff's go-betweens, the two men on the levee, and to get back the bags of drugs the sheriff had been accumulating. Problem now? Catriona had shown up at the clinic at the same time Little Frankie was waiting to meet the doctor there for the switch. Little Frankie would return the drugs he'd gotten off the dead men to the doctor for the $10,000 Catriona had seen in the safe. The same money Little Frankie had stolen while Catriona was making copies of the papers. Dr. Kirby still didn't know who had stolen the money, but he must suspect Little Frankie. Most likely suspects the sheriff's involved too. Little Frankie has the drugs. The doctor thinks the sheriff has the money, but actually, Little Frankie has the drugs and the money hidden, probably at his house trailer.

Now, the sheriff knows Dr. Kirby hired Little Frankie to kill the two men, Dale and Walter, so he knows the doc's aware of the double scam. No doubt about it, the doctor and the sheriff are out to get rid of each other. And Catriona? Well, the doctor didn't seem to know anything about her being in his office, at least not yet, and Little Frankie hadn't said anything about it, so she was as safe from him as she had been before. But the sheriff had seen her there. He'd seen her in the building with Little Frankie Dalton. The sheriff would have every reason to believe Catriona was in on Little Frankie's end of the scam, thinking both of them were scamming the doctor. *That's the trouble with thieves and murderers*, Adrienne thought. *They think all people are slime balls like themselves.* She was very aware again that Catriona's life was in immediate danger from the sheriff. He'd think there was a need to get rid of her and in time the doctor, too. No doubt he'd have to get rid of Deputy Harold.

But what about the dead women and the baby selling racket? Adrienne had listened to the inside scoop from Dr. Kirby, Sheriff Johnson, and Little Frankie Dalton, all three, this day. Not one of them had mentioned anything, not one word about Susanne Jasper or Drusilla Gifford. Not one word about babies or adoptions. That told her that Dr. Kirby was handling that little side business all on his own.

Poison in a tiny vial. It was so simple. In a split second Dr. Kirby had taken care of Little Frankie Dalton. Adrienne wondered if Little Frankie would survive. She'd check that out later. Right now she'd stake her reputation that Dr. Kirby had poisoned Susanne and Drusilla too. *I don't know where to go with this baby black market thing. I can't see a tie to any of the other crap. I'll have to figure that one out by coming in the back door. Nothing obvious about its connection to the drug scam unless somehow these women became aware of the scam and threatened to use it against him or to expose him somehow. Maybe some form of blackmail. My bet is that it's connected to the doctor's ego more than to money, his psychopathic belief about his own superiority. But any way you look at it, the man's a serial killer. What's different about him and other serial killers is that most of them have one mind set, one overall justification for the murders they commit. To control women, or sometimes just for the thrill of violence but usually against a specific group of people. Women in a certain age group or with similar physical features. There are the Jeffrey Daumers, a homosexual who preyed on young boys. Dr. Kirby's violence is toward men and women, possibly even toward children. With him, it's just whoever gets in his way or doesn't fit the part he sees for them in his plan. Anyone who gets in his way is disposable. Whatever the reality about the women and the baby black market, investigating that crime has to be put on hold until I know Catriona is safe, and there's no way she can be safe until we get the doctor and the sheriff behind bars.* . Adrienne pulled into Reward Yourself and was relieved to see Catriona's SUV in the parking lot.

Adrienne stood in the doorway and looked around the coffeehouse. A couple of business men were sitting at a table along one wall, but she didn't see anyone else. The giant lump in her throat hardened. Catriona's SUV was out front. *Oh my God. Maybe the sheriff!* The bathroom door at the back opened and Catriona came into view. Adrienne breathed a sigh of relief.

"You scared me to death," she said, walking toward her.

"I'm sorry, Adrienne. My nerves are on edge. It's been hard just sitting here waiting for you, not knowing what's going on."

"I know. I'm sorry. I couldn't tell you any more on the phone. Are you sure no one was following you?"

"As sure as I can be. I came the back way like you told me. I've been here for quite awhile and I haven't seen anyone suspicious. Adrienne, what's happened?"

"Let's sit down toward the back so we can talk and watch at the same time." They moved to a table in the back along the wall where the lights were dim. The waiter approached. Adrienne ordered black coffee and Catriona, another cup of green tea. "Look. It's all pretty complicated," Adrianne began to explain the scam that was going on between the sheriff and Dr. Kirby. She explained that she'd gotten Frankie Dalton's name and address from the Department of Motor Vehicles through his license plate number. She told Catriona how she'd gone to Winnsboro to stake out Little Frankie's house and try to find out what connection he had to the doctor, and that while she was there, the sheriff had arrived. She'd been able to film the two men through the back window of Little Frankie's trailer house, and the walls of the old trailer were so thin, she'd been able to hear every word they'd said. The Sheriff threatened to kill Little Frankie if he let Dr. Kirby know they'd talked, then he left, very possibly to go look for Catriona.

"So the prisoner who called me afraid for his life was right."

"Yes, but he only knew a small part of it." Adrienne went on to explain how the sheriff had begun to work a little drug deal of his own on the side, using the doctor without his knowing it. But somewhere along the way an informant told Dr. Kirby what's going on.

"An informant? Who?"

"According to Little Frankie Dalton, the informant is the sheriff's deputy, Harold, and the sheriff knows he's been crossed him, so Harold's in danger too." Catriona looked horrified. Adrienne went on.

"While I was watching through the window at Little Frankie's house right after I called you, Dr. Kirby put something, I think it was poison, in Little Frankie's drink. Then he left. He said he had an autopsy today at two o'clock."

"Galen was there? He is supposed to do the other autopsy today."

"Yes, he was there. He showed up just a few minutes after Sheriff Johnson left. It was like Grand Central Station out there on that old farm road. Thirty minutes after Dr. Kirby left, Little Frankie was passed out on the floor. He may be dead. I called 911 and left before they arrived. He was still breathing when I left, but barely. I didn't want to have to answer any questions." Adrienne wasn't sure how much more the visibly shaken Catriona could take, but she had to continue. "Look Catriona. There's a lot still missing. I haven't figured out what part the dead women and the child play in it all, but I'm convinced that Sheriff Johnson and Little Frankie Dalton don't have anything to do with that part. I don't think they even know anything about it. Whatever is going on there is your husband's game. We've got to put it on hold until we get the rest of this mess under control, then we'll go back to it. Right now, I know for sure that your husband and the sheriff are dealing illegal drugs on a large scale and committing fraud against the Medicaid and Medicare systems. I know for sure that your husband hired Little Frankie Dalton to kill the men on the levee and that he probably just killed Little Frankie Dalton with some kind of poison. I have a gut level feeling that Dr. Kirby is a serial killer and the two dead ex-girlfriends may jus be a tip on that iceberg." She stopped for a moment and gave Catriona a chance to respond, but she only sat in silence, staring into space. "There's every reason he's going to want to kill the sheriff next. There's every reason to believe the sheriff will want to get rid of Deputy Harold, and because Sheriff Johnson saw you and Little Frankie coming out of the clinic the other day, he thinks you're in on double crossing him. He can't just go marching into the Sheriff Department and kill Harold. It's going to take time for him to figure out a safe way to do that, so the most likely scenario is that he's looking for you. The problem is it's all circumstantial evidence. Some of it, most of it, would just be our word against theirs. We still don't have proof."

Catriona sat silent and motionless, trying to take it all in. Her husband, a fraud, a drug dealer, a murderer, in Adrienne's words quite possibly a serial killer, and the worst was yet to come. She looked Adrienne dead in the eye.

"Your name was never mentioned between Dr. Kirby and Little Frankie Dalton," Adrienne continued. "I don't think your husband has any idea that you were in his office. Little Frankie is probably dead, but Sheriff Johnson knows you were there, and once he puts two and two together, he's probably going to confront Dr. Kirby with that piece of information too. The bottom line is, we've got to find a way to keep you safe until we can get the District Attorney's office on our side."

"You got it all on film. You heard every word. That's enough evidence to convict them all. We have to get to the District Attorney's office. He's got to have Galen and Sheriff Johnson arrested," Catriona hoped the solution could be that simple.

"Look Catriona. While I was driving here to meet you, I called my detective friend in Baton Rouge. There are no voices on the film I took. It shows the men together in different scenarios, but what I overheard, according to Mike, could be taken as my word against theirs. He doesn't think we've got enough for the D.A. If Little Frankie's dead, and he probably is, we've got a better chance, but it's going to be a while before we know about that, and we've got to get you somewhere safe right now. I want to take you to my house. It's a lodge hidden off in the woods. A person has to know exactly what they're looking for to find it. You'll be safe there until we can think this through."

Catriona was barely blinking. The numbing fear had come full circle, had shifted, and was now keeping her calm.

"We have to fix it ourselves, Adrienne. We have to make it safe." She sounded much too calm for Adrienne's liking. "We have to get back to Galen's office and get the puffer fish toxin, the Zombie powder."

"What are you talking about?"

It was Catriona's turn to explain. "For quite some time now Galen has been experimenting with a toxin that comes from an exotic fish called the puffer fish. The medical community is examining the possible use of the puffer fish toxin in a dramatically diluted form as a potent painkiller for terminally ill patients."

"I've seen them in pet stores. Real cute little guys. Swell up all round. Look like miniature floating porcupines. I remember you saying Dr. Kirby had some and was using them in some kind of study."

"Yes, but a toxin contained in the bodies of some kinds of puffer fish is the most poisonous substance known to man. If that's what Galen put in Frankie Dalton's drink. Well, used in the form of a toxin, it's always fatal."

"What do you mean when used in the form of a toxin? What are you suggesting? We can't go around poisoning people Catriona. Even if they do deserve it."

"No, of course not. But there's another possibility." She looked at Adrienne with serious eyes. "There are three known uses for puffer fish toxin. One, as a fatal poison. The second, in the right combination with other chemicals as a powerful painkiller. And the third, the one Galen's been experimenting with for quite some time now, is referred to as Zombie powder. I wouldn't have known he was doing it if it hadn't been for an ethics charge someone filed against him a few years ago. He was using a recipe he'd discovered in the medical research and experimenting with Zombie powder on neighborhood cats. The idea was to put them in a comatose state without killing them. Some died, but he was finally able to perfect the technique."

Adrienne thought back to the court house records and law suits against Dr. Kirby. She vaguely recalled something about cats.

"A few months ago," Catriona continued, "Galen came to me and wanted me to help him with an experiment he couldn't do by himself."

Adrienne looked at her in shock. "Catriona, please tell me you didn't participate in Dr. Kirby's experiments!"

"I didn't want to. I argued with him about it, but he was so insistent. And the experiment was on him, not on anyone or anything else."

"He wanted you to give him puffer fish poison?"

"No. Zombie powder made from the puffer fish toxin. Remember, Adrienne, I have a degree in biology, and a strong chemistry background. I considered going to medical school, but married a doctor instead. Galen was so sure he had the formula right. He wanted to take a dose so that he could experience first hand the way an adult human being would react to it. The powder is supposed to cause total paralysis. Total inability to move or to communicate, yet everything else stays the same. The person is completely aware of everything that's happening to him, but can't move or talk. I refused, but he kept on insisting. He showed me step by step how to do it. The exact way to measure, the exact way to administer, the exact response to expect. The experiment was perfectly done. Listen to me Adrienne. If I can get to that Zombie powder, we can put Galen out of commission, on hold so to speak, until you can get the rest of the evidence we need, or get someone somewhere to believe us. He made thousands of doses of Zombie powder. Enough to keep him paralyzed for years if need be. It's the only way."

"That's crazy, Catriona. I can't let you turn your husband into a Zombie while I try to get him convicted of a crime."

"It's not just a crime, Adrienne. He's a serial killer, and it's most likely just a matter of time until he'll kill me. I can't just sit and wait, and I can't run and hide. I have to do it!"

"What about the sheriff? You gonna make him a zombie too?"

"No. But we might be able to use Galen's condition to control Sheriff Johnson."

"What do you mean?"

"Sheriff Johnson knows Galen will be out to kill him."

"Yes."

"But he can't risk killing Galen. Or most likely, he won't want to risk it."

"Possibly."

"His only need when it comes to Galen is to get him safely out of his way, and the Zombie powder will do that. We make a deal with Sheriff Johnson. Let him get the drugs that are hidden at Little Frankie Dalton's trailer, and the money too, if he can find it. Then he just keeps everything else calm. The drug scam he and Galen had going is over and done with anyway. Sheriff Johnson needs me to keep Galen in the zombie state, and I need him to keep people from asking too many questions. I forget about the drug scam and he forgets he knows anything about my husband's condition. You and I forget about trying to get the District Attorney's office involved in the drug scam, and we pursue the black market baby selling game. When there's enough evidence to convict him, Galen will suddenly come out of his coma. Just like a miracle. Sheriff Johnson knows I'll keep quiet about the drug scam because I'll go to prison too if he talks about the Zombie powder. It's an even trade off."

"And how do we keep the sheriff from killing his deputy, Harold?"

"We can't, but if we can get to Sheriff Johnson in time, maybe he won't feel a need to."

Adrienne looked at Catriona in amazement. As crazy as the idea seemed, it might just work, but Catriona would have to do it completely on her own. And if she didn't get it right?

"If I don't get it right, actually if Galen didn't perfect the powder, he'll either die and I'll probably be discovered and go to prison so your next case will be trying to get me out, or he'll be in a tranquil state instead of a comatose state. Either way he'll know what I've done, so he'll probably kill me and make it look like an accident. But you'll know Adrienne. You'll know. What car are you driving today?"

"A nice family Suburban," Adrienne answered.

"Good. No one in Destiny will recognize it." Catriona was starting to sound like the private investigator. "We've got to get to Galen's office while it's empty."

Catriona paid the check and told the waiter that she was going to leave her vehicle in the coffeehouse parking lot for a couple of hours. Then the two women climbed in Adrienne's Suburban and headed for Destiny.

As soon as they got in the car, Adrienne rolled the window part way down and lit a cigarette. She looked over at Catriona and Catriona smiled, her acknowledgement that the cigarette was OK with her. Adrienne picked up her cell phone and checked calls. Mel's cell phone number. She drove back over the Lea Joyner drawbridge while she called his number. Three then four rings. Mel said hello.

"This is Adrienne," she tried not to sound too official, but, Catriona was in the car.

"Adrienne, where are you?"

"I'm in Monroe heading to Destiny. What's wrong?"

Mel's voice sounded shaky and weak. "It's Camille. We're at the hospital."

"The hospital? You're both at the hospital?"

"Yes. I don't want to talk about it over the phone. She's in critical condition."

Adrienne's heart froze. "I'll get there as soon as possible. I have a client with me. We have an urgent matter to finish in Destiny. Will you be all right until I can get there?"

"I'll be waiting." Mel hung up the phone.

"Is everything OK," Catriona asked. "You look terrible."

"Another client. He's at the hospital. I'm not sure what's happened. We've got to keep our mind on you." Adrienne pushed the accelerator to the floor.

Chapter Twenty-Seven

"Welcome to Destiny," the sign said. Adrienne slowed down to 35 and then to 25 as they entered the little town. She didn't want to draw any attention to her car now. It seemed like so much unexpected happened every time she even thought about circling the block. She was afraid to try it, but she needed to be sure no one important was around before she let Catriona out. They drove around once, then Adrienne let Catriona out in the alleyway without even coming to a complete stop. Catriona was only feet away from the back door to the clinic. Adrienne kept going until she reached the parking lot of the Family Dollar, then wove her way in among the cars and positioned herself where she could see. The minutes seemed like hours, but finally she saw Catriona come out the back door and head back to the line of bushes in the alleyway. Adrienne drove to the hiding place and stopped long enough for Catriona to get in, zombie powder in hand.

"You got it?" she asked Catriona.

"I got it. Let's get me back to my car so I can get back home before Galen does."

They headed back to Monroe. On the other side of the divided highway as they left Destiny, both women gasped as they saw Sheriff Johnson go by headed for the Sheriff's Department. Thank God he didn't know Adrienne's car.

Chapter Twenty-Eight

"Let's go outside," Mel's soft but shaken voice said to Adrienne as he took her arm and guided her away from the hospital emergency room. In the parking lot with tall, muted lights surrounding them, he leaned against the car and handed Adrienne the letter his wife had left laying on the bed beside her. He watched Adrienne's eyes move across the page, and as the meaning of each line found its place in her mind, an overwhelming concern began to fill his heart. A kind of knowing, a fear that nothing would ever be the same between them again crept slowly like a rising, drowning water, that this love of his life would now be distanced from him forever, that there was nothing he or she could do to make things right, that there would be no possible way to go on. Not now. After all the years of aching to have feelings like this, of trying so hard to keep his heart alive, of taking every possible avenue to try to sustain the ability to love, Camille had won. She'd nearly destroyed his heart in life, and now she would destroy it forever through her death, through laying blame, through holding onto him for eternity through guilt, through suicide.

"All the years of blaming me," the letter said, "of making everyone, my family your family, all of our friends, even me, believe that the problem was my drinking when all the time you've known that the real cause has been the hardness in your heart. My adultery! How long can a person survive without even a sign of warmth? You've given me a lifetime of loneliness, a lifetime of emptiness while you pursued your books and your poet friends instead of pursuing the life we planned, the dreams I longed for. You've refused to know me. You've not just been unable to be close, you've refused to be close. No matter how hard I've tried to open the door to who I am, you've put your weight against it and forced it shut, slammed it shut in my face. And now, you, the "oh so righteous" one, the "do no wrong have no weaknesses, commit no sin" one. How long have you had a girlfriend? How long has she been your motivation for distancing yourself from me? How many nights have you spent together contriving ways to prove my sins, sins of loneliness and emptiness, while you grew your own adulteress hearts? Yes, the humiliation is complete. You've found the way. No doubt all who know us will shake their heads and blame the bourbon, and will be disgusted at all the evidence you've presented of my sins. My suicide will be just one more sad part of my wasted life. They'll elevate you and feel sorry for you and support you in your new life. But then, they don't know what I know about you and Adrienne Hargrove. A cheap, chain-smoking bleached blonde with a boob job, private investigator that caused the accident, if you want to call it that, that made her own husband an invalid. The same woman whose child died of abuse while she claimed to be somewhere else. Are you surprised that I know? Did you think I'd just be sitting around doing nothing while you tried to destroy me? Her for me? Her for me! After all these pain-filled years. I've seen you holding her hand. I saw the heat generated between you as you sat drinking wine. I saw you kiss her goodnight. Your warmth for me. You gave it to her then swore I was the cause of the coldness. There will be no divorce. I won't give you the satisfaction. You won't get rid of me. I will leave you. I am gone."

Adrienne looked up from the letter and out into the darkness in total disbelief. She avoided Mel's eyes. Even her skin trembled. The words might easily have been a description of her own marriage, of her own loneliness, of her own isolation from the man she'd married and the loss of his ability to dream. Camille had known there were feelings between Adrienne and Mel. She'd witnessed it from the very beginning, had evidently followed them just like Adrienne had followed Andrew and his girlfriend. Adrienne remembered reading a line somewhere that said what a person thinks about in his or her heart is who they really are, what they actually become. How could Mel possibly ever have respect for her now? In Adrienne's mind, she had now committed the same crime that had cost Andrew his wholeness, the same crime she'd cursed time after time in her work and in her life. The crime of which she'd always considered herself to be a victim. The perpetrator? Her? According to Camille, Adrienne was an adulteress no different from herself, and Mel, too. She died, took her own life believing that and wanting to know they believed it. *How can Mel and I ever have anything now?* She wondered silently. *How could something good ever come from something this bad?* Camille would always be between them eating away at their respect for one another. They had discarded Camille, mentally, and Andrew, too, just as surely as if they'd tossed them into a trash can. Had it really been wrong for them to give up on Camille and Andrew? *How can a person ever know when the motivation is honest or when it's just a manipulation of the way we want things to be?* Adrienne didn't know the answer to her own question, but she did know that the moment, that one moment when the whole world stood still for them was all they would ever know, would ever have. It was over now. She'd been a fool to think there could ever be a happy ending for her, not when it came to love.

Adrienne handed Mel the letter and slowly turned away. He moved close to her; she could feel his breath on the back of her neck, but he didn't reach out for her, didn't touch her. Adrienne could sense the laying of the first bricks in the wall that had already begun to build itself. A wall that would be solid and strong, one that could not be torn back down, no matter how hard she and Mel might try.

"She blamed us," Adrienne was the first to speak. "She killed herself because she knew we were lovers."

"Adrienne," Mel said softly. "She's been mentally unstable for years. Her drinking's played a huge part in bringing it on. She was unfaithful over and over again. You above all people know that."

"When does it count, Mel? When is an affair the wrong kind or the right kind?"

"What we have is so much more than an affair." Mel was desperate.

Adrienne turned to face him. "She was right. She knew where we were headed. I lied to Andrew every time I told him you were just another client. You lied to Camille every time you met with me after the very first time you realized you had feelings for me. From that very first meeting at Cottonport, it's all been a lie. From the moment of your phone call asking me to come. From the moment I first considered it, knowing that I wanted it to be more than friendship." Adrienne took a deep breath. "I have to go," she whispered, touching his face gently with her hand.

"Adrienne. Not now. Not after all we've been through," Mel pleaded, taking both her hands in his and pulling them to his heart. "We've both got to give it some time. There's too much between us to just turn and walk away. Too much of the kind of thing that really matters. We're not responsible for her death. We are responsible for what we do with the rest of our lives. We can work through this in time."

Adrienne stared into Mel's pleading eyes. *My heart never quite opens the door all the way,* she reminded herself. Without another word, she turned and walked away into the night.

Chapter Twenty-Nine

Adrienne saw Dr. Kirby sitting at the bay window in his wheelchair staring expressionless through the glass as she pulled up the long, winding driveway. She slammed the car door, and stood for a moment before ringing the doorbell and looked out across the lake behind the mansion. The long, blue fingers of Spanish moss hanging from the Cypress trees made the scene seem so peaceful. Cranes with their snow white, feathery wings rose gracefully from the water, dripping its silver droplets back into their source as the magnificent birds rose into the sky. The scene seemed surreal to Adrienne, like something out of a novel, or a dream that turned into a nightmare. Catriona opened the door and invited her in.

"How is he?" Adrienne asked, looking at Catriona with the unspoken knowledge that existed between them obvious in her eyes.

"He's fine," Catriona replied. "His health is fine, anyway. As long as I administer the drug in exactly the right dose, he'll stay in the comatose state. No one in this community doubts that he's lost his mind. His daughters came from Shreveport to visit. They thanked me for being here for him and for taking such good care of him. Even they don't suspect." The male nurse came into the room just as Catriona finished the sentence. "You may go now, if you'd like, Cameron," she suggested. "We'll see you tomorrow." The two women were silent as he left.

"You know he's completely cognizant, Adrienne. He hears everything we're saying. He knows everything that's going on. There's no way for him to communicate. He's completely paralyzed and speechless, but he hears and understands everything that I'm doing to him and why."

"I've failed you, Catriona. If only there was enough evidence to bring him to trial." She stared at the mannequin of a man sitting there completely aware that she and Catriona had tried everything in their power to convict him of his crimes and put him away for life.

"But there's not, Adrienne. Not as long as this town is owned by men connected to Sheriff Johnson. And without a conviction, Galen will keep on destroying lives, killing people whenever he sees fit. Anyone who doesn't fit into his ideas of genetic supremacy, any one who gets in the way of his fraud. He's a psychopath. He doesn't care what he's done. He'd do it all again if given a chance. He can't be fixed. Remember? You told me that."

"But it's so dangerous for you, Catriona. Not only that you'll be found out, but what if you give the wrong dosage and he wakes up, comes out of this condition. You know he'll kill you. It could happen without you even being aware. All he'd have to do is pretend, and he's an expert at that. Please, Catriona. Just leave. I'll help you get your things and get to another city where he'll never find you. Just go. Leave this corrupt little hell-hole of a town to its own vices. They know what he is. Leave it up to them to do something about it."

"It's a chance I'll have to take." Catriona looked serious. "How could I ever be free of him even if I left, knowing all he's done? Sooner or later there will be an opportunity to share my story with someone who will believe me, someone I can trust who will take the facts and do something with them. Thanks to you, Adrienne, I have 476 pages of violence he's caused, of harm he's done, just waiting for the right person to come along; someone who can and will help me. Until then, no one is safe from him, not even me. You've done all you can do. I'm the only one who can do something about it now. I can't leave. If I leave, more people will die. It's enough knowing you're there for me. Knowing that you know and understand will give me strength. Sooner or later, you'll get the evidence, maybe through the baby black market scheme, I don't know. But I know you will."

Adrienne thought back to when she'd first met Catriona Kirby. She remembered being offended that a woman would live with an adulterous mate for the sake of material things. She remembered, too, being aware, even then, that there was something she liked about Catriona, something intangible that was not reflected in what she shared about herself. Adrienne knew now how strong and intelligent and courageous Catriona was. She was putting her own life in danger, and watching her own life tick away one day at a time, for the sake of keeping Dr. Galen Kirby from causing harm to anyone else. She wondered how many babies he'd destroyed or sold that they'd never know about. How many homeless and derelict people had just disappeared from the planet because he didn't consider them worthy of existence, how many faceless entities he had destroyed mentally and emotionally, who could not or would not speak for themselves out of fear for what else he might do. There was no one who could do anything about it. No one except Catriona. Adrienne's respect for her had grown on a daily basis, unlike respect for herself, which had come completely undone since the suicide of Mel's wife.

Adrienne gave Catriona a hug full of warmth and sincerity and respect. "Someday there'll be a way. I'm meeting with Mike Morris early next week. We'll have the DNA results by then. We'll pick up where we left off."

"I know, Adrienne. I do know."

* * *

Andrew sat on the porch in the dark, his breathing tank beside him. "I wondered if you were coming home anytime tonight," he said.

"I had some loose ends to tie up," Adrienne answered. She sat down on the porch swing and looked out at the stars.

"You've always got loose ends to tie up. Always got something more important to do."

"Do you ever think about us, Andrew, and wonder what we might have been if we'd both tried hard enough?" Adrienne asked.

Andrew looked across the porch at her. "Love's nothing but an illusion," he answered. "I'm going to bed."

Adrienne listened as the click of Andrew's cane became distant behind her. She looked out across the darkness where only a slice of moon was shining. Clouds drifted across Venus and dulled her light.

Chapter Thirty

Adrienne and Mike sat across from one another at Bubba Luigi's Restaurant on 18th street in Monroe. Adrienne smiled as she watched her friend and career buddy from the past pull a cigar from his shirt pocket and moisten the end, then place the thick, brown roll of tobacco, short and squat like himself, between his front teeth. She didn't remember ever seeing Mike light a cigar, but it seemed a part of his personality to need one hanging from his lips. Adrienne had already lit her Virginia Slim cigarette and tossed her Zippo lighter back into her purse, and as she looked at Mike, she thought how nice it was to have lunch with a friend who was willing to sit in the smokers' section of the restaurant. She was glad, too, that he'd been willing to help her with this case. Today they were meeting to discuss the DNA evidence he'd accumulated for Adrienne. DNA they both hoped would show that Dr. Galen Kirby was the father of a baby boy whose mother, Susanne Jasper, Adrienne believed, had been murdered by the doctor. That DNA would be the first step to proving Dr. Kirby was involved in a black market baby selling scheme, and that he was very possibly a serial killer. Even more shocking, it was the first step to proving that he was producing and selling his own offspring. The bazaar behavior of a true psychopath.

Mike pushed his chair back a little further from the table so that his rotund stomach wasn't quite touching it. His suspenders curved around instead of hanging straight, their elasticity pushed to its limit. He folded his arms over his chest and released a contented sigh. After all, where else in the world could you find one restaurant that served the finest in Italian cuisine and good ole Louisiana Cajun food at the same time except Bubba Luigi's?

It'd been a long time since Mike had spent much time in Monroe. Today, he had really enjoyed his food, a mountain of shrimp linguini followed by an even larger mountain of fried alligator strips. Adrienne watched Mike eat in amazement as she nibbled on her Italian salad with extra black olives, anchovies on the side, and bread sticks with marinara sauce. In his mid-sixties now, thinning brown hair splotched with gray, and wrinkles that seemed deeper than before, more like crevices, Mike's smile still had its charm, but his eyes had lost their sparkle. Their shine seemed false, a thin veil covering years of pain now settled in and well-rooted. His skin was weathered and tired.

Adrienne blew smoke in the air, and pushed her blonde-frosted, long curly hair back behind her shoulders. Her turquoise eyes still shone soft and gentle, but in them, too, was an accumulation of life's disappointments imbedded even more deeply by witnessing so many tragedies in the lives of the people who hired her. That was one of the definite drawbacks in her profession. Now, she sniffed then pushed her gold-rimmed glasses back up on her nose. Five feet nine inches tall and slender even at the age of forty-five, it sometimes seemed to Adrienne she had lived several lifetimes, and she wondered when, if ever, the lifetime would arrive that would allow her to feel alive and vibrant again. A life that felt worth living. Reincarnation? She desperately wanted to believe in it. Tried with all her heart and soul to believe in it. But to her way of thinking, advancement in the living order of things would mean coming back in another life as anything but a human. In all of Mother Nature's kingdom, Adrienne had concluded, there could be nothing more low-down than human beings. All other living things acted out of instinct. Humans acted out of selfishness and greed and pride, no matter what the emotional cost to others. Her partial-invalid husband, Andrew, and his adulteress past briefly entered Adrienne's mind, but she quickly pushed all thought of him away and tried to get back to the moment.

Mike reached for the briefcase sitting on the floor beside him, and as he clicked it open, another thought clicked into Adrienne's mind. Professor Mel Brighton carried a briefcase just like Mike's. Nausea welled up in Adrienne's stomach as Mel's dark, shoulder-length hair splotched with silver and his hauntingly blue eyes forced their way into her consciousness and intertwined with that seemingly fluid guilt that pulsed its way through her veins. Adrienne's life had always been plagued with guilt. Andrew's accident was just one more link in the long chain that seemed to follow her wherever she went. From the earliest childhood memories of sexual abuse by her stepfather, to physical abuse from her first husband and the death of their infant son at his hand, Adrienne's life seemed strung together, one incident of sorrow and regret after another, right up to Andrew. And now, there was Mel and his wife's suicide.

Yes, Mel and Adrienne had fallen in love. No, that wasn't why Mel had filed for divorce. Yes, Adrienne's marriage to Andrew was a farce. No, that wasn't why she'd become involved with Mel. Yes, Mel's wife had found out he and Adrienne were seeing one another romantically, even though it had been only once. No, Adrienne wasn't sure she could actually ever bring herself to leave Andrew. Yes, Mel and Adrienne were going to continue to see one another and Mel was determined that she would divorce Andrew and marry him someday. No, it wasn't their fault Mel's wife had committed suicide even though she'd left a note that said it was revenge for Mel and Adrienne's affair. But the suicide ended any possibility of Mel and Adrienne ever finding real happiness together. Yes, yes, yes they'd been in love, were still in love. No, no, no her suicide was not their fault. Another link of guilt, strong and unbending, hung securely in the chain of Adrienne's life.

"Adrienne, you OK?" Mike asked.

Adrienne blinked, staring back at Mike. "Sure. I'm fine. What have you got there?"

"For a minute you looked like you were somewhere in outer-space," Mike smiled. "This is the DNA report on Suzanne Jasper's baby son from the hairs you brought me. It's conclusive. Dr. Kirby is the baby's father."

Adrienne stared at the piece of paper in Mike's hand, the information it contained so important. There was nothing much that could be kept hidden from today's technology, especially when it came to the field of medicine and DNA. She took the piece of paper from Mike's hand. "The markers are 99% conclusive," she said. "The little boy is Dr. Kirby's son."

"Right. And did you see the other information?" Mike pointed to a line on the paper. "The little boy is Down Syndrome. Mentally retarded."

Adrienne looked at the genetic marker that labeled the baby's defect and then back at Mike. "That explains why this baby wasn't adopted like all the others Dr. Kirby produced. It doesn't explain why, if Dr. Kirby murdered the baby's mother like I think he did, he didn't kill the baby too. There are ethics charges accusing him of intentionally causing stillbirths of infants he believed would be inferior because they were the offspring of people who he believed were inferior. Poor people, people of other races who, in his sick mind, had more children than they needed. There was enough suspicion to file an ethics report with the State Medical Board who took away his license to deliver babies, but not enough evidence to press criminal charges. Everyone involved knew he did it. They just couldn't prove it. The man is definitely not above murdering an infant. We know he performed abortions on his own teenage daughters." That one seemed almost impossible to believe even to Adrienne. The man killed his own grandchildren. "What kept him from killing this little boy?"

"You're sure the baby was in the house when his mother was killed?" Mike questioned.

"That's where he was when the police found her body."

"Your theory is that he poisoned the mother, this Susanne Jasper, with some kind of toxin he's been experimenting with."

"Yeah, puffer fish toxin. He raises puffer fish in an aquarium at his house. They contain the most potent toxin known to man."

"I read something about puffer fish poison just recently," Mike recalled. "Seems like it was something about researchers making a pain killer for terminally ill people, cancer victims I think."

"Yes. That's a pretty new medical advancement," Adrienne explained, remembering her conversation about puffer fish toxin with Catriona, who herself had a biology degree.

Catriona regretted her choice to marry Galen Kirby, but she didn't regret the biology degree that allowed her to understand completely the experiments Galen had been carefully recording using his puffer fish toxin. She'd found research articles he had hidden away, and she understood how potentially dangerous the information was in the hands of someone like her husband. Catriona knew about her husband's experiments on neighborhood cats to try to perfect the exact dose of "zombie powder," and that fact had been one more added to the list of things that convinced her he was a very dangerous man. It was either her life or his. That's how she saw it. And maybe the lives of many other people if someone didn't stop him.

"Look, Adrienne." Mike continued now. "When you first started telling me about Dr. Kirby and this black market baby selling scheme, especially the part about him selling his own illegitimate babies, I thought it was pretty far out. But after seeing the birth certificates and getting this DNA report, I took a look at the police report on the deaths of the two women. You're right. Something just doesn't make sense, and all the fingers are pointing back to Dr. Kirby. The fact that he's the coroner who certified their deaths is just too creepy. I've been thinking about it. I've got some vacation time coming. I could take a couple of weeks and come to Monroe. See what I can do to help you. You got a place out there in that log cabin lodge of yours where you could put a guy up for a couple of weeks?" he smiled. "If you don't think that old man of yours would think we're having an affair."

"I don't care what Andrew thinks," Adrienne replied, but hesitated to give Mike a concrete answer. She'd told Mike that Dr. Kirby was in some kind of a comatose state that no one knew for sure would last for any specific amount of time. She hadn't told him Catriona was inducing the comatose state with puffer fish toxin, Zombie powder. She couldn't tell him. What Catriona was doing was illegal, and Adrienne was an accessory. Mike Morris was a police detective. If he knew, he'd have to take action or be in danger of being locked up himself, or, at the very least, throwing his career away along with his pension. She couldn't tell him any more than necessary about the puffer fish toxin. Mike didn't need any more trauma in his personal life either. And, he was an excellent detective. On one hand, Adrienne was glad he was so talented and that he was willing to come to Monroe and help her. On the other hand, she was terrified his talent would help him discover the truth. Still, she could really use his help. He had access to police files and secret websites with information a private investigator like Adrienne couldn't touch. She needed Mike. She'd just have to keep him away from Catriona and Dr. Kirby as much as possible. "I'd love to have your help, Mike. When can you come?"

"Give me a couple of days to get things in order. I'll tell my boss first thing tomorrow morning. He's been encouraging me to get away for awhile, take a break. You know, a trip to the beach in Florida," Mike grinned mischievously. "Can't you just see me in a new thong bathing suit on the beach in Florida?" He didn't want Adrienne to suspect that part of his reason for coming was concern for her. She looked tired, but more than that, she looked sad, and that was out of character for Adrienne. She'd always been energetic, even exuberant. No matter what was going on in anyone's life, she always had something to say about tomorrow being a better day. Mike remembered just like it was yesterday how Adrienne had been there for him the days following the murder of his wife. Other friends brought him food and sent him flowers. But Adrienne listened to him talk. No matter how fowl his language, no matter how many threats of what he was going to do when he found the son of a bitch who'd killed his wife. No matter how many things he threw and broke, or what things he'd pounded with his fists. Adrienne smoked with him and drank with him and listened to him. She stayed with him for days so he wouldn't be alone. Mike overheard the telephone conversations between Adrienne and Andrew during that time, conversations where he knew Andrew was accusing her of everything from not caring about his needs, to having an affair with Mike, never once listening to what was really going on in her life. Now it was Mike's turn to return the favor. He wanted to help Adrienne solve this bazaar case, but he also wanted to find out what was causing the immense pain he saw in her eyes and help her the way she'd helped him at a time when no one else could possibly understand the way she did.

"How about if I make it to your place Sunday evening? We'll have a nice, friendly chat with Andrew, maybe take him out to dinner, and then you can fill me in on the case. That little guest cabin of yours empty?"

"It's empty," Adrienne smiled. Something in her heart lifted a feather's depth to think that someone who knows her and cares about her would be there to help through the upcoming days. Even Andrew with all his rottenness was easier to get along with when company was around, and in his own way, he liked Mike. "See you Sunday night."

Chapter Thirty-One

Adrienne stood thinking at the foot of the Lea Joyner drawbridge connecting Monroe and West Monroe, Louisiana. She flipped ashes from her cigarette out across the water. The bridge had been renamed the "Lea Joyner" in honor of a woman minister who had done much for the community, but who'd been murdered in her church by a drug addict one night a few years ago. This was one of the few drawbridges left in the whole country, and Adrienne loved it. For her, the Lea Joyner Bridge represented security and roots. It had been there for ages, and even as northeast Louisiana grew and developed and modernized, the drawbridge had stayed basically the same. It was a place Adrienne often came to think things through, to sort things out. The gentle ripples in the water of the Ouachita River soothed her, and on occasion while standing, leaning over the railing deep in thought, she would see a giant barge moving slowly down river taking its precious cargo to who knows where. The two cities, one on each side of the river, both used to the barges, were unimpressed with their presence, but to Adrienne they seemed representative of forward movement, some sort of hope for tomorrow to be a better day, no matter what she had contended with this day.

This afternoon there was no barge. Adrienne stood between the two pink watchtowers on either side of the break in the center of the bridge smoking her Virginia Slim and letting all the metaphors the bridge, the river, and the barges created run through her mind. The watchtowers held the buttons the engineers pushed to drop the safety arms, keeping cars at a distance as the bridge divided and rose into the sky, allowing the barges to pass under, untouched, and to keep cars from falling off the bridge and into the Ouachita.

Safety arms, she thought to herself now. *Where are the safety arms for me? Where is the person or the thing that can keep me from falling off the deep end? Why are my emotions always so close to the surface, so egg-shell thin?* She struggled to keep Professor Mel Brighton out of her mind. The entrance to Antique Alley and the road leading to Cottonport Coffeehouse where she and Mel had met to talk over wine and jazz lay at the foot of the Lea Joyner. Just a few blocks from where Adrienne was now standing was the very place Mel spent most of his time when he wasn't at the university teaching his literature classes. She wondered if he was at Cottonport right now. It was getting close to four o'clock, he most likely wouldn't still be at the university. She wondered where he was spending his time now that he must live with his wife's suicide haunting him. Adrienne thought he'd moved out of the Marriott and back into his home, but it was better that she didn't know for sure. She did know for sure she could never go to Cottonport or see Mel again. It would be much too painful for them both.

Adrienne looked out at the water and felt chilled from the November air even though the sparkling sun attempted to deceive one into thinking there was warmth. It would be Thanksgiving soon. She dreaded the holiday season. Andrew hated anything that smacked of generosity like inviting family and friends for Thanksgiving dinner, or the giving of Christmas presents. The holidays only served to remind her of the death of her only child, the tiny little boy who'd been beaten to death at the hands of his own father, nearly twenty years ago. *Jimmy would be grown now, in college maybe.* Adrienne tried to form a picture of what her fair haired little boy might look like as a man. Jimmy's father had only served three years in prison, and was free to go on with his life. But there was no freedom for Adrienne. Every single solitary day she saw the tiny boy's face and wished she could turn back the pages of her life, wished with the deepest regret it's possible for a human to feel that she had left with her baby like she'd thought about doing so many times, before it was too late. But at least the tears had subsided. There were none now. There hadn't been for years. Sometimes life's too sad to cry.

Adrienne was conscious of footsteps. The bright daylight of an autumn afternoon was all around her. Plenty of cars were crossing the bridge. There was nothing to fear. Still, the steps unnerved her, and she turned sharply to her left. A homeless man approached, hair, skin and clothes so filthy they blended into one indiscernible color. He had a cardboard sign in his hand with the words "will work for food" scribbled across it. He held it up for Adrienne to read.

Sorry," Adrienne said. "I don't even have my purse with me." She was glad she'd left it locked in her car parked at the foot of the bridge. She waited, but the man didn't leave. Instead, he stood there silently staring at her.

"My name's Smiley," the homeless man finally said, grinning as though it were necessary to show Adrienne why he'd been given the nickname. Gums devoid of teeth appeared.

His idea of a smile, Adrienne ridiculed silently. "Where do you stay, Smiley?" she asked, attempting to break the uncomfortable silence.

"Up under the bridge," he pointed to a place where the bridge connected to the land.

Adrienne bent her neck to look, and saw a large duffle bag stuffed in the very corner, up high out of the wind and rain if they were to come. "You sleep there?" she asked, amazed.

"I live there," Smiley answered.

"How long have you lived there?"

"I been living under bridges for a lot of years now. I don't have no calendar. I don't know exactly how long. I haven't been living under this bridge but just a few days. I've been traveling, making my way back home."

"Where's home?" Adrienne wondered what had happened to the mind of a man who lived like this for years at a time. She wondered what events or one final event had pushed him across that fragile line so that he'd walked away from all life's supposed promises, the American Dream, and began living like this. At the same time, she was keenly aware of the fine line all humans walk and of how close to falling off one side or the other she herself was each and every day.

"Somewhere in Missouri," Smiley answered.

"You're a long way from Missouri," Adrienne was surprised.

"Am I?" Smiley seemed disappointed. "Well, I'm gonna find it someday." He looked at the ground.

Adrienne could see clear evidence that time, weather, and probably alcohol abuse had taken its toll on Smiley's mind. He jumped from one subject to the other, spoke in disjointed sentences, and sometimes looked at her as though he was surprised to see her standing there, like he'd forgotten they were talking. She supposed it was possible he could be dangerous, but here, in the daylight, he seemed harmless enough.

"Who's in Missouri?" she found herself asking him.

"My family," he looked hard at Adrienne, trying to pull together the loose strands in his mind. "My wife and kids, I think. I keep having this dream about a woman and some kids. I think that woman's my wife and them's my kids and some of them's sick. They're calling me but I can't remember where to find them." Pain filled his eyes. "Someday I'm gonna find Missouri."

Adrienne heard despair in the man's voice and felt a lump of emotion rise in her own throat. "What's your real name, Smiley, before you got your nickname?"

"Erle, Erle Blue," the man answered matter-of-factly, without the slightest hesitation. "Erle spelled E- r-l-e."

"Erle Blue. That's a very distinctive name, and an unusual way to spell Erle. I don't think I've ever heard it spelled that way before."

"That's it. Erle Blue. That's me....someday I'm gonna find Missouri." Erle Blue turned and walked slowly away.

Won't hurt to check missing person's reports, Adrienne thought to herself, her natural detective's curiosity coming to the surface. *The name's too unusual for him to have made it up. Of course it could be a name he's heard somewhere along the way and has taken on, convinced himself that's who he really is. Who knows? It won't hurt to at least look through the missing person's reports. He looks to be in his sixties. Looks like he's been homeless a long time. Not much chance of finding anything connected to him. Still, Erle Blue's a pretty unusual name.* She flipped the butt of her cigarette into the Ouachita River and walked the opposite direction from Erle Blue to the foot of the bridge where she'd left her car, and headed for home and Andrew.

Chapter Thirty-Two

Andrew pulled a long, greasy slice of double meat pepperoni pizza from the Johnny's Pizza box and raised it high enough in the air to let the pointed tip fall limply into his mouth. Adrienne was glad you could order pizza half 'n half. Her half was filled with vegetables. Green peppers, onions, tomatoes and mushrooms, black olives and a few anchovies. She pulled a slice loose from her side of the box and bent over the coffee table to take a bite. She and Andrew sat side by side on the sofa in front of the big screen TV, his oxygen tank by his side, Adrienne's secure cell phone, Virginia Slim cigarettes and Zippo lighter by hers, even though she never smoked in the house due to the damaged condition of Andrew's lungs. This was Andrew's idea of a pleasant evening. TV, pizza, and Adrienne home at night for a change.

"Mike Morris is going to come stay in the guest cabin for a couple of weeks," Adrienne announced. "He's helping me with a case." She took another bite of pizza and waited for Andrew's reaction.

"Mike Morris?" Andrew questioned. "I thought he joined the police department in Baton Rouge after his wife died. Why's he showing up in the picture after all this time?"

"She didn't die, she was murdered." Adrienne corrected Andrew. "He did."

"So what's he doing helping you with a case in Monroe?"

"Well actually, the case I'm working on involves people throughout northeast Louisiana, not just Monroe. Maybe even some other states."

"Last time I heard," Andrew said with sarcasm, "Baton Rouge was in south Louisiana."

"The main crime lab's in Baton Rouge, Andrew. Mike had some DNA testing done for me. He has access to crime technology through the police department that I can't touch as a private investigator. I've gone as far as I can on this case without expert criminology techniques." She was irritated.

"And Mike's an expert, I suppose."

"I told you, Andrew, he has access to files and computer programs and criminal technology that has to be cleared through official police channels, sometimes even through the F.B.I., and they don't give that kind of clearing to private investigators like me. Besides, what's your problem with Mike? He's an old man."

"Yeah, well, old men are the worst kind Think they have to prove themselves," he mumbled. "What's so important about this case?" Andrew reached for a second slice from his side of the pizza.

"We think the guy I'm investigating may be involved in a black market baby selling scheme. It's even possible he's a serial killer." Adrienne was careful not to mention the doctor's name, which would be a breech of the confidentiality law governing her P.I. credentials.

"So now it's 'we,'" Andrew said. "What the hell are 'we' doing investigating a serial killer? That's way outside the realm of a P.I."

Adrienne looked at him with dismay. "Why do you have to turn everything I say into some kind of argument? And yes, it is way outside the realm of what a private investigator should be doing. I didn't know that's what it was about when I took the case, but now I'm caught up in the big middle of it, and I have to have help from someone higher up than another P.I. That's why Mike's coming," she said in frustration. "He'll be here Sunday evening. He's staying in the guest house…. He wants to take us to dinner." Adrienne tossed the thick crust from the end of her pizza slice into the box and stood up.

"Take 'us' to dinner," Andrew questioned. "Who is us?"

Adrienne's voice was getting progressively louder. "God, Andrew. Why do you have to make even the simplest thing complicated? You and me. Who do you think? Mike's a nice guy. He likes you. He thought it would be nice if the three of us went to dinner before we get too tangled up in this case. It's nice of him, considerate. Something wrong with that?" She walked toward her office, her back turned to Andrew.

"I didn't say there was anything wrong with it." Andrew yelled after her, but would not leave it alone. "Where's he want to take us, McDonald's?"

"I don't know. He didn't say. What does it matter?" Adrienne slammed the door to her office behind her, went over to the aquarium and sprinkled flakes of fish food across the water, attempting to calm herself. The orange and white clown fish, her own personal Nemo, sprinted to the top and began gulping. The two black and white angel fish took their time, gliding smoothly and consistently toward the particles of food as they floated slowly down through the water. Nemo was greedy. He gulped, gulped, gulped as fast as possible like he was afraid the angels would get it all and leave none for him. *Foolish little Nemo*, Adrienne thought. *You spend every day and night of your life in this aquarium with the angels. They never take your food. They're always polite and generous. You'd think you would know that about them by now.* Maybe it wasn't possible to ever know the mind and heart of another even in the world outside the human race, Adrienne decided as she took a deep breath and let it out slowly, thinking of Andrew, her husband, the man who's supposed to know her better than anyone else. Even after thirteen years of marriage, the things in her heart were nonexistent to him.

"You've never missed a meal in your life," Adrienne spoke to little Nemo, "but you're constantly afraid of going hungry. How insecure is that?" All of a sudden Adrienne remembered the homeless man she'd encountered at the Lea Joyner Bridge earlier today, and wondered what he'd eaten tonight. Her mind created a picture of him curled up in a ball, tucked away in the slanted seam where the bridge touched the ground, cold and damp. She turned on the computer at her desk and sat down. She pulled up internet and typed in her P.I. code. When the secure site opened, Adrienne typed in a search for "missing person's files." This was one of the crime- solving links private investigators did have access to. The screen blinked to black, then to green, then to black and white. The "missing person's link" was open. Adrienne thought for a moment about how Smiley had spelled his name. Erle Blue, spelled E –r-l-e Blue. She pushed "enter." The screen asked her to put in a time period, a decade. Adrienne thought for a moment. Smiley, Erle Blue, appeared to be in his sixties, but how could she determine how long he'd been homeless or possibly missing? "A long time," she said to herself. " If he's sixty years old, that means he was born in the 1940's or there-about. Around the end of World War II. That'd make him a 'baby boomer.' " She wished she'd thought to ask him about his age and birthday. "Assuming he was not homeless as a child takes us to the 1960's with him as a young adult in his twenties. Let's see, the Vietnam Era. He would have been in his twenties." Adrienne typed 1960 through 1970 in the search line and pushed enter. The screen blinked again and added another search line. "State or city." She typed in "Missouri." Erle Blue said he was trying to find his way back to Missouri. Adrienne pushed enter again. The screen flashed its answer. "0 matches for your search. You may broaden the search by eliminating specific pieces of information."

"Hmmm," Adrienne said out loud. "Eliminate some pieces. Let's take out Missouri." She back-spaced through the word, eliminating it one letter at a time, and pushed the enter key. Again the screen showed 0 matches. This time Adrienne back-spaced through the name "Erle," and left in the last name, "Blue," and the decade "60 through 70." She pushed 'enter.' This time, three names appeared. One was a Mark Blue who'd disappeared while vacationing in Jamaica. Originally from Florida, he was 52 at the time. "Not him" Adrienne said. "That would make him in his 80's or 90's now if he were still living." The second one was a Benjamin Blue who'd disappeared from his home in Seattle, Washington after a fight with his wife. He was 30 at the time of his disappearance. His car had been found a few miles from home. No signs of violence or a struggle. The car appeared to be simply abandoned. Money was withdrawn from the family savings account the next day, and no one had seen or heard of Benjamin Blue since. "Possible," Adrienne said, "but not likely. Sounds like that guy just made his own creative divorce and avoided the alimony and community property settlement." Too, Adrienne realized, Benjamin Blue would be in his 70's, and she was pretty sure Smiley, Erle Blue, wasn't that old. "Late 50's, maybe mid 60's at the most." She scrolled down to the third name. "Robert E. Blue." Adrienne clicked the appropriate lines and read the information about Robert E. Blue. It didn't give his middle name, only the initial "E." He'd served in the Vietnam War, and returned home to Kansas in 1968. He'd spent six months in a "post-traumatic stress syndrome" program the first year he was home from the war. The treatment had been deemed successful. He had a wife, Matilda (Mattie), and a son and daughter, at the time he was drafted into the military. They later had two other children, both boys, after his return. Two of Robert Blue's three sons, the two who were born after his return from Vietnam, suffered from Muscular Dystrophy. Robert E. Blue was born in 1945.

Adrienne lit a cigarette and sat back to think. *Robert E. Blue was born in 1945. That'd make him around sixty now. The age could be right. Hard to tell about someone who's been living outside in the elements for so long. And Smiley said he had a wife and children and some of them were sick.* "God," Adrienne said out loud. "That sure could fit. Two of this guy's sons had Muscular Dystrophy. Still, Robert E. Blue was living in Kansas at the time of his disappearance. But Missouri is just the next state over." Adrienne's thoughts turned inward. *I need to find out what the "E" stands for in Robert E. Blue. Need to ask Smiley if he remembers anything about the name Robert. But not tonight.* She closed down the program and turned off the computer. She wanted to call Catriona to tell her about the DNA results and about Mike Morris joining her to help with the investigation.

"Catriona, it's Adrienne. I hope it's not too late. You weren't in bed yet?...How are things with Dr. Kirby?.... I'll be so glad when we can get him away from you. You're sure the toxin's working as planned?.... Look, I have news. Some of it I can tell you over the phone, some I'd rather talk to you about in person. Remember I told you about a good friend of mine who works for the Baton Rouge Police Department? Yeah, he's the one who ran the DNA test for me. Well, he's gotten real interested in our case. He has some vacation time coming, and he's going to come stay at my place and help us for a couple of weeks. He's a homicide detective Catriona, and a good one. Probably one of the best in the country. He can legally do things I can't. Name's Mike Morris. He'll be a tremendous help in moving this thing along as quickly as possible. He'll be here Sunday evening. I'd like to bring him out to meet you maybe Monday, mid-morning.... The thing is.... Is anyone else around? Where's that male nurse you hired? What's his name?...Yeah, Cameron LeBlanc.... The thing is we can't let Mike know about the zombie powder. He knows Dr. Kirby's in some kind of coma and that you're being the good little wife and taking care of him. He also knows there's a good chance Dr. Kirby may try to kill you if and when he wakes up. I've been completely honest with him about the deaths of the women, the murders of the two drug dealers on the levee and the murder of Little Frankie Dalton. He knows about Sheriff Johnson and Dr. Kirby and the drug scam, and the death of the prisoner. He knows we're trying to get evidence on this baby black market thing to tie Dr. Kirby to the women's murders, but I can't let him know you're keeping your husband in a coma. It's illegal, and having that knowledge would make him an accessory. Even though Mike would probably understand, I'd be jeopardizing his career by telling him about it. He'd either have to report it or risk ending his career with the police department if they ever found out that he knew. I can't do that to him. When we come out there Monday you've got to act like you're as confused as the next person about Dr. Kirby's comatose condition.... Yeah, another Academy Award performance," Adrienne smiled at Catriona's remark. "Look. We need to be able to talk, you, me and Mike. What hours does Cameron LeBlanc work?.. So if we get there around 10:30 or so he'll be gone, or at least about to leave?...By the way, I've been meaning to ask, where'd you find this male nurse?...You checked his references? No chance of any ties to the sheriff? He's from south Louisiana. Doesn't know anyone in the community.... You're sure?.... OK. Mike and I will see you around 10:30 or so Monday morning. Be safe, Catriona." Adrienne hung up the phone, making a mental note to herself to do a little background check on Cameron LeBlanc as soon as she had time. He was only there a couple of hours in the morning and a couple in the evening, but still, that was way too much time for comfort, in Adrienne's mind anyway. And she sure wouldn't put it past Sheriff Johnny Johnson to have found a way to place Cameron LeBlanc there, right in the big middle of Dr. Kirby's 'coma.' Still, Catriona did have to have help. There was no way she could get her paralyzed, comatose husband in and out of bed by herself. Maybe Adrienne was letting her investigator's nose go a bit too far. *I'll have to make time to do a little research on Cameron LeBlanc,* she decided.

Adrienne opened the door to leave her office and walked across the den to the kitchen just about the time Andrew was turning off the television. His favorite program, CSI, had just ended. He tossed the remote on the coffee table and leaned on his cane to pull himself up from the sofa. Adrienne was putting on a pot of coffee.

"It's ten o'clock at night," Andrew said. "Why the hell are you making coffee?"

"I'm usually out on a case this time of night. I'm used to being awake. I don't feel like going to bed. How many more damn reasons do you want, and why do you think I have to explain everything I do to you?" Adrienne replied.

"Shit," Andrew answered and walked slowly to the bedroom dragging his oxygen tank on its metal pole alongside him.

Adrienne poured a cup of coffee and went outside to sit in a rocking chair in the dark on the back porch overlooking the pond. Bullfrogs croaked in the distance and an occasional fish slapped against the water. "Star light, star bright, where oh where is Mel tonight? Please, God, let him be all right," she whispered. A single tear glistened in the moonlight.

Chapter Thirty-Three

"Guinness stout and the best sandwiches in the world," Mike Morris chewed on a cigar and grinned ear to ear as he and Andrew looked at the Enoch's Irish Pub menu. Adrienne had suggested they go to Copeland's for dinner, but Mike had insisted on Enoch's. It was a popular and light-hearted place with its live Irish band playing lilting Irish tunes while people chattered and laughed, crowded around one another. But its light-hearted atmosphere was not the same for Adrienne, not now. This was the place she and Mel met for lunch the day he told her he was getting a divorce, and he wanted her to divorce Andrew, too. This small, crowded room was the very one they sat in when Mel told her he loved her and wanted the two of them to have a future together. Now, sitting here with Mike and Andrew, her heart was leaden and she felt nauseated inside. She tried not to let it show.

"A Guinness pint for me too," Adrienne smiled at the skinny, young, red-haired waitress in her short black skirt and ruffled green blouse that scooped low in the front allowing cleavage to show.

"Make it three," Andrew added.

"Andrew, your medications," Adrienne said.

"I haven't taken any in two days," Andrew said. "No pain killers, no sleeping pills. Nothing since you told me Mike was coming, just so I could have a few Guinness stouts tonight." It had been a long time since Adrienne had seen Andrew smile, but he was smiling now.

The waitress returned with a tray full of Guinness mugs and hummed the tune the band was playing while she sat them on the table.

"Hell. A few Guinness stouts," Andrew went on, "and I might drag my oxygen tank and this stupid pole out there on the dance floor and do an Irish jig." He laughed out loud and took a large gulp of the foaming Guinness. "Here's to letting your hair down," He raised his mug and bumped it against Mike's, then Adrienne's.

Adrienne ordered a Park Avenue, her all-time favorite sandwich made with portabella mushrooms, avocado slices, tomato, sprouts, Swiss cheese and a special Enoch's sauce. She just hoped her mood would allow her to enjoy it. Mike ordered a fried shrimp po-boy that Adrienne knew from having seen them before would come stuffed with shrimp fresh from the Gulf dripping out its sides, and Cajun fries with extra gravy. Andrew ordered Irish nachos, a delicious treat of thick potato wedges instead of chips and covered with all the regular nacho goodies, seasoned meat, green onions, tomato pieces, tons of melted cheddar and sour cream. Enoch's chef piled the potato wedges high and built a pyramid of goodies from the potatoes up. It was big enough to feed and fill several people.

"Another round of Guinness," Mike grinned as the waitress set the plates of food on the table. "Time to celebrate a new beginning, and hopefully a quick ending to this black market baby selling case." The three of them bumped their mugs together again, then dove into the delicious food sitting in front of them.

Even on Sunday night, Enoch's was packed. Monroe's coffeehouses and other pubs were closed, so everyone gathered at Enoch's. It was a rather intimate situation, since there was no way to walk through the room without touching chests and stomachs or backs and butts to other people trying to pass. Someone bumped Adrienne's elbow as she took a big gulp of Guinness, causing her to miss her mouth and spill the rich, brown liquid down the front of her blouse. She grabbed a napkin and started dabbing.

"I'm so sorry," a man's voice said. "Please excuse me."

Adrienne looked up to reply, and found her self looking into Mel's eyes. She sat speechless, motionless.

"Adrienne! What a surprise!" His voice trembled.

"Professor Brighton," Adrienne answered, shocked to see Mel standing there, close enough to touch. "How nice to see you." She lay down the wet napkin and picked up a dry one to continue the dabbing. "This is Detective Mike Morris from the Baton Rouge Police Department." Mike wiped the gravy from his face with a napkin and extended his hand.

"Mel Brighton," Mel said to Mike with a smile, shaking his hand.

"Andrew Hargrove," Andrew said to Mel and extended his hand.

Mel stood quietly for a moment and glanced from Andrew to the oxygen tank standing next to his chair, then back to the man it was attached to. That this was Andrew, Adrienne's husband and they were out for a pleasant evening on the town, having dinner with a mutual friend became instantly clear to him. His heart sank. He tried to compose himself.

"Nice to meet you, Andrew. Adrienne's told me a lot about you and your hunting lodge." He shook Andrew's hand. Andrew eyed him suspiciously and said nothing.

"Dr. Brighton's one of my clients," Adrienne announced, looking straight at Andrew. "Or I should say, was one of my clients. Just finished his case a couple of weeks ago." She looked back at Mel. His beautiful, deep blue eyes were heavy and tired. "How are things going for you, Mel?" The question seemed so flat, so ordinary. Oh how she wanted to ask all the important questions, the ones she could only hope were obvious in her eyes. *Who was there with you at Camille's funeral? Please tell me you didn't have to go through that alone. Did her family support you or blame you? Are you sleeping well? Eating well? Are you living back in your house now? Do you know how much I ache for you? Want to comfort you? Miss you? Love you?*

"Everything's as good as can be expected, under the circumstances," Mel replied, then silence again. Suddenly, he reached for Adrienne's hand. "It's nice to see you again," he said softly. Then to Andrew and Mike. "Very nice to meet you both. I'll let you get back to your dinner." *Her life's moving steadily on*, he thought. *Was I really just another client?*

The band began playing, "When Irish Eyes are Smiling." Mel swallowed hard and pushed himself hurriedly through the crowd and out the door to the parking lot.

Chapter Thirty-Four

"Mike, this is Catriona Kirby."

"Pleased to meet you Mrs. Kirby."

"Please call me Catriona."

"This is Detective Mike Morris, Catriona, my friend I told you about."

"I'm glad to meet you detective. I'm so glad you've come to help us." Catriona extended her hand.

"And this must be Dr. Galen Kirby." Mike walked toward the wheel chair positioned with the bay window behind it, and stood looking into Dr. Kirby's expressionless eyes. "You mean to tell me he can hear and understand everything we say?"

"We believe so," Catriona answered. "But he's totally paralyzed. He can't move at all, or speak. Cameron, our home health nurse, has to bend and unbend him to get him in and out of his chair. It's not an easy task."

Mike took hold of the doctor's wrist and lifted. It was stiff and unyielding. The man looked and felt almost like a mannequin. "And what are the doctors saying about his condition?"

"That it's most likely temporary," Adrienne spoke before Catriona had a chance. "Remember, Mike, Dr. Kirby knows we're trying to convict him of murder. He knows we know about his black market baby-selling racket. It's just a matter of time, and we don't have any way of knowing how long that will be, before he gains his mobility back. Catriona's life will be in danger when that happens. We've got to move as fast as possible to get our proof and get an indictment so we can protect her from him."

"How could something like this happen," Mike quizzed. "This comatose thing, I mean? There's got to be some kind of explanation."

"Some kind of neurological poison," Adrienne explained while Catriona watched and listened. "Possibly from a plant or an animal. Possibly something he's eaten that's extremely toxic, or an insect bite of some kind. They just don't know for sure. But they're telling us there are no signs of permanent damage. It's just a matter of time and he'll come out of it."

Mike looked hard at the doctor. "You son of a bitch," he said. "We're gonna get you, and we're gonna get you good. Gonna put you away for a long time, maybe forever." He turned toward Catriona. "Adrienne told you the DNA came back?"

"Yes," Catriona replied. "And?"

Mike looked at Adrienne then back to Catriona. "It's a positive," he answered. "Your husband is the father of the little boy." He paused a moment. "There's more. Are you OK with this?"

"I'm OK," Catriona said, looking down at the floor. "I got over any misconceptions about my husband's decency and integrity a long time ago. Does the little boy have a name?"

"His name is Joey," Adrienne answered softly.

"The tests also show that the baby is Down Syndrome. Mentally retarded." Mike turned quickly. He could have sworn he saw Dr. Kirby jump. "He bent over the wheelchair and looked straight into the man's empty eyes. "Yeah, he's retarded you jerk, and he's your son. Is that why you killed his mama, cause she produced a defective child? That why you couldn't sell him? Your own flesh and blood, and he's retarded. That eat at you, you psychopath? A baby you produced is defective? Retarded? You think you're God, producing perfect babies and selling them. We're gonna get you and put you away where you belong, you...Either in prison or the nut house." Mike stopped just short of saying the "F" word in Catriona's presence.

"Can we sit down a minute, Catriona?" Adrienne asked, a little concerned with Mike's emotional reaction, and wanting to get him back on task. "I want to let you know the general plan of action." The three sat down at the breakfast room table a few feet away from Dr. Kirby. "As soon as we leave here, Mike and I are driving over to the house where Susanne Jasper and her son were living. Where she was found dead. We're trying to figure out why Dr. Kirby didn't kill the baby too. You can easily tell a Down Syndrome child from its physical features. He has to have known. Do you have any ideas about that, Catriona? Anything we can go on?"

"I'm not sure," Catriona answered. "But you're right. Down Syndrome children have very distinctive features. Galen's a physician, he would have known at a single glance, from the moment of the baby's birth. With all the other things we know for sure he's done, I can't imagine why he would have spared the baby's life."

"Well, we know it's not out of compassion," Adrienne added. "The man's a certified psychopath, and they don't have emotional ties to other human beings. People are just objects to him. Another thing we know for sure is that all his actions are egocentric. Everything he does is to promote his own interests, and to have total control of everyone who's a part of his personal environment and life. Let me ask you one more thing, Catriona. We know now why he couldn't adopt the baby out, but we don't know why he allowed it to survive. It's hard to believe, but it's crossed my mind that Dr. Kirby might have kept the baby alive to have a human guinea pig to practice his experiment on. You know, the one he used on cats." Adrienne looked carefully at Catriona and prayed she'd remember not to say too much in front of Mike about the puffer fish toxin, but she had to ask the question. It was the only thing that made any sense.

Catriona looked as though she would get sick. "I hadn't thought of it, but you're right Adrienne, it makes sense." She looked over at Galen. "How could I have been so wrong about him? How could I have lived with him, slept with him, looked evil in the eye and not recognized it?"

"I think that's a good theory to start with," Mike changed the mood. "Adrienne can tell me more about the experiment you both seem to be aware of while we're driving to Susanne Jasper's house. Another thing to think about though. As the coroner, he signed the woman's death certificate stating her death the result of natural causes. He couldn't have done that if the woman and baby had both been found dead. It would have created too much suspicion."

"You're right, Mike." Adrienne nodded. "He must have been planning to either take the baby with him when he killed her, or to come back and get him later when less suspicion would be aroused. Maybe he was interrupted before he could finish things out." She smiled at Catriona. "See why I'm so glad he's here? Two heads are definitely better than one, especially when you've got them both thinking out loud." She stood. "We'd better get going. We've got a lot to get done."

"Pleased to meet you, Catriona." Mike shook the woman's hand. "Keep your chin up. We'll have him out of here before you can count to a hundred," he smiled, then turned toward the doctor and gave him the bird.

Catriona walked Mike and Adrienne to the door. "I hope so. For everyone's sake," she said.

Chapter Thirty-Five

"What's the experiment the doctor's been working on? What's it got to do with cats? What's it got to do with the baby?" Mike turned onto the highway, pushed the accelerator to seventy-five, and set the cruise control. "Why is this the first time I'm hearing about this experiment? You've got to keep me filled in, Adrienne."

Adrienne tried to think how to explain as much as possible without getting too close to the truth about the doctor's paralysis.

"Dr. Kirby raises puffer fish," she started, "in a giant aquarium in his den. We didn't go in that room or you would have seen them. There's a lot of research going on right now in the medical community about puffer fish toxin. Supposed to be the most potent and deadly toxin in the world, but when it's mixed just right with some other kind of chemicals, I don't have a clue what kind, there's reason to believe it can be an extremely effective painkiller for terminally ill cancer patients. At least that's the way Catriona explained it to me. By the way, Mike, I don't remember whether or not I told you that Catriona has a degree in biology. She was getting ready to go to medical school before she met and married Galen Kirby. Anyway, Catriona's been aware for quite some time that Dr. Kirby's been experimenting with the puffer fish toxin. Somehow, she found out he'd captured some neighborhood cats, one at a time over a period of time, and used them to try his formula. The cats died." She looked at Mike to see his reaction. "There's some stuff about the incidents on file at the Bayou Parish Court House. Some of the cat owners found out Dr. Kirby had killed the cats and pressed charges. He was fined a few dollars. A letter was sent to the State Medical Board. He was reprimanded for unethical behavior, but nothing else ever came of it. It's entirely possible he kept his Down Syndrome child alive so he could experiment on him, a human, instead of cats. When you think about it, it makes sense that someone with his psychopathic mind would tell himself he had a right to the child since he's its father. That since the child was already defective and he's a doctor, he had the right to try medical experiments on him. And to him, whether or not the baby died would be no more important than the deaths of the cats. Remember, this is the same man who performed abortions on his own daughters. Also, that theory might explain why Dr. Kirby killed Susanne Jasper. Maybe she refused to give the baby up. She would have known that no one was going to adopt it. Maybe she figured out what he was going to do. Of course Dr. Kirby would blame the baby's defect on its mother, which would make her easily disposable too. He wouldn't want to use her for breeding purposes for his black market baby racket any longer. All of this would be just another way to separate himself from reality."

"Anything else I might need to know about these experiments?" Mike questioned. "I don't much like surprises."

Adrienne hesitated. "Nothing else I can think of." She turned her face away from Mike and looked out the window. She hated lying to him, and worse yet, she wasn't good at it. If she looked him in the eye, he would know she was holding something back. But she couldn't allow him to become an accessory to the fact that Catriona was doing something illegal and that she, Adrienne, knew about it and in some ways was helping Catriona to accomplish it. Maybe someday after it was all over and Dr. Kirby was behind bars or locked up in a mental institute she'd be able to tell Mike the whole truth. Right now, it would only add to the burden life had already dealt him, and it would accomplish nothing toward solving the case. Right now, she needed to get him off the subject.

"Mike, do you know anything about the black market baby business? Seems like that's an old- time racket. Haven't heard of such a thing in years."

"You'd be astonished, Adrienne. After you and I first talked about this case and the possibility of the doctor being tied to a black market baby selling racket, I did a little cyber checking to see how difficult it would be for a person in this day and age to create a baby black market. I found websites to help adult victims of black market adoptions try to find their biological parents and to have a chance to discover why this happened to them. Just imagine what it would feel like to discover that you had been sold without your biological mother knowing, probably believing that you were dead. On one black market website that advertised they help people find their roots, to date there had been over 20,000 hits. I found another website that is a black market adoptee's registry. There are several articles available if you want to read them, and they're pretty interesting, but I'll give you the jest of them.

"Black market baby rings were common in the 1930's through the 1960's. They aren't as common today as far as we know, but they definitely do exist, and there are many more of them than just Dr. Kirby's. One common denominator is that they are usually run by doctors. Today, healthy Caucasian babies bring $100,000 on the illicit market. One of the people involved in helping black market adoptees find their past is a 60 year old New York psychotherapist who is himself a black market baby. He says it's easy to find black market babies to buy on internet.

"I found a case where a small town Kansas physician named Dr. Mary Townsend-Glassen signed birth certificates for babies she delivered in her office in Phillipsburg, Kansas. She filled in the names of the people adopting the infants as the birth parents, which eliminated the need for legal adoption. That brings up another question, Adrienne. Dr. Kirby filled in and signed the original birth certificates showing that he delivered the babies, and he used the real mothers' names. As the babies were adopted out, the new birth certificates were issued with the adoptive parents' names. That means there's an attorney involved. I checked a couple of the birth certificate copies you showed me. The original birth certificates and the revised birth certificates are on file with the Louisiana Vital Statistics Department in Baton Rouge. They're legal. That means they had to be filed by an attorney. Have any idea who that might be?"

"I don't have a clue," Adrienne answered, but you're absolutely right. Dr. Kirby couldn't have filed the adoption papers. An attorney had to do it. I don't know why I hadn't thought of that."

"You would have in time," Mike smiled. "Anyway, before she died, Dr. Townsend-Glassen actually wrote a book about how she had helped unwed mothers find good homes for their babies at a time when contraception was uncommon, abortion was virtually unavailable, and the social stigma of illegitimacy was overwhelming. Of course she didn't mention in the book the amount of money she earned from the 'placement' of babies. She totally refused to see or acknowledge the harm she had done or the pain so many mothers must have suffered. She died in the 1970's.

"The most notorious black market baby selling ring operated out of the Tennessee Children's Home, run by Georgia Tann. A 1950 investigation determined that Tann had grossed an estimated $1,000,000 supplying babies to out-of-state residents. There was an article in a 1991 issue of Good Housekeeping Magazine written about Georgia Tann. It's called, 'The

Woman Who Stole 5000 Babies.' And Mary Tyler Moore starred in a movie about Georgia Tann called, 'Stolen Babies.' It seems many of the babies were taken from the mothers without the mother even knowing her baby was alive. Ms. Tam and the physician who helped her would tell the young mother that her baby had died or was stillborn, depending on whether or not the mother had heard the baby cry. She would then ask the mother to sign the papers for her to take care of burial of the infant, but the papers were actually a form giving up custody of the infant to the Tennessee Children's Home society which Georgia Tann operated. Tann made the moral judgment that these women were unworthy of motherhood.

"You'll find this interesting, too, Adrienne. Your theory is that Dr. Kirby is producing his own babies from women he believes are inferior. But pitiful, insecure, dependent women are the only ones he can get involved in affairs with him. He rationalizes that his superior genetics will make the children superior if they're raised right. So he's adopting them out to select, rich, highly intellectual families. That whole scenario is not too far off from the genius sperm bank that existed here in our country until just five or six years ago. A couple of doctors decided that our country was becoming overpopulated with low-intelligence people, and that the only way to avoid disaster in the future was to produce geniuses on a larger scale. This sperm bank only accepted sperm from Nobel Prize winning men, and only allowed women who were qualified to become members of MENSA, the organization for geniuses, to become pregnant by the genius sperm. These people actually convinced themselves that this combination would most likely produce genius children. There are journalists and researchers looking for the offspring of these 'breedings' as we speak. According to what's known, there were over two hundred children produced through this sperm bank. Some of them are just now becoming teenagers; some are still pre-adolescent."

"How can otherwise OK people convince themselves of these awful things and think they have the right to put themselves in the position of playing God? Are they all a bunch of psychopaths?" Adrienne was in shock.

"That kind of thing has been going on for a long time, Adrienne. It just gets done more scientifically as the medical technology gets more advanced. It was the same basic principal in Georgia Tann's time. Tann organized the Tennessee Children's Home Society in Memphis to remove children from the slums and put them into the hands of the rich who would educate them. She took children out of homes, parks, anywhere she could find them. Any poorly dressed or dirty child, and sold them to the wealthy. The article says

Georgia Tann left behind a legacy of hate, broken families, stress, disease and other disruptions that would have put her in prison if she hadn't died before the Tennessee Attorney General's Office could finish the investigation."

"That's exactly why we've got to finish this investigation, Mike, as soon as possible. The Louisiana State Attorney General's Office has given up. To them it's all on the back burner with Dr. Kirby. They have bigger fish to fry, and they've never been able to find anything conclusive. They're willing to listen if we can bring them anything concrete, but they're not pursuing matters connected to him any further themselves."

"Yeah, it's funny who can actually know, and yet nothing be done about it. You know there were actually Hollywood celebrities who adopted children through Georgia Tann? Joan Crawford, for instance, who was accused by her children of severely abusing them in the book, "Mommy Dearest". And June Allyson and Dick Powell.

"There's another angle as far as the attorney idea goes we need to look into, too, Adrienne. During the investigation of Georgia Tann, local attorneys and justices were found to be part of the network that allowed adoptive parents to be out-of-state residents. In other words, they were respected public officials running shady deals in the back room. The selling of babies for profit."

"Well, we already know Sheriff Johnny Johnson is corrupt and capable of anything, including murder. But there are absolutely no signs he knows anything about this black market baby racket of Dr. Kirby's. As a matter of fact, I think he was pretty angry to find out the doctor had a money-making deal on the side that he hadn't told him about and included him in."

"So, it's not the sheriff. There are plenty of others, and at least one of them has to be a lawyer. Everything I read showed doctors and attorneys working together to get rich selling babies.

"There was another real interesting case, too. A Dr. Katherine M. Cole, a physician, ran one of the largest black market adoption rings in the country from 1927 to 1963 in Miami, Florida. Cole destroyed her records after leaving behind an estimated one thousand adoptees with falsified birth certificates. Dr. Cole was arrested seven times in her life for everything from manslaughter, to unlawful possession of barbiturates, to failing to have a birth certificate filed.

"So see, even from the idea of the drug angle with Dr. Kirby and Sheriff Johnson, none of what you've told me is really that far out. Except the fact that the babies Dr. Kirby is selling appear to be his own.

"It was estimated that Dr. Katherine Cole delivered somewhere between 2000 and 4000 babies during her twenty-eight years experience. Investigators believe Cole handled hundreds of adoptions. In one case, she took two babies from separate mothers and registered them as twins. There was nothing she wasn't capable of doing to make a dollar at someone else's expense. She had no conscience whatsoever about the harm she was doing."

"That does sound like something we'd expect of Dr. Kirby, doesn't it," Adrienne added. "Not an inkling of a conscience."

"Yeah, well wait til you hear this one." Mike pulled a cigar out of his shirt pocket. "There was a black market baby broker in Brooklyn in the 1940's. Her name was Bessie Bernard, and she was just a housewife. She charged as much as $2000 per baby. That was a lot of money back then. Two attorneys, an Irwin Slater and Harry Wolfson were tied in with her. This was a big time business done on an assembly line basis. Unwed mothers were found in the Miami area and once their babies were born, they were brought north and sold in New York and nearby states. Slater and Wolfson drafted formal agreements just like a bill of sale for a piece of property. Slater was in charge of production, and Wolfson was his office manager. Bessie Bernard was in charge of placement and transportation of the babies. Girls giving up their babies were given from $100 to $300. Adoptive families paid between $1650 and $2000. In 1949, Bernard was charged with conspiracy and illegal placement for adoption. And get this, Adrienne. She was sentenced to one year in jail. When she got out, she took up practice under the name of Elizabeth Weiner, her maiden name, and continued selling babies until as late as 1970. All this stuff is on internet. Anyone can read about it. Who knows, maybe that's where Dr. Kirby got some of his ideas."

"My God," Adrienne said. "We can't let Catriona know that. To think that Dr. Kirby could get off with a slap on the wrist? We can't let that happen, Mike."

"That's why we've got to prove the murders, and anything illegal he might be doing with those experiments of his," Mike said. "Evidence that he's actually selling his own babies will really help prove he's a nut case, and should help us get Susanne Jasper's death turned over to homicide, once they're shown the evidence that he's her baby's father. At the very least, it shouldn't have been him doing the autopsy."

Adrienne cringed. Catriona could actually end up spending time in jail for keeping her husband in a coma, and Dr. Kirby could go free. They couldn't let that happen. No matter what, they had to get the evidence. And Adrienne was more convinced than ever that Mike had to be kept in the dark about the Haitian's and their zombie powder.

Chapter Thirty-Six

"You two finally made it home," Andrew commented as Adrienne and Mike came in from their trip to Susanne Jasper's house. Mike had slipped a credit card through the lock, a trick Adrienne never had been able to master, and they'd explored the house together. Nothing. They'd talked to the elderly woman who made the call to the police, and she'd been more than happy to cooperate. Mike hadn't even needed to show her his shield. Again, nothing they didn't already know.

"Something smells good," Mike commented.

"Red beans and rice. I put a big pot on this morning. Big chunks of Cajun sausage and sweet Vidalia onions cut in quarters Threw in a few chicken wings for good measure. Ought to be ready whenever you're ready," Andrew smiled.

"Well, I'm ready, "Mike said.

"Come on then." Andrew pulled his oxygen tank along and Mike followed him to the kitchen.

"That cornbread?" Mike looked at the giant pan with its golden contents.

"Sure is," Andrew said. "Grab you a chunk." He ladled enormous bowls of red beans and rice, making sure to put lots of sausage chunks and a couple of chicken wings across the top, then pushed it across the counter to Mike. "Can't beat red beans and rice and a big pan of cornbread on a cold November night. Adrienne, you gonna eat with us?"

"You two go ahead," Adrienne answered. "I think I'm going to soak in a hot bubble bath first. Want to think about all the research on black market baby rackets we talked about, Mike."

"Sure thing. How about tomorrow morning we start looking at the list of babies adopted out in this part of the state? See if we can talk to some of the parents?"

"Good idea," Adrienne answered, pretending to be interested, but wanting to forget about the case for tonight. In reality, she was looking forward to a few moments alone to think about Mel, and to wonder where he was tonight and what he was doing at this very moment. She gathered her pajamas, a robe and slippers, and headed for the bathroom. She started the water running and put her hand under it to be sure the temperature was just right, then poured a cap full of Secret Garden bath oil in the water. While it was running, she went to the den and opened the liquor cabinet. An open bottle of Merlot stared back at her. She took it and a crystal wine glass and went back to the bathroom. She could hear pleasant, manly voices in the kitchen, Mike and Andrew enjoying the red beans and rice together, as she walked back through the room. Locking the door behind her, Adrienne lit the Love Spell candles sitting on the foot-end of the garden tub, then dimmed the overhead light. She let her clothes fall to the floor, and stepped lightly into the foaming hot water. She slid down until the water touched her chin, then allowed its warmth and the candles' aroma to move her, float her gently away from the reality of her own personal world into the world of fantasy where she could find peace, and freedom, and Mel's sweet smile and gentle touch.

Chapter Thirty-Seven

"The first address is on Deborah Drive," Adrienne gave directions to Mike as they headed for the home in an elite part of Monroe where one of the children adopted out by Dr. Kirby hopefully still lived. "It will be easier this time, Mike. I don't know what I would have done if the parents of the boy I was checking out before had actually asked to see my identification up close. At least now, with you, I'm completely legal."

Mike grinned. "Yeah," he said. "It's a pretty good idea to do all this legal, Adrienne. We don't want to get to court and have the whole case thrown out because of some little item we overlooked. Of course, if they wanted to press the issue, I'm out of my territory, but evidence is evidence. We just have to be sure we turn it over to the right people. And if we find any of these black market kids in Baton Rouge, well, we're home free. " Mike had a feeling Adrienne knew something she wasn't sharing with him. He hoped it wasn't something important; he hoped they were good enough friends that she wouldn't hold anything back, not from him. "Tell me what you know about the family we're going to see."

Adrienne pulled out a legal-sized pad of notes. "The family's name is Field. Bob Field is president of a Hibernia bank. Marsha Field spends most of her time with the City Improvement Committee deciding where to plant flowers and how to organize parades. They have two children. One is the twelve year old girl they adopted through Dr. Kirby. It appears they adopted their other child, a nine year old boy, through an out of state agency. Nothing to show the boy is connected to Dr. Kirby, at least at this point. I'll check it out more thoroughly later, after we finish our interview with the family."

Mike asked, "Do we have any information telling us how they got involved with the doctor?"

Adrienne replied, "None so far. I'm hoping we'll find out this morning, and maybe that information will give us more to go on. Someone knows who the lawyer is that's tying the strings together for Dr. Kirby. Don't you think it would seem strange to the adoptive parents to sign papers with just the doctor present, and no attorney?"

"Yeah," Mike answered." And another thing, Adrienne. Whoever this attorney is, it seems logical he'd be asking questions, at least to himself, about the deaths of the women connected to Dr. Kirby. He's had those women right in front of him to sign their babies away. He knows about the deaths of at least the women we know about."

"Yeah, Mike. You're right," Adrienne cringed. "He has to at least suspect the doctor, even if he doesn't know for sure. Maybe he's afraid the doctor will get rid of him too. If the women are being forced to give up their babies, or are being deceived so they'll give them up, the adoptions are illegal. Maybe he's afraid he'll be exposed. Maybe he's just in it for the money. Who knows? One thing I'll bet he doesn't know though. I'll bet he doesn't know the sicko doctor's fathering the babies himself."

"Let's make that a priority for today," Mike said. "Let's see if we can get the name of the attorney. That will fill in a tremendous gap."

"There's the house," Adrienne pointed to a three-story mansion sitting far back away from the road. "Two golden retrievers met them at the gate as they stepped out of Mike's car. Mike pushed a buzzer on the gate that rang a bell in the house. The front door opened, and a woman stepped onto the porch.

"May I help you?" an attractive middle-aged woman asked.

Mike showed her his shield. "Detective Mike Morris," he said. "Baton Rouge Police Department. This is Investigator Adrienne Hargrove. Are you Mrs. Marsha Field?"

"Yes. What's wrong?" Mrs. Field sounded concerned.

"Maybe nothing. We'd like to ask you a few questions about the adoption of one of your children. Is it all right if we come in? No use getting the neighbors involved." Mike hoped that little comment would encourage the woman to invite them inside the house. Mrs. Field pushed a button just inside the front door, and the gate opened. Mike and Adrienne walked to the porch.

"Please come in. Would you like something to drink?" she asked as she guided them to the sofa.

"No thanks. We'll just be a few minutes," Adrienne answered. Mike shook his head "no."

"What do you want to know about my children, and why?" Marsha Field asked as she sat down in a chair across from Mike and Adrienne.

"Are the children home?" Adrienne asked. "We wouldn't want them to overhear our conversation."

"No," Mrs. Field said. "I'm the only one home right now."

Mike started. "Mrs. Field, according to our information, your two children are adopted, but through different sources. We're interested in asking you a few questions about the private adoption that was assisted by Dr. Galen Kirby."

"May I ask why?" Mrs. Field said, obviously concerned.

"We have reason to believe Dr. Kirby has been involved in a black market baby-selling ring for a number of years," Mike saw no reason to tread lightly, "and it is very possible the adoption you participated in through Dr. Kirby was done illegally."

"No," Mrs. Field shrieked, standing up suddenly. "There's no way. We made sure everything was done legally. Dr. Kirby matched the baby with us and made sure there were no health issues. Everything else was handled by a licensed and experienced attorney."

Mrs. Field had no idea how glad Mike and Adrienne were to hear those words, or how much easier their goal of finding out today who the attorney was had just become.

"Mrs. Field," Adrienne continued, hoping that her woman's voice would help calm her. "We don't believe you or your husband did anything illegal, but there's a chance that Dr. Kirby had no legal right to place the child you adopted for adoption. It would help us to sort through all this if you'd tell us the name of the attorney who handled the paper work. Will you do that?"

"I, I guess that would be all right," Mrs. Field was visibly shaken. "I wish my husband was here. I'll call him."

"If you don't mind, Mrs. Field," Mike said, "you can do that later. We'll need to talk to him too, but right now we need to know the name of the lawyer. That fact alone can help us determine whether or not we need to look further into the history of the child you adopted. We'll arrange to come back another time when your husband is here, after we have more of the facts. In the meantime, there's no reason to disturb your children or husband in any way. Maybe it will all turn out to be a mistake. The name of the lawyer is what will help us determine that fact." Mike was persistent. He and Adrienne needed the name of that lawyer. It would make everything so much easier.

"George Hathaway," Mrs. Field said. "His name was George Hathaway. His office was in Destiny. I think he lived in Destiny, too. Although I remember hearing several years ago that he'd moved to Monroe. I'm not sure where he is now. I do know he's a licensed attorney. My husband checked his credentials very thoroughly."

"We're not questioning his credentials, Mrs. Field," Adrienne said. "Having a license to practice the law doesn't necessarily keep a person from breaking the law, especially if enough money is involved. Can you tell us how you and your husband got involved with Dr .Kirby and George Hathaway?"

"My husband knew Mr. Hathaway. I really can't remember how. It seems like it was through the bank. Mr. Hathaway knew we were interested in adoption, and that we really didn't want to be on an adoption list for years like some of our friends. He knew a doctor in a small town that handled private adoptions. I really don't remember much of the rest. My husband handled that part."

"What kind of fee was charged?" Mike asked. "How much money actually changed hands?"

"Oh I have no idea," Mrs. Field answered. "My husband handles all our financial matters. I've never been good at that kind of thing."

Another kept woman, Adrienne thought to herself, *southern bell conditioned not to think or ask questions. No telling what kind of double life Mr. Field lives.*

Mike stood and reached out his hand toward Mrs. Field. "Thank you, Mrs. Field. We'll be in touch with you in a few days." Adrienne smiled at the woman as she and Mike left.

Adrienne and Mike pulled into a Sonic. Adrienne got the Monroe phone book off the back seat while Mike ordered cherry limeades. She looked under attorneys. There he was. George Hathaway, still in Monroe. Now all they had to do was find out exactly how he was connected with Dr. Kirby. That shouldn't be hard to do. The day was turning out to be a very productive one.

"OK, Mike," Adrienne said. "We've most likely got the attorney now, and I'm willing to bet it will be easy to find the paper work that ties him to the doctor. What I'm thinking is it's going to take a long, long time to look up all these families that adopted kids through these two, and we don't have a long time. Every day that goes by, Catriona Kirby's life is in more and more danger, and her emotional stability. No one can live like that for long without breaking down. We've got to go faster."

"I was thinking about that too," Mike said. Once we've got what we need to connect the doctor and the lawyer, and we can probably do that tomorrow, we need to contact each set of parents and have them meet with us all at once.

They don't have to know there'll be other parents there. That way we can have sort of a group meeting and interview them all at once. That should speed things along. Help us find common threads I think it's very possible we can have this thing wrapped up before the week's over, maybe. Then we can approach the district attorney's office and get them on the case. After that it should be smooth sailing, at least as far as getting him to trial goes. Pretty rough sailing for the families involved though, especially if some of them knew or suspected what was going on. Like this banker. I have a bad feeling about him."

"Yeah, me too," Adrienne said. "Still, it seems like we're on a roll. I'll call Catriona tonight and give her the good news.

"Mike, before we head home, I need to make one more stop. Won't take but a minute."

"It's fine with me," Mike said. "Where we going?"

Adrienne cut over to Louisville and headed for the Lea Joyner Bridge. "I need to check on someone," she said. She pulled up to the bottom of the bridge and parked the car. "If you don't mind, Mike," she said, "it'd be better if you stayed here." She walked to the edge of the bridge where it hooks to the land and looked up into the shadows. Sure enough, he was there sound asleep on a piece of cardboard using his back-pack for a pillow. Adrienne walked slowly toward him, calling his name as she went, hoping not to alarm him. "Smiley?" she called. "Smiley?" The man sat up.

"Who are you?" Smiley asked, slowly standing up. "What you want?"

"I met you on the bridge the other day. You told me your real name is Erle Blue. Remember? You told me you were trying to find your way back to Missouri?"

"I don't remember you," Smiley said. "What you want?"

"Maybe you'll remember me if we step out in the sunshine where you can see me clearly," Adrienne said.

"What you want?" Smiley asked again.

"I want to ask you about your name, your real name. I think I have a couple of dollars with me today if you'll walk over to my car with me."

Smiley perked up. "I'll work for food, "he said.

"I know," Adrienne answered. "But today, I'll just give it to you as a gift." She thought to herself that even this homeless man whose mind is half gone has some sense of pride, a need to feel useful. "Maybe another day you can do some work for me. Today I just need a little information." Smiley walked toward her and Adrienne walked out from under the bridge and toward her car where Mike was waiting.

'Who's this?" Mike asked as he rolled down the car window.

"This is Mr. Erle Blue, Mike," Adrienne answered, "better known as Smiley."

"Hello Smiley," Mike said as he climbed out of the car. He didn't know what Adrienne was doing with this homeless man, but he didn't like the disadvantage of being seated in the car with Smiley standing outside by Adrienne if something went wrong, his automatic sense of police suspicion kicking in.

"Would you hand me my purse," Adrienne said to Mike. Mike looked at her like she was crazy, but reached across the seat and got Adrienne's purse and handed it to her.

"Smiley," Adrienne started. "I'm a private investigator. Sometimes I help find people who've been lost. I might be able to help you find your family in Missouri. Maybe not, but I'd like to try."

Smiley looked at her in disbelief. "You gonna help me find Missouri?" he asked excitedly.

"Maybe, Smiley, but don't get your hopes up. Not yet anyway. I need to ask you a couple of things. Were you ever in the military? Do you remember anything about the Vietnam War?"

"I was a soldier," Smiley spoke slowly, focusing on some pain off in the distance beyond Adrienne and Mike. "They wanted me to shoot people." He looked at the ground, the sorrow obvious in his face. "I couldn't do it. Somebody shot me. I was sick a long, long time."

Oh my God Adrienne thought to with excitement. *This may really be the guy* "Do you remember anything about the name "Robert?" Adrienne asked.

Smiley lifted his eyes and looked at Adrienne with confusion. "That's me," he answered. "Robert Erle Blue. Can you find Missouri? They need me in Missouri?"

"I don't know, Smiley," Adrienne answered, handing him a ten dollar bill. "I'm not sure, but I'll try. You get yourself something good to eat, no alcohol," she warned. "I'll let you know in a few days." Adrienne thought she saw tears in his eyes as he looked at the ten dollar bill. "They need me in Missouri," he said as he turned and walked away, back into the shadows under the bridge.

* * *

Andrew was sitting in a white, plastic lawn chair on the dock with a fishing pole in his hand as Adrienne and Mike pulled up to the lodge. "Grab a pole and come on out," he hollered at Mike.

"Don't mind if I do," Mike hollered back. "I'll be right out."

Adrienne smiled at Mike. "If I didn't know better I'd swear you actually like Andrew."

"I do like him," Mike answered. "Look Adrienne, we're all just people stuck on this giant ball rolling around together in space. I don't like the things Andrew's done to you, and I don't have a clue why you've stayed with him all these years, but I do know that all people have their own personal struggles going on inside of them. And sometimes those struggles can be more than a man can bear. It looks to me like Andrew's burden is just about as heavy as a man can handle." He smiled and gave her a quick hug. "I'm going fishing."

Adrienne sat in the rocking chair on the back porch, lit a cigarette and watched Mike, fishing pole in hand, walk across the yard to where Andrew sat fishing on the dock. She wanted to clear her mind of cases and evidence and Andrew, and just think about Mel. She just wanted to think about Mel, right or wrong. She just wanted to think about Mel.

Chilled by the cool evening air, Adrienne went inside and turned on the light in her office. She walked over to feed the angel fish and little Nemo. Like always, Nemo greeted her with his silly clown fish smile, darting back and forth through the water while the angel fish watched him in disgust and waited proudly for their evening meal. She sprinkled fish food across the water and watched it drift slowly, slowly downward, each grain snatched by a hungry mouth before it could reach a hiding place in the colored sand. Everything in the fish tank moved in slow motion. Nothing ever got in a hurry or seemed confused except little Nemo who gulped the food like he was afraid there would be none tomorrow.

"Smiley," Adrienne thought. "Let's see what we can find out about Smiley." She walked away from the aquarium and sat at her desk at the computer. She typed in her investigator's code and pulled up the "missing person's" link. She typed in Robert Erle Blue and read the story again. It sure read like Smiley could be the same man. She closed the site and pulled up the Kansas City, Kansas phone directory. Robert Erle Blue was first reported missing in Kansas, right across the state line from Missouri. She found the number for the police department and dialed.

"Missing Persons," she said when a man's voice answered. She was transferred. "This is private investigator Adrienne Hargrove calling from Louisiana. Look, we've got a homeless man here in town living under a bridge who says his name is Robert Erle Blue. It appears a Robert Erle Blue was reported missing by your department back in the 1980's. There's a chance it might be the same guy. I was wondering if you could fax me any information you have about him, and a picture if possible. Sure. My fax number is 318- 968-5252. I'd appreciate it. I'll watch for it this evening. Thanks." She went to the kitchen and took a look in the refrigerator to see what might be available for dinner, then picked up the phone on the counter and called Bar-b-que West. "I'd like to order a family feast for four, please. Beef, ribs, chicken, potato salad and baked beans. How long before it'll be delivered? That's fine." She hung up the phone and went to her rocking chair on the back porch again to smoke a cigarette. Only Mike and Andrew's silhouette's were visible on the dock. She could hear their voices but couldn't make out what they were saying, only that they were having a good time. She thought about Mike and the awful burden in his life, the murder of his wife. She thought about Mel and the suicide of his wife, yet he seemed to moving forward with his life, too. Why did she always seem to be hanging in mid air, never able to quite be content, to quite find peace or joy or fulfillment in her life? Why couldn't she be like the angel fish instead of like Nemo, always in turmoil? She walked back into her office to wait for the fax.

Chapter Thirty-Eight

Adrienne and Catriona sat across from one another in a booth at the IHOP restaurant right off the exit road from I-20. Mike stayed at the lodge and was using Adrienne's office as his work station for the day. His job was to take the list of phone numbers and addresses and contact each household in Louisiana where a child had been adopted through Dr. Kirby and his attorney friend, George Hathaway. He was going to invite or intimidate the parents, whichever it took, to meet with him, Adrienne, and the assistant district attorney at the Ouachita Parish Public Library on 18th street the following evening at seven o'clock. Later in the day, he would trace, backward to forward, anything he could find about George Hathaway's legal career in Destiny, and look for links to the doctor. Adrienne's job was to meet with Catriona and see what she might be able to tell her about George Hathaway's connection to Dr. Kirby. Adrienne ordered an omelet and coffee. Catriona ordered German pancakes with lemon butter and hot tea.

"Look Catriona" Adrienne started. "I don't want to get your hopes up too high, but it looks like we're getting really close to pulling this thing together. Yesterday afternoon, Mike and I were able to find out the name of the attorney that handled the birth certificates for your husband."

"Oh Adrienne," Catriona said. "I'm afraid to hope it could actually be over soon, that I could be free and safe. Who do you think the attorney is?"

"Name's George Hathaway," Adrienne answered.

"George Hathaway? You must be kidding. We bought our house from George Hathaway. Well, sort of, in a roundabout way."

"Tell me about that," Adrienne stared hard at Catriona.

"I don't actually know all the details. It was done rather quietly. George Hathaway built the house. The rumor was that he got into financial difficulty and needed to sell it to avoid bankruptcy. Galen had fallen in love with the house. We went to see it. He bought it. That's all I know." Catriona realized again that she really knew very little about her husband at all, and virtually nothing about his financial affairs. "I remember Galen laughing later. Saying that George Hathaway had been run out of town. There was a rumor going around he was gay."

"And was he?" Adrienne asked.

"I have no idea," Catriona answered. "He was married at the time, but I heard he was divorced not long after. In later years I heard that he had remarried and was living in Monroe. Nothing about him seemed gay to me, but then, I never knew him very well. I can tell you that the house always seemed to me to have a darkness about it, a kind of heaviness that's hard to describe. Almost like bad luck and misfortune are just hanging in the air waiting to happen. I've felt like my guardian angel is working a double-shift since the day we moved in"

"I'll have to say, Catriona, every time I've been in that house I've had the creeps. I thought it was just because I know how evil Dr. Kirby is, but I can sense how it could be even more." Adrienne cringed. The waitress brought their food and refilled their drinks.

"From the first time I saw it," Catriona went on, "it seemed to have an aura of evil about it, even from the road long before I went inside. But there was no stopping Galen. He had to have it. I think it was some sort of status symbol to him."

"As soon as we finish breakfast," Adrienne said, "I'm going back to my house to see what Mike's been able to find out. It's all starting to come together pretty quickly now."

Adrienne and Catriona stood in line at the cash register waiting to pay for breakfast. Adrienne reached inside her purse for the money, but Catriona wouldn't hear of it. As Adrienne was thanking her, she heard a man's voice.

"Adrienne, is that you?" She turned around and stared into the face of Mel. Flushed and tongue-tied Adrienne said, "Mel, how nice to see you. This is my friend, Catriona Kirby."

Mel took Catriona's hand. "I'm glad to meet you," he said, peering into her lovely eyes, and noticing how very soft her delicate hand was, holding it a few seconds too long.

"It's nice to meet you, too," Catriona answered awkwardly, her eyes drawn like a magnet to his hypnotic ones.

"Mel is an English professor friend of mine," Adrienne explained. "Professor Mel Brighton." Adrienne saw an immediate attraction between the two, and she felt a sense of urgency to get Catriona and herself out of the room. "Sorry to be in such a hurry Mel, but we have to meet someone."

Never taking his eyes off of her, Mel said again, "It's so nice to meet you, Catriona. What was your last name?"

"Kirby," Catriona answered. "At least for right now."

Mel smiled. "I'll see you again."

Over my dead body, Adrienne thought to herself as she felt a lump rise in her throat.

"A fax came for you," Mike said as Adrienne walked into the study. "I laid it over there," he pointed to a small table.

"I was expecting it last night," Adrienne answered.

"It just came," Mike said. "In the meantime I found some pretty interesting stuff about the doctor and the lawyer."

"I found out a couple of pretty interesting things myself," Adrienne said, feeling a little depressed about seeing Mel. "According to Catriona, Dr. Kirby bought their house from George Hathaway when Hathaway got in some kind of financial trouble. She also heard some kind of rumor that Hathaway might have been gay."

"Right on," Mike answered. "But there's even more. Evidently Hathaway did file bankruptcy, but he'd made an arrangement with the doctor ahead of time. See, only by filing a chapter seven bankruptcy could he get completely out of debt, but by doing that, he'd lose all the equity he had in his house. He worked out a little deal with the doctor under the table so to speak. The doctor would get the house for practically nothing at the sheriff's auction, and he'd pay Hathaway a lump sum under the table so the bankruptcy court wouldn't get hold of it for the equity in Hathaway's house. It'd still be a really good deal for the doctor, and Hathaway would lose nothing. The doctor wouldn't have to worry about being outbid, or the price skyrocketing. In the meantime, you know who else had to be involved in setting it up to be sure the doctor got the house and not someone else who was bidding on it?"

"The sheriff," Adrienne said.

"The sheriff," Mike mimed "There were accusations by another lawyer in the community who had hoped to buy the house at the sheriff's auction. There was a deposition, but of course Dr. Kirby, George Hathaway, and Sheriff Johnson were all in on it together, so they all just lied. The deposition is a part of the public record. That's how I was able to find this out."

"And the accusations that George Hathaway is gay?" Catriona asked.

"There's nothing on record about anything like that," Mike answered. "But that could very well be the hold Dr. Kirby had over George Hathaway to get him involved in selling him the house, and possibly this baby black market thing too. That, or he's just plain corrupt and would have done it for a cut of the money anyway. That'll be up to the district attorney to determine. Our job is to link both men to the selling of babies."

"Looks like that won't be too hard," Adrienne answered, still feeling down.

"What's a matter?" Mike asked, turning the chair and looking directly at Adrienne for the first time since she'd come in. "You look like crap.'

"I'm just tired," Adrienne answered. "Feeling a little confused."

"Some way I can help?" Mike asked.

"You're doing enough already, Mike," Adrienne said.

"I've got pretty big shoulders," Mike said, "especially for you."

"Nothing I can talk about," Adrienne said. "Nothing I have a right to be feeling." She picked up the fax and began to read. "It's got to be him," she said.

"Who?" Mike asked.

"The homeless man, Smiley. Robert Erle Blue. He's really a Vietnam Vet, decorated for bravery when he rescued some soldiers, then was wounded himself. He got shot. Lived with his wife and four kids in Missouri. Was hospitalized several years later in Kansas in the psyche unit .for post-traumatic syndrome. They thought he was better. According to this, he checked himself out of the hospital and was never heard from again. Left her alone with two dying sons and two teenagers to support. She got sick and died from cancer while she was still young. Neighbors said she worked herself to death trying to take care of her family, and trying to track down Erle. Last anyone knew about him was after her death. Someone reported seeing him in Tom Thumb, Texas, remarried and with a young daughter. He disappeared from there, and no one's seem him since. New wife's name was Dequetta."

"You're sure it's him?" Mike asked.

"No," Adrienne answered, "but it all makes sense. I just need to find out if he remembers the name Dequetta, or the name of his first wife, Anna. This gives his kids names too. A couple of them, one by each of the wives, were named Mary, and his mother's name was Mary. His grandmother too."

"You gonna tell the man he abandoned his wife and kids and that his wife worked and worried herself to death looking for him?" Mike asked. "That two of his kids died?"

"I don't know what I'm going to tell him," Adrienne answered. "Maybe I won't tell him anything at all. What's the point if it only makes his life worse? They're all dead and gone now, anyone who would care anyway."

"What about his kids who weren't sick? What about the second wife and their child?"

"I don't know, Mike. Would it be better to tell him and watch the last eggshell-thin fragments of hope and sanity he has left be washed away forever? Or is the right thing to do to leave him alone with his illusions and his dreams that he's working his way back home? That someday he's going to find his family and all will be OK. Do I have the right to destroy that?"

"You're an investigator, Adrienne. You have the obligation, if he's the missing person, to report it to the authorities and let them decide who to tell and what action to take," Mike answered.

"I don't know, Mike. I just don't know."

Mike changed the subject. "I arranged our meeting with the parents for tomorrow evening at seven at the public library. The assistant district attorney will be there to do the questioning. He'll determine if there's a strong enough case to take to the district attorney. I was able to contact eight of the families. I told them to bring all the legal work on the adoptions, and to be prepared to discuss everything they know about Dr. Kirby and George Hathaway. They know they'll be subpoenaed if they don't come, so they'll be there. I think we've got him, Adrienne."

Worried sets of parents sat in a large circle in the meeting room at the Ouachita Parish Public Library. Mike and Adrienne had gotten there early to be sure the parents didn't have any private time to talk about things just in case some of them were actually involved in the illegal part of their kids' adoptions. Assistant District Attorney James O'Brien walked in a few minutes after seven. Mike had prepped him on the phone the previous day about what to expect.

"Let me make this perfectly clear," Mr. O'Brien started. "No one here is interested in destroying your families by taking your children away from you if they were adopted legally, or without your knowledge of anything illegal. Any family whose child was adopted illegally but without their knowledge will receive legal counseling on how to pursue the legal adoption of your child. We're interested in finding the truth so that you can go on with your lives without shadows hanging over your heads. Each of you was asked to keep copies of all legal work done concerning your child's adoption, including birth certificates, and to bring the originals to be turned over to me. I've brought a deputy along who will be responsible for taking these items from you individually, and documenting the materials as evidence. As we look into each individual case and clear you from direct and knowing involvement in the illegal purchasing of a child, the originals will be returned to you. I must inform you, however, that this is an ongoing investigation, and we expect it to be a lengthy one. At this time, we believe we have enough evidence to tie Dr. Kirby to the murders of some of your children's biological mothers, and to the illegal selling of at least two children. We have already processed materials that will help us locate the biological mothers of your children, and in those cases where the biological mothers gave up their children, the procedure will be simple. If the birth certificates and adoption papers were legally filed, the only other matter to be considered will be the amount of money paid, and who it went to. In some cases, we believe the biological mothers were threatened and forced to give up their children, and in at least two cases, possibly more, the biological mothers were murdered when they refused to give up their children. Who the children were will be discovered as we go along. In the meantime, there is one fact we are reasonably sure of in some cases, and positive of in others. Dr. Kirby was fathering his own illegitimate children through these women with the sole purpose of selling them to wealthy families. Money was not his motivator. Proving his own intellectual superiority was his purpose. He believed his genetic makeup would produce children who, if raised in privileged homes, would be geniuses. It's important for you, as parents, to know too that Dr. Galen Kirby is a classic psychopath, and that he is most likely the father of the child each of you adopted."

You could have heard a pin drop in the room. Then suddenly, a woman burst out crying. Adrienne looked closely. It was the mother of the first child whose home she had visited. The fourteen year old boy who was a dead ringer for Galen Kirby, the one who was already receiving psychiatric counseling and had been expelled from school. Adrienne felt numb. What would happen to these families, to these people who had wanted to love and raise a child like any normal family? Was the psychopathic personality inherited or environmental? The old argument, nature or nurture, dependent wholly on who you talked to. Were these people raising the next crop of full-fledged psychopaths who would someday be let loose on society, or were they simply raising children who had a strike against them when they were born? How could anyone be sure?

"Homicide Detective Mike Morris will be assisting me this evening with the questioning," Mr. O'Brien continued. "Private Investigator Adrienne Hargrove will help with any questions you may have while we talk with each family one-on-one. We appreciate everyone being here. Let's start with you first," he pointed at the crying woman, "and see if we can't get each of you out of here as quickly as possible."

It was nearly midnight by the time Mike and Adrienne left the library and headed for the lodge. Both of them rode along silently, thinking about the nightmares Dr. Kirby had caused in the lives of all these people. How awful it must be to get up one morning and have breakfast with your family, thinking your world was normal and secure, and in the twinkling of an eye have that same world collapse around you, everything you believed to be true about yourself and those you love challenged in every way possible.

"Well," Mike broke the silence, "there's no doubt we've got enough on Dr. Kirby to put him away for a long time. Looks like there'll be some jail time for the attorney, too. Mr. O'Brien felt pretty secure about the doctor being prosecuted for the murders of at least two women, and probably more. They're going to bring in profilers from Baton Rouge to take a good look at him. I don't think anyone believes these two women are the only ones he's killed."

"How are they going to go about arresting him, Mike. With him in a coma and all?" Adrienne asked, wondering silently how to prepare Catriona for the event.

"The D.A.'s office will issue a warrant tomorrow. They'll go to the home and arrest him with an ambulance assisting. He'll be taken to the psychiatric ward at the hospital with round the clock guards until the case goes to court, or until his health improves. Then, he'll be held in jail or at the hospital until the trial's over. Mr. O'Brien thinks they'll be looking at locking him up in a hospital for the criminally insane rather than just prison. Any way you look at it, Dr. Kirby will never be a free man again." Mike added, "You'd better let Catriona know. They'll probably be out there pretty early tomorrow."

"Yeah," Adrienne said, still feeling almost numb as she pulled out her cell phone and dialed Catriona's number.

* * *

Catriona Kirby walked into the breakfast room where Galen sat staring, in his wheelchair. It was early morning, and Cameron LeBlanc had just started the doctor's morning routine. He covered the doctor's legs with a blanket and turned to face Catriona.

"That will be all for today, Cameron," Catriona said. "I'm expecting company this morning, and they'll be here to help me with Dr. Kirby."

"Are you sure, Mrs. Kirby?" Cameron asked. "I can stay til your company arrives if you'd like."

"I appreciate that, Cameron, but it's really not necessary. There'll be at least two strong men. I'm sure all will be fine." She wished Cameron would hurry up and leave before the officers and the ambulance arrived. She really didn't want to do any explaining this morning.

"See you tomorrow," Cameron said, looking over at Dr. Kirby. "I was just about to give him his medicine."

"I'll take care of it," Catriona said, "not to worry," as she closed the door behind him.

Catriona walked over to Dr. Kirby. She picked up the dropper of zombie potion Cameron had left on the table, and moved toward her husband. "Last dose you'll need," she said. "By this time tomorrow, you'll be starting to come out from under the drug's influence. A little weak probably, maybe a little disoriented, but that won't last for long. A few days from now, and you'll be just like you were before. Look at all you've done, Galen, all the pain and suffering you've caused and will continue to cause for a long time to come. Would you have killed me too, in time?" Emotions welled up inside and she felt like crying, but there was no time for that. "As soon as they leave with you, I'll have to get rid of all evidence that the zombie powder ever existed. Your reign of terror is over, Galen. All the years I've lost to you, a thing of the past, finally." She placed the dropper in the corner of his mouth and pushed the syringe slowly in. She was careful not to waste a single drop. Minutes later, two police cars and an ambulance pulled in her drive.

"Mrs. Kirby?" a strong-built, young police officer asked as Catriona opened the door.

"Yes," she answered.

"I have a warrant for the arrest of your husband, Dr. Galen Kirby, on two counts of murder, and for the illegal marketing of children. I have another officer and an ambulance with two attendants to assist me."

"Please come in," Catriona answered. "The detectives called to tell me you were coming. I think you'll want these," Catriona handed the policeman a stack of magazine articles. "I found them in his personal files. They're articles about a genius sperm bank. I suspect these articles had something to do with my husband's idea for what he's been doing all this time."

"I'll see that they get into the hands of the right detectives," the officer said. "It's time for us to get him out of here now, if you'll excuse us, Mam."

Adrienne moved aside and watched as the ambulance attendants came in and carefully removed Galen from his wheelchair to the gurney. They laid him on his side in a fetal position. All emotion seemed to come to the surface for Catriona as they took her husband of ten years out the door. Was she really safe? Was it really all over? For the first time in a long time, she felt like she could breathe without fear again. But it wasn't quite over yet.

Catriona watched as the police cars and ambulance pulled out of the driveway. No doubt the house would be searched soon for any evidence related to Dr. Kirby's crimes. She'd need to get rid of the zombie powder right away. She turned the oven on 450 degrees, and got a cookie sheet out of a kitchen drawer. She went to the cabinet in the bathroom and brought out the two ounce vial of zombie powder. Very carefully, she spread the powder on the cookie sheet with a spatula. She set the sheet with its deadly contents in the oven and set the timer for thirty minutes. The heat would detoxify the deadly poison, rendering it as harmless as a spoonful of sugar. She held the spatula over a burner until it was scorched, then threw it in the trash.

Catriona opened a bottle of cabernet sauvignon and filled a wine glass. She thought about all the evil her husband had done, all the pain he had caused and would still cause as the truth about him came out. Dozens of families destroyed, no telling how many naive young women who thought he could be trusted because he was a doctor, betrayed, some, no telling how many, dead. Even in the midst of her own confusion, she realized it was actually a time for celebration. She went to the den and lit a scented candle, then put on the Rolling Stones, "I Can't Get No Satisfaction," album. .She went back to the kitchen, took the cookie sheet out of the oven and scraped part of its contents into the glass of wine, stirring it thoroughly with her finger. Slowly sipping the contents like any other glass of fine wine, she took the cookie sheet with its remaining contents, walked to the den, and stood in front of the aquarium watching the round, spiny puffer fish as they swam toward her, making eye contact as they moved slowly, questioningly through the water. She sat the wine glass down and carefully scraped the remaining zombie powder into the aquarium. "Ashes to ashes," she whispered. "No more evidence." She poured another glass of wine, swished it around to be sure any residue of the powder was absorbed, and sat down to think. No need to dispose of the zombie powder at Galen's office. When the police searched there, they would discover his experiment and think he'd caused his own toxic poisoning by accident, especially when they read the medical reports about his condition saying he was suffering from some sort of neurological allergy or poisoning. They'd assume it was an accident he'd caused himself.

No more to be done. It was all over.

Chapter Thirty-Nine

Mike and Adrienne sat in the early morning air on the back porch of the lodge with coffee mugs in hand.

"Hard to believe it's all over," Mike said. "The weeks have really flown by. It's great to get the news that Dr. Kirby will never see the light of day again. Even the D.A. said he'd never seen anything so bazaar, but the evidence is clear-cut."

"Yeah," Adrienne answered. "It's hard for regular people to understand the kind of things that can go on in the mind of a person who has no conscience...I hate to see you go back to Baton Rouge, Mike. I'm really going to miss you."

"Gonna miss you too girl," he smiled. "That apartment of mine can get pretty lonely sometimes."

"You don't have to be here on a case to come and visit, Mike," Adrienne said. "Come and stay from time to time, whenever you can." They heard Andrew coming, dragging the pole and his oxygen tank alongside him. Mike stood to pick up his bag and gave Adrienne a big hug.

"Hate to see you go, man," Andrew said, extending his hand to Mike. "Gonna miss my fishin buddy. I hope you'll come again soon."

"I'm going to do that Andrew. Thanks for all the hospitality. You take care of yourself." Mike winked at Adrienne and stepped down off the porch.

Adrienne and Andrew stood watching as Mike pulled out of the long, winding driveway and disappeared around the tree line.

"I've got to go check on a client," Adrienne said to Andrew, walking past him and into the house.

"It's seven o'clock in the morning," Andrew said. "Who do you have to check on at this time of the morning?"

"An old man. Name's Erle Blue."

"Why don't we have a little breakfast before you leave?" Andrew said.

"I've got to get there while I know where he is," Adrienne answered, grabbing her shoulder-strap bag and throwing in her silver Zippo lighter and an extra pack of Virginia Slims.

"Shit," Andrew said as she brushed past him and picked up the keys to her car.

Adrienne parked at the foot of the Lea Joyner Bridge and locked her purse in the car. She started down the embankment to the part of the bridge that made a pocket as it touched the ground, the part where Smiley, Robert Erle Blue, lived. The shadows made it hard to see. She walked closer. He wasn't there. Neither was his duffel bag…. "No," Adrienne said out loud. "No, Smiley, don't be gone." She almost felt like she would cry. She walked back and forth, back and forth. "Don't be gone, Smiley. Don't be gone."

Adrienne climbed back up the embankment and walked to the watchtowers on the bridge. She lit a cigarette and blew smoke in the air. Down river, she could see the silhouette of a barge making its way to some unknown destination. Slowly, she walked back to her car and drove home.

* * *

The message line on the phone was flashing as Adrienne sat down in her office in front of her computer to think. She took a deep breath and pushed the button.

"Adrienne, this Catriona," a gentle voice spoke. "I was hoping to say good-bye to Mike and to thank you both again for all you've done to help me. There's no possible way to explain how good it feels to be able to look forward to the future again after ten years of this nightmare. There's even the possibility of love for me, Adrienne. Remember that professor you introduced me to when we were having breakfast at the IHOP? Mel Brighton? Well, I ran into him at Reward Yourself Coffeehouse. He said his old coffeehouse, Cottonport, had closed down, and he was looking for a fresh start and a new beginning. He invited me to have dinner with him. He's absolutely gorgeous, Adrienne, and he seems so genuine." Adrienne thought she heard Catriona giggle. "I'll let you know how it goes." She hung up the phone.

Adrienne went to the back porch and lit a cigarette. She laid her head back, closed her eyes and listened to the water in the pond gently slapping against its banks, and to the gentle creaking of the rocking chair.

Printed in the United States
59200LVS00005B/280-297